AND SO IT BEGAN. . .

The lieutenant and the English woman were running neck and neck as the bus began to move. They reached the corner at the same time—too late.

They stopped and turned, and Halloran really saw her for the first time: unruly hair, pert nose, full and humorous mouth, and those eyes. With war-heightened perception, he knew every detail in an instant.

"You missed your bus." He felt himself grinning, stupidly.

"I don't own a bus."

"I'll buy you one," he promised, expansively.

She took in the sandy brown hair and loose, easy style. So unmistakably American, she thought to herself.

"How about a cup of coffee?" He was sure. She must feel it, too.

"I don't drink coffee."

He shrugged. Perhaps he was wrong. Far down the street another bus was approaching and she could see it.

"I drink tea," she relented, a smile beginning to curl at the edges of her mouth.

And so their affair began . . .

Columbia Pictures
Presents

A Lazarus / Hyams Production
of a Peter Hyams Film

Harrison Ford
Lesley-Anne Down

and

Christopher Plummer

in

HANOVER
STREET

---

also starring
Alec McCowen
Richard Masur
Michael Sacks

•

Music by John Barry
Produced by Paul N. Lazarus III
Written and Directed by Peter Hyams

HANOVER STREET

MAUREEN GREGSON

BASED ON THE SCREENPLAY BY
PETER HYAMS

HANOVER STREET
A Bantam Book / June 1979

ISBN 0–553–12413–7

Published simultaneously in the United States and Canada

Bantam Books are published by Bantam Books, Inc. Its trademark, consisting of the words "Bantam Books" and the por-
trayal of a bantam, is Registered in U.S. Patent and Trademark
Office and in other countries. Marca Registrada. Bantam
Books, Inc., 666 Fifth Avenue, New York, New York 10019.

PRINTED IN THE UNITED STATES OF AMERICA

HANOVER STREET

1

Evening settled over London as if it weighed more than the afternoon. Unrelieved by the flare of street lighting, it slowed the traffic and pushed down on the crowds choking the sidewalks. The slight smog was thickened by dusk mingling with its yellow air and the blackout screens and curtains shrouded the windows of the city.

People turned up their collars. The muddy film which clung to their skin and hair was hazardous, but familiar, a legacy from their industrial great-grandparents. It was the blackout which made them bunch their shoulders defensively and hurry home.

David Halloran was pushing his way along Hanover Street, the wrong way against a tide of bodies swirling toward the Oxford Circus subway station. He weaved through the mass like a tailback looking for his blockers, waiting for holes to open up, then sliding through. It was still slow going, but he moved that way from habit.

On the whole he found Londoners were jokey and cheerful. It was always strange for an outsider to see them treat the war like a job, going to it each morning, steadily ignoring the terrible gaps in groups of colleagues and friends, and laying it aside before sleep, with the hope that there would be no late-night calls. Practical, stoic, stubborn. The scars in the brick and concrete from the blitz and the fact that most men and many women were wearing uniforms were the only signs that anything was wrong.

Laconic, cat-voweled catch phrases picked up from the radio shows met him as he collided with passing strangers.

"Ginger's back."

"After you, Claude." "No. After you, Cecil."

"Don't forget the diver."

Shrewd glances took in his battered leather jacket with the Eighth Army Air Force patch with its first-lieutenant bars, and the tough, tired faces were friendly. It was as though they were celebrating a home win. And perhaps they were.

The lineup at the bus stop was tidy, like all British queues. Its components rolled off the moving assembly into the allotted spaces to form that meticulously straight row along the edge of the curb.

Halloran did not fit in too well with crowds, always appearing to be in more of a hurry than the others. Tall, lean, with a casual buoyancy, he was one of those guys who never pays attention to the clothes he wears, yet always looks good; pants cut well, as in Brooks Brothers ads and the rest casual and expensive-looking like it was purchased on Fifth Avenue.

The double-decker bus rumbled down the clogged street and he started to inch forward, registering that it was almost full even before it came to a halt. The line pressed together with a concertinalike gasp of effort and people began to cram themselves onto the rear platform.

Halloran felt a pain in his ankle, followed by a prod in the back. As he turned, automatically, a woman elbowed past without looking up and without even bothering to say "Excuse me." The serviceman pushed against her and received a vigorous shove in return. He pushed harder and so did she, using her shoulders to hold her position as the line edged on. But the bus was beginning to pull away, the queue curving around after its packed decks. There was room for maybe one more, someone with no need to inhale.

Halloran and the woman saw the space at the same time. He reached around her, grabbing her far shoulder, and she instinctively wheeled in the direction of his hand. That was all he needed to slither through, grab the pole at the end of the bus, and swing on. The brakes hissed and the vehicle grunted into the crawl of traffic.

The woman left on the pavement glared at him—dark indignant eyes, small angry features. He grinned.

Suddenly her eyes rolled up and her face went rigid, hands clawing spasmodically at her stomach. She began to sway, her voice strangled, as if a hand was clutching her throat.

"My God . . . it's the baby! It's the baby!"

The bus jolted. Halloran watched in abject terror as she went limp against the bus-stop sign and began to slip to the ground. The queue was scrambling past her, too intent on the appearance of the next bus in the distance to notice.

Halloran jumped off the platform. Someone else immediately leaped into his place. He reached her side. Her face was down in her hands, and he gently turned her over. She looked up . . . grinning . . . stuck out her tongue, and sprang to her feet.

"I'm frightfully sorry. It appears you have missed your bus." It was one of those cool, well-bred English voices.

Halloran blinked in disbelief. The bus was now turning into Oxford Street. She sneered in triumph, and a ball of anger hit him in the gut. He gave her a long, cold stare, then turned and walked off.

His left leg dragged slightly along the asphalt as he went, and he pulled his jacket closed against the cold, self-conscious about the stiff-legged limp, but unable to hide an infirmity of that magnitude.

The woman watched him stumble away. The second bus had drawn up to the curb, and she looked from it to his limping figure again. People were already clambering on. She stood, torn between a guilty desire to escape with them and an urge of pity for the injured officer. She hesitated a moment longer, clearly harrowed, then ran after him, darting from the sidewalk onto the street alongside the cars to avoid the crush.

Catching up, she reached out and put her hand on his arm, in some way trying to apologize.

Her voice was halting. "I'm . . ."

The word "sorry" never stood a chance. Halloran pivoted and raced back toward the bus with long, graceful strides. It took her a second, and then she was after him, tearing down the street, face flushed with rage.

Halloran was gliding through the crowd ahead, but what she lacked in speed and size she made up for in obstinacy, tunneling through impossibly small gaps and slamming against wedged forms. Out of pure self-defense they gave way before her, whereas Halloran was held up by a boulderlike body, which refused to be shifted.

They were side by side as the bus began to move off, each trying to push the other out of the way. The bus gained speed. Two people were already hanging perilously onto the pole at the back. The lieutenant and the Englishwoman reached the corner at the same time. They were too late. The bus had gone.

They stopped and turned together, which was when Halloran really saw her for the first time—unruly hair, pert nose, firm chin, full and humourous mouth, and those eyes. With war-heightened perception, Halloran knew every detail in an instant and felt the tightening in his stomach. He tried to breathe deeply, but there seemed to be a shortage of air. Those clear and strong and defiant eyes gazed back at him.

"You missed your bus." He felt himself grinning stupidly.

"I don't own a bus."

"I'll buy you one," he promised expansively.

The glance was still on him, taking in the sandy brown hair and the loose, easy style. So unmistakably American, she thought to herself with approval, but aloud merely responded with stilted formality, "No, thank you."

"How about a cup of coffee?" Halloran was sure. She must feel it, too.

"I don't drink coffee."

He shrugged and put his hands in his pockets. Perhaps he was wrong. Far down the street another bus was approaching and she could see it. Its distance from the bus stop was the measure of their time. Its arrival would mean the end—or the beginning.

"I drink tea," she relented, a smile beginning to curl at the edges of her mouth.

Halloran was rocked by that inner lurch again as he looked down. It was such a nice mouth.

"There won't be another bus for quite a while," he lied, turning his back on the approaching red giant.

"Probably not," she agreed.

And they joined the crowd, allowing themselves to be bowled along unresisting for a few minutes, pleased to be hustled away from the bus stop; each mentally questioning and searching for clues, intrigued by the closeness of the other.

A sudden eddy swept her on ahead. He experienced a moment of panic until she turned her head, and slowed to let others pass around her until he was there again.

"Where are we going?" she called.

He scanned over the sea of heads. Hanover Street was a short, fat thumb of a street sticking out from the square of the same name. A surprising imbroglio of architecture littered its limited length, ranging from a couple of tall Victorian remnants to a 1930's office building. The Grand Banqueting Suite on the left was fruity with stone ornamentation beneath a Greek pediment. Ornate metal grilles covered the windows of a small diamond merchant, but the iron railings, which had once protected the basement, had been removed to be smelted down into ammunition. Dangerous wells now opened up between the pavements and the buildings.

An alley called Pollen Street ran off to the right. A door on its corner opened to let a shaft of light slide into the twilight from a small tea shop with a bay window. Halloran cupped a hand over the Englishwoman's elbow and steered her to it, into a dark wooden rectangle of a room containing more tables than seemed possible in such restricted space. The air was warm, with pipe and cigarette smoke replacing the smog in the darkness outside.

A gray-haired waitress in a black dress and token white apron showed them to a table covered by a white cloth. Her pad and pencil were attached to her clothes by a safety pin and string, but she looked as though she should have been wielding a feather duster in someone's stately drawing room.

"Yes, dear?" She regarded him expectantly.

"Tea," said Halloran bravely.

The pencil scratched. "Biscuit?"

He raised an interrogative eyebrow.

"Biscuit?" she repeated.

"Oh, yeah. Cookies." He confirmed the order with a nod and received a maternal smile.

A few minutes later, individual pewter pots of tea were placed in front of him and the woman, who reached over and filled his cup with the burnt-colored liquid. He looked at his like a kid confronted by a dose of medicine.

"You really drink this stuff, don't you?" He surveyed her with admiration as she dropped a couple of saccharin into her own cup without flinching.

"No, we just like to pour it and stir it," she retorted, leaning forward to ease out of her coat and hook it back over the chair. She was wearing the Civil Nursing Reserve uniform. Blue striped dress with short puffed sleeves, secured by elastic white cuffs. Starched white collar and apron, tied with a scarlet belt. Cute. A sip of the lukewarm tea instantly dismissed his cheerfulness.

"It tastes like boiled water," he protested.

"It *is* boiled water," she pointed out.

He sighed philosophically. "I knew there was a reason."

Two elderly ladies at the next table rose to leave in a fuss of worn handbags and old leather gloves. They tottered out, to be replaced within minutes by an almost identical pair, in mulberry frocks with crocheted collars. Hair coiled into buns under hats decorated with faded flowers. Matching faded eyes, filled with watery bewilderment at the chaotic world in which they found themselves.

Museum pieces, he thought, wry at finding himself in their company and noticing the cause of his presence watching them, too, with the concern she probably showed for the wounded men in her ward.

Their eyes met and her pupils dilated. She knew it was happening.

"Nobody's supposed to look like that in a uniform," he murmured.

Her face remained serious. "How am I supposed to look?"

A flickering image of curving female bodies crammed into squared-off wool suits, shirts, and ties invaded his mind. Women he had known recently. "Like a short man" he declared with feeling.

"Your boiled water is getting cold." She tried to avoid his unswerving stare and tugged uneasily at a strand of hair, asking where he came from in an attempt to keep communication casual.

"New York. A place called Morningside," he answered.

"That's a peaceful name," she observed wistfully.

"New York likes to play little practical jokes like that on people. I think it's for the tourists." He recalled the student-filled streets around Columbia University with rueful affection; then, following her lead: "What about you?"

"Who are you . . . ?" she hedged.

"Who are you . . . ? What are you . . . ?"

"I'm a short man. I live in London. I always have and probably always will." She steepled her fingers against her chin. "I work in a hospital, telling a lot of young men that they are going to be all right . . . and then watching them die. I want it all to end."

Her face had gone blank. The small lines around her eyes answering his. They came from seeing more than they were supposed to see at that age. It was the look they shared with all young men and women of their time.

The chink of crockery and buzz of voices around them receded, as though the nearest tables had been pushed back a few feet to leave them alone by the window.

He had to break the mood. "I'll win the war for you."

Her expression remained bleak. "That will be nice."

She ran a finger around the rim of her teacup, composing her features into a mask of remote politeness, and asked, "Are you stationed in London?"

He shook his head, explaining that the base was about an hour and a half out, and hinting hopefully, "I normally get a day every two weeks."

"You're a pilot?" This was safer.

"B-25's."

"Do you like flying?"

"I hate to walk." He was careful not to smile at her innocent phrasing, and studied the contours and textures of her face with pleasure. "What's your name?"

"Tell me about New York." The English had this trick of creating unspannable distances with their voices. He had been disconcerted by it before. But not this time.

"I think you are lovely," he persisted.

Her head gave a little shake and her voice faltered. "Tell me about Morningdale."

"Morningside," he corrected. "It's where the George Washington Bridge is."

He leaned forward urgently, impatient to cut through the prudent game, and stating it slowly and loudly: "Something is happening here."

She shot him a tortured glance. "Please . . . don't."

"Please don't what?" he insisted.

"I have to go."

He reached across the table with both hands. "I don't want you to go."

"I shouldn't be here." She was without hope in a way he could not understand.

"Yes, you should." Nothing was more certain.

Both of them looked down at the table at the same time and realized her hand was clinging to his. She jerked back, trembling, and stood up.

"I have to go." Grabbing her coat, she ran from the table.

The other people in the tearoom watched with mild curiosity as Halloran flung a handful of coins on the white cloth and dashed out after her.

By the time he reached the street, the woman had crossed it and was running toward the bus stop. The sidewalks were less crowded now, and it was easy to catch up. He seized her arm and swung around to stand in front of her, blocking the way.

"Please . . . I have to get the bus," she pleaded, her face flushed.

"Don't go like this." It was more of a command than a request.

"I have to," she stressed.

He moved both hands up to her shoulders and looked down. "I want to see you again."

"I can't . . . I can't." She sounded close to tears.

"Please . . . There's only a few more hours before I have to go back." Now *he* was desperate.

"I have to go," she repeated woodenly.

"Why? Why?" Halloran yelled, pulling her to him.

For a moment she stayed against him, the clean smell of her hair dispelling the soot-heavy smog. Then, flinching away in dismay, she fled toward the bus stop.

Halloran stood, watching her go, staring at her diminishing figure. The subconscious, never admitted knowledge, that each day could be his last, intensified every experience and brought key moments into razor-edged focus. But even without such magnified awareness, there was no mistaking this. What had taken place in Hanover Street that day, that hour, would have been life-shattering in the most peaceful circumstances. She was almost at the bus, which was coming to a stop. It was like watching someone die unnecessarily. He felt bereaved and enraged—and completely helpless. Then he lost sight of her.

The explosion ricocheted again and again off the buildings and the air was filled with echoes and splinters of glass. There was a fractional pause, as though the street gasped, and then the bus blasted apart, dissolving into a ball of orange fire. The sirens set up their pagan wail and the tongues of the searchlights licked the sky for Heinkels. Another bomb fell at the far side of the square. Screams and bells and the roar of aircraft accumulated into a bedlam of sound. Halloran had been batted against a wall and winded by the concrete-hard shock wave.

A heap of twisted metal, alive only with lambent blue flames, was all that remained of the bus. The American lieutenant stared across at it numbly. There could be nothing left of anyone on board.

The bay window of the little tea shop where they had been sitting moments before cascaded onto the pavement. The building shuddered, and then the bricks collapsed in a waterfall of debris. His eyes moved from the vehicle to the ruin and back. Nothing left. He felt sick. And then he caught sight of her for an instant, framed against the charred shrubs of the square, mouth open and eyes wide with fear through the smoke. She had not reached the bus after all, but must have been hurled right across the road.

She saw him in that same second and stumbled forward, arms outstretched. Halloran careened into the sobbing people surging toward the security of the subway.

The traffic had jammed behind the wrecked bus; the roadway was clear. Suddenly the small shop on his right flared with a meteoric glitter of light, the pavement heaved, and the smell of gas mingled with the scorched smog. There was an avalanche of masonry, and his legs were knocked from under as it hit him.

Caked with the dust of powdered stone, he found himself crawling up the street on hands and knees. Heavy shoes thudded into his back and ribs as the crowd trampled unseeing over him in a wild scramble for shelter through the dark. He felt disoriented, somehow detached from his own body, and only knew that he must reach the spot where he last saw her.

A man fell over him, cursing, and filled the space in front of him with a freakish expression of mad eyes. The lieutenant struggled to his feet. The oval gardens of Hanover Square were shriveling in a red cloud. She was not there.

He spun around. Fire fighters were struggling to put out the flames now offering the whole of the West End of London as an invitation to the German bombers overhead. A middle-aged couple huddled over a still figure in a hospital service uniform. Her uniform.

Halloran staggered frantically toward them, clearly seeing only the slim legs on the pavement. They were not moving. An air-raid warden, fat, elderly and brave, in a tin helmet and uniform, was shouting at everyone to clear the area and take cover in Oxford Circus Station. The pilot pushed past, reckless with thoughts of hatred for the enemy above and anguish over the body on the sidewalk; no longer sane, a crazy man.

The warden, too, raced toward the couple crouched over her, and pulled them back, trying to lead them away. As they stood up, Halloran saw her face. She was dead—a woman about forty-five years old—her broken glasses lying on the pavement.

He felt weak and dizzy. He wanted to sit down on the asphalt and howl noisy tears like a child. She was all right. She was somewhere in Hanover Street, somewhere nearby. Currents of people buffeted him backward and forward.

Two more bombs caught the square, the first crashing by the burning carcass of the bus and the next blowing out the second story of a brownstone. Halloran was beyond wincing. He could see twisted bedroom furniture exposed as the outer wall fell to the street; an obscene glimpse into private lives. Small, inconsequential objects caught his eye, a hairbrush falling, feathers from the pillows floating upward to the attackers. White feathers. Wasn't that what they used to give cowards? His mouth twitched involuntarily.

A small, wicker-seated chair, like the one in Van Gogh's painting of the bedroom at Arles, slid down the sloping floor of the raped room and fell in slow motion. Halloran's gaze followed it to the sidewalk, and he saw her, standing in a doorway behind a curtain of falling stone, covering her head.

Nothing else mattered, only reaching her. The terror and the devastation and the mob gave way before him. A three-foot barrier of broken rubble was massed across the entrance. Halloran dived over it just before a section of the parapet fell as a huge slab of concrete crashed and blocked the way. She was cowering in the shadows.

There was not even any question of what to do or what to say. Their arms went around each other. Their mouths pressed together. She held on to him as if to life itself, her mouth hard and desperate against his, demanding rescue, grasping for strength. It was a kiss of sheer despair. He drew her closely and protectively into the shelter of his body, curving deliberately over her, sensing how small she was, kissing her eyes and her wet cheeks, tightening his hold to stop her shaking. She buried her head under his chin, her hair billowing against the side of his face.

The doorway was deep and dark. They slowly settled onto the floor in the corner. Halloran eased open his jacket and pulled her against him. They lay quite still. He smelled of bombs and burning and smog, but he also smelled warm and human. She felt strangely drowsy. He stroked her hair, catching a faint fragrance from the nape of her neck. It evoked formless feelings of peace and home, a mixture of past and future, as though she had been with him always. He drifted in their shared closeness.

The war raged a few feet away, people shrieked for help, sirens howled, airplanes growled real threats of death, yet it all seemed very far off. Halloran and the Englishwoman were in another dimension. In the middle of hell, they were safe.

A reedy braying penetrated their seclusion at last, forcing them back to the angry planet. It was the "All Clear" being sounded. Reluctantly they opened their eyes. For a moment he tried to pretend they were still in that capsule of timelessness, but she stirred and drew back.

She was smoothing her clothes and beginning to look embarrassed as he struggled to his feet and held out a hand. Together they clambered up the heap of rubble and stared over into the night. The world was coming back after being out late. Mangled cars and buses were strewn on the street, like overfilled ashtrays on the living-room rug. People were emerging stiffly onto Hanover Street from their hiding holes, dazed and oddly silent.

The woman half-turned, as though wanting to escape back to the dark corner of the doorway. Halloran took her hand. They climbed over the fallen parapet and stepped onto the pavement.

Her face had already stiffened into the wary expression it had worn earlier, outside the tearoom. He put his arm around her, but her body was tense. They did not know what to say to each other.

It's like summer camp. You never think it's going to end, he thought miserably to himself. And then, suddenly, you're on the bus back home, singing songs that nobody else gives a damn about.

He looked down into her taut small features, reading her thoughts easily. "You're trying to go away again . . . and I'm not going to let you," he asserted, turning her toward him.

She was wide-eyed and starting to cry, lips trembling in an effort of control.

He pinned her gaze tenderly, shaking his head with a wry smile and saying again, "I'm not going to let you."

A man and a girl turned the corner from Oxford Street. They had obviously just arrived in the West End and missed the bomb attack. The girl was fashionably dressed in a padded-shouldered, short-skirted suit, and sling-back shoes. She was laughing, and as they passed by, her companion gave her a friendly pat on the butt. They brought normality back with them.

"I can't think." The Englishwoman looked confused by them and halfheartedly tried to pull away. "I . . . I have to go home."

"I'll take you," he declared, keeping a firm hold on her shoulders.

"No . . . You can't . . ." She bit her lip as twin tears escaped.

Halloran instinctively drew her back into his arms and kissed her, tasting that heart-stopping mouth yield willingly to his. It was all right. It had to be.

"My name is Halloran . . . David Halloran," he murmured against her face. "I'm from New York—right near the George Washington Bridge." His arms tightened again. "And I won't let you go."

She was gasping against him. "Please . . . I have to go . . ."

"What's your name?" He had a deep, warm voice, the kind most women love.

"I'm sorry . . . I'm sorry." She shook her head violently and started to back away.

Halloran refused to relax his embrace and grinned down quizzically. "You're in my arms, and you won't tell me your name!"

Those eyes looked back, pleading and intensely vulnerable. "Please let me go."

He decided to bargain. "I have to see you again. I'll have another day, two weeks from today—Thursday."

Now she was definite. "I can't."

So was he. "I'll meet you here—right here."

"No." She turned her face away, in a gesture of fierce determination.

Halloran ignored it. "On the same corner—Thursday. I'll be here." It was a statement.

"I won't be here," she retorted.

They were standing in the middle of the road. A fire engine came jangling around the corner and was almost upon him before they realized and jumped to one side. But the lieutenant kept a grip on her arm, stopping her again on the pavement.

"I will be here," he confirmed. "And I'll wait all day."

"Don't . . . don't . . ." She became distracted. "I won't come."

"I'll be here." He said it again, and with sudden urgency gave her a slight shake. "There's not enough time. You can't act like something hasn't happened. . . . There's not enough time!"

All the pressure of past months sounded in his insistence. It must be the same for her too. The stark knowledge of mortality, of having maybe only an hour more to live. She must wake each morning, just like him, knowing that she might not reach the evening, that night might never fall. There was no time for waiting games. The good things were miracles. You had to grab them with faith.

"It's too late," she cried, angry with regret and twisting out of his grasp.

Halloran reached to stop her, seizing her hand, but she pulled back, leaving her glove behind. In the light from the burning buildings, the gold ring shone scarlet on her third finger. Halloran stared at it and then at her face. Their eyes met, hers filled with infinite hopelessness, his blank.

"It's too late," she repeated very quietly, and turned away.

This time he made no move to prevent her. In the shadowed doorway where they had lain together, he had taken her, in his mind, on a journey. Now he was surprised to realize he had taken her through a lifetime, and he felt cheated. When he focused again on Hanover Street, she had gone.

Firemen were still working on the smoldering building. Ambulances, with little blue lights on top, surrounded the overturned bus. The street was wet with water. Halloran stumbled bitterly along it. The body of the nursing-reserve woman had been taken away. Her shattered glasses were still on the pavement.

2

Although the rush hour was over, Oxford Circus subway station was crammed with people carrying rolled-up bundles and carpetbags. Swarms of kids rushed about, screaming with excitement, while harrassed-looking mothers struggled with babies, strollers, and baskets, and fathers yelled ineffectually. The families bombed out of their homes were making for their nightly positions on the station platforms.

Halloran decided to head back to base and bought a ticket. As he waited for the next train, people were already laying out blankets and unfolding canvas chairs. The lucky ones had sleeping bags, and all had come prepared with thermos flasks and meager food supplies.

They staked out their territory as though it was real fun, unwrapping unappetizing sandwiches and shouting to other families.

" 'Ere, pass the caviar, then."

"Wot, no clotted cream!"

"I'll 'ave rump steak, mushrooms, and chips, love."

"You'll have bully beef and like it, Dad."

Halloran gaped. These people, who had lost everything except what they carried now, behaved like they were on a picnic.

Two small boys, catching sight of his U.S. uniform, marched up, saluted, and began to shout a song to the tune of "Colonel Bogey":

> Hitler
> Has only got one ball!
> Goering
> His balls are very small!
> Himmlers'
> Are something similar,
> But Doctor Goebbels
> Has no balls
> At all!

A surrounding group cackled with laughter and cheered. Halloran found himself chuckling and slipped them a couple of sixpences as the train came in.

There were more families in the carriage, and at Piccadilly, the next stop, the doors slid back to reveal another platform turned into an overnight campsite for refugees.

"Hi, Joe!" a fat woman called from the middle of a large brood.

Okay, he thought. If that's the way it is.

He jumped clear just before the doors slammed closed again, and made for the surface. Minutes later he was turning off Shaftesbury Avenue into the narrow streets of Soho. He hesitated in front of the photos of the strippers at the Windmill Theater, then strolled into the pub opposite. It was empty except for a couple of old-timers in the far corner and a pressed-and-polished RAF officer.

The bartender gave him one of those slow, wised-up stares and asked pointedly, "Been cleaning out the cellar, Joe?"

Halloran caught sight of himself, still smeared with the dirt and dust of the explosions, in the mirror behind the bottles.

"Camouflage," he responded. "I'm hiding from your Mr. Churchill. He keeps trying to pin this medal on me."

The bartender nodded humorlessly and advised, "Keep moving and you'll be marked absent."

"Can an absent man have a bourbon on the rocks?" queried Halloran.

The man shook his head. "That's an absent drink. You can have a Scotch and water."

He jabbed a glass against an optic a couple of times, slurped in too much water, and slid it across the puddled surface of the bar.

Halloran eyed it without enthusiasm. "When's someone going to invent ice over here?"

"Wouldn't be no use, guv." The other leaned toward him conspiratorially. "Our warm cockney natures'd melt it away."

Halloran took the first sip and grimaced. "Perhaps your warm cockney nature could now put some Scotch in this water."

The barman smirked, unabashed. "Just thought I'd test your taste buds, seeing you've had a few already."

"First today, Mac," Halloran corrected, deliberately passing the glass back.

"Have it on me." Britain's answer to Errol Flynn in RAF uniform had come up to the bar and drawled reprovingly, "Other bottle, Fred."

The barkeeper shrugged and pulled a bottle of Haig from under the counter, poured two solid unmeasured slugs into fresh glasses, and pushed them across.

Halloran was aware of cool gray eyes studying his battered appearance with interest. He raised his glass politely.

"Celebrating?" queried the other.

"Escaping," he responded. "From one of your English tea shops."

"Good God!" The squadron leader gazed at him with a mixture of horror and sympathy. "It must have been a woman."

"Right," agreed Halloran, noting the wings and DFC ribbon.

"Well, old man, the cure for that starts at Mabel's."

The Scotch disappeared down his throat like an oyster. "Charles O'Donnell. 'Chod' to friends."

"David Halloran." The American flier shook the outstretched hand. "Lead me to it."

Mabel's turned out to be a club, dimly lit by red bulbs which gave everyone an artificial glow of health. Halloran's became genuine on discovering that they actually stocked bourbon.

"Smooth landings, Bud."

"Bung ho!" responded the Englishman.

It was the start of a night of serious and dedicated drinking. Mabel's Club, the Studio, the Wellington, the Red-Eye, the Blue Angel. Some smart, some not so smart. Halloran lost count, but for a country at war, the supply of seventy-proof liquor was phenomenal. As they walked into each smoking dive, Chod flashed his even white teeth in a hypnotic grin and barmaids dimpled and weakened, producing the forbidden bottles from shadowy corners and secret closets. The limey squadron leader knew them all and was apparently loved by most.

Prohibition in the States must have been something like this, Halloran thought as the varnished counters blurred into one long bar without end, and Elsie and Gracie and Vera and Ruby merged into a single pneumatic, drink-pouring blond.

At one point they found themselves in a ritzy basement restaurant, Halloran eyeing the menu and asking, "How's the pigeon pie?"

"Happier in Trafalgar Square, sir," replied the elderly waiter in tones of doom.

They settled for whale-meat steaks, which would have made a good pair of boots, and a couple of bottles of red Algerian wine, tasting like it should have been poured over the french fries.

The pianist played all the right tunes. He and Chod sang along drunkenly.

"Tearooms, eh?" Chod had quizzed. "Sounds serious."

"A lost cause," he answered morosely.

"Not at all, old boy." Chod thumped him firmly on the back. "Try a bit of throttle?"

The American brightened. Why not!

A great night. Halloran did not even remember leaving it.

The mattress felt like a moving sack of potatoes. Halloran rolled over to find a more comfortable position and slid down a hole. He woke with a jolt, and sat up. It *was* a sack of potatoes and it *was* moving. Freezing night air deluged over him. He clutched his head and moaned. Where the hell was he?

He tried to peer over the side of the truck; the hooded headlights showed up nothing and the black rushing countryside knocked him back with a wave of nausea. He struggled over the lumpy cargo to tap feebly on the driver's cab window. The man half-turned and gave an amiable wave without lessening speed.

Halloran slumped back and gave up the struggle, but it would have been easier to sleep in a bowling alley, so he gave up that struggle, too.

About half an hour later the truck drew up in the middle of nowhere, the driver leaning out of his side window to shout, "You're here, Joe."

"Where the hell's 'here'?"

"Home sweet home. Your mate told me to drop you off at Letchworth."

Good for Chod. Halloran stumbled onto the asphalt. Returning to base was like walking into the middle of the Los Angeles freeway at 1800 hours. A detonation of lights, roaring engines, and yelling voices ran over him and left him for dead. His disembodied spirit staggered to his quarters. Lieutenant Lennard, looking disgustingly bright-eyed and clean-shaven, surveyed his ghost wordlessly at the door, scribbled on a scrap of paper, and held it out.

The message read, "Briefing—0700 hours." That meant now.

The briefing room was a corrugated Quonset hut. It looked as if it had fallen from someplace and spread slightly as it hit bottom. Its domed roof came all the way down to the ground. The ceiling was ribbed by exposed apparatus officially termed heating pipes, which gave as much heat as a subzero freezer unit. Conical metal lampshades, each housing a bare light bulb, were attached to these by a series of poles. There was no insulation. Badly fitting windows had been inserted into the sides of the hut about three feet from the ground, with the result that they faced upward, and winter snaked, unhindered, through their drafty gaps. It was a savage place. No man could relax there and live.

Someone had made an attempt to put a collection of wooden school chairs in rows facing the end wall where there was a raised wooden platform.

Last to arrive, Halloran slumped next to his co-pilot, Second Lieutenant Martin Hyer, and received an open-faced smile, the radiant freshness of which was painful. He was a blond, blue-eyed, handsome kid whose father, a builder, had successfully predicted the land boom in California and the start of World War Two—and profited equally from both. Hyer had glided through his rather privileged twenty-six years of life without ever trying at much, or failing at anything. His was the face that put mothers' minds at ease when he came to pick up their daughters for a date, but not the face to greet a hangover like Halloran's.

The pilot turned weakly from it to the more understanding features of Jerry Cimino, the bombardier. His was the face that made fathers reach for their shotguns. The alert, cynical son of a Chicago bartender on the North Side, he could break enough tackles to be recruited by the University of Illinois and was a man with a deep appreciation of Halloran's sensibilities at such a time.

Colonel Ronald N. Bart marched into the hut as though heading an entire division, mounted the steps of the platform, and assumed authoritative stance, legs astride and head flung back in front of the large map of northern France. He cast what he hoped was an eagle eye over the assembled flight crews. It fell on Halloran with all the repugnance of a born civilian company man at the sight of an unwashed, unshaven face. It skipped over Cimino and took in the rest of the men with curt approval.

Then the colonel seized a long pointer and rapped briskly at the position on the map.

"The objective this morning is this airfield—north-northeast of Rouen," he began, small puffs of cloud punctuating his words in the cold of the hut. "Reconnaissance shows we didn't do too well there last time."

He moved to several aerial photographs of the area pinned on a board to the right of the map. "These dark circles here are fuel-storage tanks. They are under concrete, so it will take more than one direct hit to knock them out. Again, the recon photos show they didn't take even one direct hit last time."

He stepped forward, tapping the cane against the palm of his other hand. "We should approach from the east. We'll have the sun at our backs and in their eyes."

"How come he says 'we'?" Cimino whispered with a distinctly baleful glance in the direction of his commanding officer. "He's not going. *We're* 'we.'"

"They have two fighter wings and a medium bomber group. If we come in fast enough, they won't be able to get them up fast enough."

Bart always addressed his men in the same keen note of leadership he believed would inspire them to respect. He was one of those men who had never risen above the bottom of the middle echelon of life during peacetime. World War Two, through a process of bureaucratic, as well as alphabetic attrition, had moved him upward to his present rank. He would not rise above it, and with the unfortunate declaration of peace, would return downward—and fondly remember these few years as the highlight of his life.

"We can expect light to moderate flak. We'll approach at twelve thousand. Cloud cover is six to eight thousand. We'll drop at six thousand."

Basing his style on that of General Patton, he gave the crews a square-chinned, military nod and added with gruff sincerity, "I wish I could be going with you."

Halloran leaned groaning to his bombardier. "We'll stay and he can go."

The colonel heard and swung around, glaring. "Lieutenant Halloran. Is there something you want to say?"

"No, sir," drawled the flier.

Bart glared at him in hatred. He had not forgotten the time Halloran had undermined his pet scheme for the men to run a daily five miles across country, by bribing a local farmer to pick them up half a mile from base and drop them at the nearest village bar.

"I'm sure none of us would want to miss whatever it is you have to add, Lieutenant," he insisted sarcastically.

"Yes, sir," agreed the other.

And then there was the time Halloran had broken all regulations by taking a woman to Scotland for the weekend on a mail plane. The whole camp knew of it, but Bart hadn't been able to prove a thing. It was time that smart-ass was put down.

"Yes, sir, what?"

"Yes, sir, none of us would want to miss whatever it is I have to add, sir . . . except I have nothing to add, sir . . . so there is nothing for us to miss, sir," countered Halloran in bored tones.

There was a silence as the colonel tried to figure out whether he had won or lost. Cimino and Hyer were having difficulty keeping straight faces. Bart would have liked to find a legal way of murdering Halloran.

He straightened his shoulders, swallowed. "Takeoff is at 0800. Good luck, gentlemen."

The men were dismissed.

The wind charged head-down across the tarmac, colliding squarely with Halloran, who lowered his own head and battled his way to the plane. A day as overhung as he felt himself had crawled out of the night since the start of the briefing.

Cimino was grumbling behind, "Light to moderate flak . . . what the hell is light to moderate flak?"

"Less than heavy flak." Halloran's attempted optimism was lost.

"It's more than no flak," Cimino stressed.

"You've got a point there."

The B-25's were standing in a line, a series of protrusions, transparent domes, rivets, machine guns, aerials, and bomb-bay doors. They were all painted dark green. The crews in khaki and dark brown jackets ambled toward them in groups. The runway surface stretched like a sheet of dull metal to the heavy sky. Even the hills to the left were gray-furred with cloud. There was almost no discernible color.

"He wishes he could go with us," snorted Hyer, still rankling over Bart's send-off.

Halloran was tense. "Somebody has got to stay behind and volunteer us."

They had reached their aircraft and he was the first to crawl up through the belly hatch. Hyer followed.

"Shit!" Cimino, as always, had hit his shoulder climbing in last.

The pilot and copilot squeezed into their cockpit seats, put on their headsets, and began their preflight check, testing the microphone first.

Halloran called up his crew chief, John Lucas, who was wedged in the transparent turret on top of the airplane, checking the two machine guns that pointed aft.

"How we doing?"

"Ready, sir," confirmed the sergeant.

Halloran automatically scanned the interior behind him. The metal walls were bare, exposing the seams and bolts of the fuselage. A jungle of cables and wires ran along each side.

"Giles?" he called.

The young corporal, testing his equipment in the retractable turret protruding from the belly of the aircraft, replied instantly, "All set, sir."

Cimino had wriggled into the glazed fairing on the nose. He had one machine gun with three hundred rounds and one hand-held gun with six hundred rounds, and, as bombardier, he also had the navigation and bomb-bay release equipment. There was not enough room, and he did not stop muttering to himself as Halloran's voice called his name.

"I don't understand it. They make it so goddam hard to get in these things—and I don't want to be here in the first place."

The pilot and Hyer were turning various dials and flipping their respective toggle switches. Cimino's running commentary burbled in their ears.

"I mean, I can understand them making it hard to get out—because everybody wants to get out . . ."

The first plane had just taken off. Halloran's aircraft revved both its engines. There were eight planes behind, all straining as their brakes held them back. The lumbering path down the runway began.

"You know these things are made of metal . . . right?" Cimino's question was rhetorical.

The aircraft began to gather speed. "Did you ever try to pick one up? You can't. You know why?"

The aircraft was going faster.

"Because it's made of metal, and metal is heavy. Very heavy. . . . You don't believe me? You should see my brother trying to lift weights before a fight. A Jalapeno chili couldn't produce that much sweat."

His reflex bellyaching merged with the noise of the engine, and became almost comforting, a kind of invocation to fend off fate.

"Just try to pick one of those things up. You'll see —you'll wrench your back, that's what you'll do."

The nose began to lift slightly.

The bombardier began to expand his theory with increased animation. "Air isn't heavy. This pile of junk is heavy. This pile of junk weighs 33,500 pounds. That's heavier than air. Much heavier. Don't you see? This thing isn't supposed to be up in the air."

The plane took off reluctantly, right on cue.

"Oh, Jesus . . ." moaned Cimino. "I hate these things."

Cloud wrapped around them, thick and dark as wire wool and condensing into water as it met the cockpit windows. Then they were through it, suddenly into a glorious blue sky and floating over a gleaming white endless cloudscape, bubbling and popping under the hot sun.

For the first time that day Halloran felt good. It always happened when they broke through the earth's drab pelt. The danger ahead concentrated his thinking but did not prevent him from looking around with pleasure. The flight was flying in formation. Relative to each other they hardly seemed to move, except to make slight corrections. To an outside eye, they would have appeared motionless, as though hanging there by invisible wires, an elaborate mobile in a small boy's room.

"Pacer one to Pacer group. We are twenty miles from target. Descending to six thousand." The leader's voice sounded through Halloran's headset.

"Roger, Pacer one," he acknowledged. "Descending to six thousand."

He was already easing forward on the stick as he spoke, and they began to descend through the clouds again. The windows were blank for a few moments; then the plane spurted out under the ceiling of cloud.

Halloran felt the familiar squeeze of tension, that excitement spiced with fear he experienced on all bombing operations. His senses became acute as adrenaline flowed. The almost physical sensation of his mind growing colder and sharper was enjoyable. Peak alertness. It was impossible to be more alive.

The airplane shook violently with the sound of the first explosion. A puff of black smoke appeared outside the windows, then another, and then a series. The shock of them shifted the plane straight up a few feet, like hitting an air pocket in reverse.

"Hey!" Cimino's pained voice carried up. "They're shooting guns at us."

"Pacer one to group. Maintain position. We are ten miles from target." The leader sounded like he was directing a line at a hot-dog stand.

Low booms resounded, beating an increasing tempo all around them, a drum solo in quadraphonic.

The antiaircraft fire was now so heavy it was difficult for one pilot to see another plane. In the nose cone, Cimino was trying to fix the approaching target on his bomb sight.

"Somebody forgot to tell the Germans they're only supposed to have light to moderate flak today," he complained, refocusing and pressing a switch, before reporting, "Bomb bay open."

The formation was becoming ragged, but all the bomb-bay doors had swept open. The aircraft to the right was hit. It shuddered upward as part of its oversized tail broke apart in flames.

"Dick Lennard!" A second of pain in Halloran's consciousness was guillotined by the need to concentrate on the job ahead, on getting through.

Lennard's plane was out of control, zigzagging. Then the nose pointed earthward. The plane tumbled downward, flames streaking behind it. Out of sight.

Eight miles from target.

There was a violent bombardment, rocking the two pilots forward as the plane banked sharply to the right. It was hit. The starboard engine belched thick black smoke. Halloran fought to regain control, his brain directing with robotlike precision.

"Feather number one."

Next to him, Hyer was gaping out of his window at the big burning fourteen-cylinder engine right beside him. At the sound of his captain's voice, he reached for the switch automatically. The propeller stopped spinning and came to rest.

He took a deep breath before confirming, "Number one feathered."

"Let's turn the hell back," yelled Cimino from below.

Halloran could just see the lead plane, surrounded by black smoke, ahead.

"How far is the target?" he queried.

"Five miles," Cimino answered. "Let's turn the hell back!"

"He's right," put in Hyer.

"We'll have to slow down to two hundred," Halloran pointed out.

Hyer groaned. "We'll be sitting ducks at that speed."

He glanced out at the dead engine beside him, wavering with indecision.

Through the glass nose Cimino could see the puffs of smoke coming straight at him. They seemed soft and unreal, but he was not fooled.

"We're going to get our asses shot off," he wailed.

"How far from the target?" Halloran's voice demanded again.

"Three miles." Cimino looked upward in wild appeal to a hidden listener. "Am I the only one who's not crazy here?"

Halloran grinned at the controls. "Hey, Cimino. You ever take a good look at Hyer?"

"I've seen him naked, if that's what you mean," came the answer.

"No," retorted Halloran. "Take a look at him sometime. Hey, Hyer. How rich are you?"

The copilot swung around, forgetting to be scared in a moment's indignation. "What kind of question is that?"

"He's rich . . . and blond . . . and really neat," Halloran summed up into his mouthpiece. "If there's a God, he doesn't spend all that time making someone neat like Hyer, and then let him do something messy, like die in an airplane. So, as long as we're in the same plane as Hyer, God will have to figure out another way to get us."

"I'm messy enough to take Hyer down with me," retorted Cimino, unimpressed and doom-ridden. Then he yelled, "We're over the target! We're over the target . . . and the wing's gonna fall off. Now drop the goddamn bombs and let's get out of here."

"A few more seconds," the pilot maintained.

"You son of a bitch! We're over the target! The engine's gonna fall off," Cimino was screaming.

Halloran stayed cool. "Hey, chief. What do you think?"

Above them, Sergeant Lucas was watching out for enemy aircraft through the dorsal turret. The curly hair on the back of his hand was damp with sweat, but his answer was steady.

"I think it'll hold out, sir. You want to wait . . . I'm with you."

"Terrific. We got Sergeant York on the plane," lamented Cimino. "I hate you, Lucas. Goddamn it. Let me drop the goddamn bomb. We're over the target. I swear it!"

Flak was tossing the plane around like a toy; the whole structure was beginning to vibrate. Hyer looked glassy, staring at the black smoke from the engine. Halloran could see it too, from the corner of his eye. Deliberately he turned his head enough to block it out.

"My guess is you may be sighting just a little bit early—because you think the wing's gonna fall off," he drawled to his bombardier. "So I'm going to wait just a few more seconds."

"If anyone is interested, I hate Lieutenant David Halloran," Cimino ground out. "What's your serial number?"

"057327969."

"Serial number 057327969," repeated Cimino's voice with venom.

"For God's sake . . ." Hyer sounded shaky. "Let him drop the bombs."

"If we don't hit the stupid target now, we'll just have to come back again," Halloran explained patiently.

"Okay, okay," Cimino shouted again. "Now we're *really* over the goddamn target."

"Drop them!" ordered Halloran.

The bombs fell. He banked sharply, stuttering up through the cloud, jolting into the safe blue above. A few shells exploded harmlessly on the surface of the shining white ocean of cloud below, leaving small black humps of smoke, which soon sank back to the hell beneath, where they belonged.

The wounded plane began to limp home.

"Jesus. I hate these things," murmured Cimino.

There were regular missions over the next two weeks. Halloran and his crew seemed to spend almost as long in their B-25 as in their bunks.

The Mitchell was an efficient, adaptable machine, with particularly good handling characteristics, for which he often sent telepathic messages of thanks to North American Aviation, as it roared them up to safety at 1,110 feet a minute. He even began to feel affection for it.

Cimino suffered no such reversal. His hatred of the airplane remained implacable and was expressed with vitriolic fluency on every flight.

They were all bonded, both as a team and as men, by a shared schizophrenic life, which veered crazily between imminent destruction at six thousand feet and longevity at sixteen thousand.

At night they drank hard, roaring around Stevenage, where the two second lieutenants womanized in their individual styles—Hyer initially appealing to higher, finer feelings, and Cimino adopting a much more basic approach.

Until the night in Hanover Street, Halloran had taken an equally active part in this assault on the susceptibilities of Britain's females. Now the face of the Englishwoman he had met at the bus stop haunted him constantly, clear as a photograph over his bunk each night, slightly shadowed during the day, and disappearing only during those frenetic games with his own mortality. In his mind, they met and mated, married, returned home to the States, had kids, and grew old together during those two weeks.

Then it was the day. A borrowed jeep was secured, after the donation of a couple of bottles of Scotch encouraged the transport duty sergeant to turn a blind drunk eye. Halloran was on his way before dawn, rattling through the black town and singing at the top of his voice down the empty roads to the capital. By eight A.M. he was bounding across the oval gardens of Hanover Square.

The sun was shining one of those bright spring yellows. Hanover Street had been tidied up, the holes in its tarmac filled with new light-colored cement. It looked like someone's favorite pair of old pants, patched and patched, until it was hard to tell which was the original material. Thin, slatted boards had been hammered across the gap where the bay window of the little tea shop had been, and the bedroom furniture had gone from that exposed second-floor room. There was still a faint oil and carbon stain where the bus had burned, but no one even looked down as they walked over the spot where the middle-aged volunteer nurse had died on the pavement.

Halloran strode toward the Oxford Street end, his jacket open, the khaki shirt neatly pressed, and the silver first-lieutenant bars glinting on the collar. If someone had told him it was cold, he would not have believed it.

The street was filled with people, and the bus pulling up was bright and shiny. London had washed away that other day, and even rinsed off the suds.

He crossed to the doorway where they had sheltered. It had been swept clean, and thick beams nailed together formed a protective arch. He could almost smell her scent in the recess, and sat down on the steps to remember that evening and wait.

A second butt joined the one by his feet, and he lit a third cigarette and stood up. An hour had passed. His right leg had fallen asleep. He walked to the square, hesitated by the shrubs charred by the bombing, considered crossing the diagonal path of the garden, changed his mind, turned around, and slowly returned to the doorway, to lean against the side of the building and look up and down the street. After another few minutes he buttoned up his jacket, sat down on the steps again, and drew deeply on the cigarette.

By ten o'clock the pile of cigarette butts had grown. He crumpled an empty package, the cellophane making a crackling noise. He unwrapped a second pack, took out a cigarette, and lit it, exhaling the smoke in a way that showed it did not taste good anymore.

By now he knew every inch of the motley buildings of Hanover Street, from the diamond merchant's tucked behind a porch at one end, to Davies and Son, impressively and mysteriously "By Appointment to His Majesty George V," at the other.

He had examined the statue in the square, of "William Pitt, died MDCCCVI," and pondered on the incomprehensible Roman numeral. Business at the Grand Banqueting Suite must be down, he guessed. One egg, a quarter of butter, and two rashers of bacon did not make a weekly blowout, even with the imaginative addition of a tin of sardines. But there was nothing about the place to suggest that glamorous crowds of bright young things had ever stormed its dingy brown entrance before the war. Business had probably never been better.

A figure in voluntary nurse's uniform turned the far corner and began walking toward the doorway. Halloran jumped to his feet, stamping out the cigarette.

His whole body changed from watchful glumness to anticipation. The woman came closer, then turned into a stationery shop.

The curl disappeared from the corners of the lieutenant's mouth. He slumped down on the steps again and lit another cigarette. It tasted no better than the one before.

By noon his face had frozen into an expression of weary stubbornness. Hands in pockets, he was shifting from one foot to the other, plainly cold. The clear early morning had been defeated by solid gray cloud.

He had been counting the bricks in the wall, when a chilling breeze scattered the pile of ashes by his feet. Absently he watched one of the cigarette butts roll off the sidewalk and onto the street. All at once he was not cold anymore. There was no reason for it. He was simply staring at the CAM of CAMEL printed on the paper of the lifeless cigarette when, suddenly, he was not cold anymore. His face was different. He could feel the change. He glanced up.

She was at the bus stop, looking down the street at him there in the doorway and clutching her purse in both hands for something to hold. The uncertainty in her eyes was visible, even from that distance.

He started forward. At first, she did not move, just stood there. Then she began to walk to him, slowly. But she was the first to break into a run, and Halloran was not far behind. They met halfway.

She was in his arms, her head burrowing under his chin, just like before. Except that it was not just like before. It was different. Halloran's eyes closed in relief.

3

"A half of beer, please," she said as they walked into the pub.

Halloran decided to try that too, but thought he had better order a pint. It looked inviting in the heavy, dimpled glasses, and he raised his to her, with an openly appreciative gaze, which made her color and appear slightly flustered. Flat, lukewarm liquid filled his mouth.

"Christ!" It was like drinking dishwater. Laughter exploded from her, crinkling her eyes and tossing back her head to reveal a long and graceful neck. Halloran wanted to lean forward and kiss its warm, creamy surface in front of everyone. Her laugh was infectious, causing people at the bar to turn around and smile along, too. He tried again, taking another gulp and choking over the unbelievable substance, which successfully destroyed all romantic impulses.

A shout went up from a group of sailors in the far corner, as the bartender put a loaded tray of full pints down on their table. The lieutenant watched in disbelief as each man seized a glass and emptied it with huge, bull-like swallows. He shook his head and turned back to the Englishwoman, to see her do much the same, but with more delicacy.

"I give up," he said, raising his hands in surrender before returning to the bar for a large Scotch.

As he waited for it, he could see her reflection in

35

the mirror, her skin faintly luminous and eyes blue
and shining in the dim room. She was wearing a soft
green dress with a white jacket, and the other city
women in their brown and gray utility garments
looked pathetically drab alongside.

"You've been dealing on the black market," he
accused, sitting beside her again. "No one wears
clothes like that these days."

"It's true," she confessed, glancing furtively around
the crowded bar. "I confess all. I am Madam X, head
of Contraband Inc., and I illegally smuggled this
frock into London in 1938."

"Fifty percent of the action, or you finish up in a
serge suit," threatened Halloran.

"Oh, no! Not that! Not a serge suit!" Her hands
flew to her face in alarm.

"A serge suit!" he insisted ruthlessly.

"You win, Al," she said, lifting her glass and waving toward his almost full pint of beer. "Let's drink to
it in our national drink."

The pilot squinted. He knew when he was beaten.
"Okay. Okay. The partnership's dissolved. You're the
boss, but just leave my liquor habits alone."

She giggled, her glossy hair stirring against her
face. He reached out to catch a curl, and she rubbed
her cheek against his fingers in an instinctive feline
response to his touch. It was like coming home. Halloran took a deep breath of contentment and relaxed.

The waitress laid their lunch order down, then hurried to the next table. He looked at the steaming
food with interest and asked, "What is it?"

"You're not supposed to ask what anything is. Don't
you know there's a war on?" the Englishwoman repri-
manded.

"Right. I won't ask what it is, if you just tell me
what it is," he offered.

"Snook."

"Snook?"

"Snook."

"Oh, that snook." He nodded, and followed her example by attacking the unknown fish.

It turned out to be a booby trap of needle-sized bones baited with barely visible shreds of flesh. Halloran philosophically accepted that his relationship with this delicious lady was not going to be highlighted by appropriate experiences of gastronomic fulfillment. He finished the plateful manfully.

An hour later they were bouncing out of London in the borrowed jeep. The sun had returned and there was little traffic because the basic petrol ration for car owners was too precious to waste on inessential journeys. A few trucks, the occasional bus, and little flights of cyclists were all they passed as the jostle of houses thinned and finally ended where the hills of Kent began a gentle roll.

They drove by ancient oasthouses standing like dunces under their distinctive chimney caps in the middle of fields stuck with rows of poles. The American gave her an interrogative shrug.

"This is where they grow the hops," she answered with a mischievous grin. "For our national drink, you know. The oasthouses have kilns for drying the hops."

He put his arm around her and she rested her head on his shoulder. The village went by, whitewashed and old-world as a calendar picture.

He slowed down as the road climbed through an overhanging wood. Daffodils grew in clumps along the grass verges, and as a clearing opened up, he stopped the jeep and climbed out, lifting her over the side before she had time to step down.

Last year's leaves were luxuriously thick under their feet, covering a springy loam built up over half a century of autumns. Beech trees rose massively from it, to open into arabesques of branches over their heads, and pale green flags were beginning to unfurl from the pointed buds disguised as brown twigs. A gray squirrel darted out of a hole in a tree trunk and stared at them sleepily. The Englishwoman was delighted.

Halloran felt like he was back in high school and wanted to do handstands and shoot goals and beat records and get engaged to her on graduation day.

Soon they were clambering up a steep incline, the woman leaning back on his hand and panting a little with the exertion. Suddenly the trees ended and they were at the top, with the whole of the south of England beneath them. Fields of the greenest grass in the world; woodlands still pale dun from winter life suspension, with only transparent mists of green betraying the faltering emergence of spring foliage; soft brown acres patterned by the plow—all threaded together by countless miles of hedgerows in startling cubism.

The country from the sky always appeared one-dimensional, but the view from this hill was alive with the voluptuous folds and textures of the land swelling to the distant Sussex Downs.

They had spoken very little since leaving London. The weather, of course, the countryside, the lighter aspects of his job and her job, some of their likes and dislikes; mundane subjects which did not matter, because words did not matter.

The voice of a man singing carried up from the farm below.

"When I was a little girl, I used to spend summers at my grandfather's," she said, gazing at the stone farmhouse and its cluster of shippens and barns.

"You worked on a farm?" Halloran looked across, surprised.

Her face was still flushed from the climb, but there was a polish and elegance which made it hard to imagine her laboring in the fields.

"I can milk a cow," she said proudly.

"You can milk a cow?"

"I can milk a cow." She nodded her head vigorously.

"With your very own hands?" He glanced skeptically at the oval scarlet nails.

"No, with my feet," she retorted defensively. "Why
do you find it so incredible that I can milk a cow?
Lots of people milk cows."

He thought about it, trying to picture her as the
adored grandchild of an old man on a farm like that,
in hot, peaceful summers, lifetimes ago.

"Did you ever milk a cow?" she was asking.

"I opened a bottle once," he admitted.

"Really?" Now she was dubious.

"Yes," he affirmed.

"By yourself?" she probed.

"With one hand," he boasted.

A lane led from the little farm, and his eyes followed its riverlike course for about a mile, until it
reached a village. On the edge of the village he could
see the thatched roof of an inn.

"Are you hungry? There's a place to eat down
there."

"I'm famished again," she replied eagerly.

"Good. So am I. I want some tea." He hauled her to
her feet. "Did I ever tell you I love tea?"

"No," she declared.

"Well, I do," he vowed. "I drink it all the time."

A heavy skeleton of timbers visibly supported the
white plaster exterior of the Tudor inn. The carefully
tended garden, massed with spring flowers, led to a
stream into which a willow tree trailed its flexible
branches. In such a place it was nonsensical to think
there was a world war going on, the only reminder of
that other face being the dirty jeep which had
brought them there.

The restaurant was small and beamed, containing
only six tables, on each of which stood a glass vase of
freshly cut flowers. At one end there was a deep
medieval fireplace with an inglenook and an iron basket full of great burning logs.

Halloran experienced that mixture of amazement

and glee that hits Americans in the presence of any object over two hundred years old. It was worth drinking tea just to sit in such a place, before such a fire. In fact, tea was the only possible drink.

A row of small china basins hung from the great timber running across the center of the low ceiling: Christmas puddings, heavily laced with brandy and hung there to mature since long before the war, the landlord explained. Each year the oldest had been taken down, eaten, and replaced by a newly made one. There must have been twenty-five of them, but none would be touched again until peace returned.

A comfortable-looking woman with an incomprehensible rural accent bustled in with sandwiches and cake, obviously made by herself.

As she left, Halloran's appetite vanished. He could feel tension growing, but tried to act casually, helping himself from the laden plates with simulated hunger. The Englishwoman did the same, avoiding his eyes and playing with morsels of sponge cake instead of eating them.

"This place looks like something out of a British movie." He glanced around with false cheerfulness.

"I was sitting in the garden in Hanover Square, behind the shrubs, for over an hour," she confessed unexpectedly, turning pink with embarrassment. "I was just watching you. I was afraid, so I just stayed where you couldn't see me."

He looked over with a rush of gentleness and asked, "Are you still afraid?"

"Yes." It came as a whisper. Her fingers nervously moved the crumbs on her plate into little heaps. "I wasn't, a few minutes ago . . . when we had something to do, like driving, or walking." The phrases came out in hesitant bursts. "Now I feel awkward again. I don't know what I'm doing here."

"Yes you do," he said with quiet insistence.

"Yes I do," she murmured back, still not raising her eyes.

"I'm not hungry anymore." He made it sound like a decision.

"Neither am I." She looked up at last, with that clear, strong, almost defiant stare he remembered from their first meeting.

The sun had dropped down the sky and sent its yellow glow directly through the lattice window by the time they climbed the stairs to the inn bedroom. Halloran closed the door, and they looked at each other without touching for a lingering minute. The shades of her husband, his squadron, their friends, passersby, and the rest of the world, which had accompanied them everywhere, were suddenly shut outside. They were alone and it was as if they had not really seen each other before.

The rays of light glinted in her dark hair, and her eyes glistened brightly. Halloran took her in his arms and they kissed a soft, long kiss, searching and promising.

She was so small, it was like holding a fantasy that might disappear if he opened his eyes. Her hands moved across his shoulders and the muscles of his back. They kissed again. It was not as soft a kiss as before.

Then they were lying on the quilted bed, with her hair sprayed on the white pillow. Slowly they undressed each other, with a kind of wonder, as though they had never seen the contours and hollows and silk, smooth planes of a human body before. The shoulder straps of her slip slid away, and it was as though he was seeing a woman's breasts for the first time.

He drew her closer, and her head tilted back. Their movements became fluid and wordless and possessive. Deep rhythmic breaths parted her lips. Her eyes were half-closed with a look he did not know, of unseeing hunger and abandon. She was only conscious that her life had been waiting for this moment with this man.

Outside the window, the light had turned deep ocher. A flock of airplanes flecked the sky with black dots as they headed across the Channel, soundlessly.

At last he drew the covers over her with unusual tenderness. She curled into the crook of his arm and rested a drowsy head on his chest. He felt joyous.

Halloran had always enjoyed women, their company and their bodies. They had been playmates in a good game, in which he had participated without much cheating. He could make them laugh, which scored more points than his good looks. He liked their shapely figures, neat walks, and incredible legs. High-spirited blonds with quick wits were his type.

One or two had managed to reach beyond this good-humored approach and convince him he was in love, by hovering about in his mind all the time and having qualities that stirred a certain protectiveness. Jennifer Mullen's great blue, shortsighted eyes had done it, and Anne Drucci's sadness after her brother died, and Kate Kennedy, because she looked like a waif and had the fastest tongue since Dorothy Parker. Now he knew that none of them had lasted because it was not enough to love a pair of eyes, or a mood, or a defenselessness. It had to be the whole person, and the Englishwoman beside him was the first. He loved everything about her, even the things he did not know, even her angers and her failings. She was the part of himself that had always been missing.

He stroked her head, and she smiled dreamily. Happiness tingled in his muscles, and he let himself drift with her.

Then the afternoon was gone and they were driving back in the jeep, still in a kind of trance. The night air blew coldly across the open windscreen and she tucked in behind his shoulder, trying to keep warm. For some miles they did not speak.

"Next Thursday," Halloran said at last. "I can get back next Thursday."

Minutes of dark countryside passed before she answered "Yes."

Only black walls and hedges marked the unnaturally dark villages on the way, and a heavy continuous rumble, drowning the noise of the jeep's engine, came from the allied bombers setting out on their nightly missions to Germany.

"What's your name?" Halloran asked.

She did not reply, but pushed her face closer to his shoulder.

"I bet your name is really Fred—and you're embarrassed," he teased, grinning.

The muffled headlights scarcely illuminated more than a couple of meters ahead, so Halloran could not take his eyes off the road to look at her, but he could feel her, warm through his jacket, and her scent of grass and love was the scent of the whole day.

"Hey, Fred ... I think I love you," he exclaimed.

She tightened her grip on his arm. "Yes," she agreed in a voice full of love.

Halloran went through the next few days in a daze, listening to briefings and lectures and going through all the right actions, both in flight and off duty. But he, himself, was in abeyance, waiting. It was as though he could no longer function fully without her.

The impact of the war receded, and with it, his trained hostility toward the enemy and his easy acceptance of official reasoning.

"Pacer one to group. We are twenty miles from target. Begin your descent. Bombs away at eight thousand."

It was Wednesday. The leader's voice droned in his right ear. He registered the words mechanically and pushed forward on the stick, taking the plane down through the clouds again.

Hyer was watching the altimeter and offering periodic readings as they descended.

"Fifteen thousand . . . twelve thousand . . . ten thousand . . ."

"Open bomb bays," ordered Halloran without much interest.

"Bomb bays open," confirmed Cimino.

The first burst of antiaircraft fire was low, causing only distant popping noises, but the second bursts were closer, creating a turbulence of their own, and the aircraft began to bounce in the choppy air. Halloran became sharply aware of his surroundings once more.

"They're shooting guns at us again," Cimino was shouting indignantly. "How come every time we fly over them, they shoot guns at us?"

"Because we drop bombs on them," Halloran pointed out succinctly.

The plane was lurching about in the buffeting of flak as though being flown by a drunk.

"They've no sense of humor," commented Cimino.

A burst of shells hit directly before the left wing, and the aircraft pitched violently. The bombardier, who was looking through the bomb sight, almost had his eye knocked out.

He glared through the nose cone and screamed down to the ground, "Can't you guys take a joke?"

The pilot was fighting hard to keep control.

"Nine thousand," Hyer gave the altimeter reading.

"Five miles from target," Cimino reported.

Flak used to be nothing more than an inconvenience to Halloran, but now there was a tension in him. He held the control tighter than before and blinked at every burst of fire.

"How many miles now?" He was impatient.

"Three miles."

"Altitude?"

"Eight thousand five hundred," Hyer responded, not used to Halloran's new manner. He was slightly puzzled.

He studied his captain and noticed the tightness around his mouth. The plane recoiled again.

"Hey, are they just shooting at me up front here? Or are you getting shot at too?" queried Cimino in aggrieved tones.

"Must be just up front." Hyer was carefully low-key. "It's quiet back here."

"Son of a bitch! I knew it," commented the voice in the glazed nose. "We're just about over target."

"Altitude," demanded Halloran.

"Eighty-three hundred . . . eighty-two hundred . . . eighty-one hundred . . ."

He listened to the readings and scanned ahead. Those bastards below were not going to stop him getting back.

"Cimino! Drop them!" he ordered suddenly.

Hyer stared at him in amazement. There was a stunned silence in the nose bubble before the bombardier's voice cracked over the question, "Now?"

Then, exuberantly, "Bombs away! Halloran, I love you. There is a God. There really is a God. Do you hear that, ladies and gentlemen? There is a God."

Halloran had already banked the plane sharply and was making for home, with Cimino still babbling vows through the right earphone of his headset.

"I'm going to church as soon as we get back . . . that's what I'm going to do."

Hyer could see small beads of perspiration forming on the captain's forehead.

"So I haven't been to church for a little while . . . so I missed a few Sundays . . ." Cimino's voice sounded in his ear, too.

Halloran was fixed straight ahead. He'd done it. He'd outwitted them. He was heading back to Thursday. Hyer could not take his eyes off him.

"It's only fifteen years since I've been to church. What's fifteen years in the infinite scheme of things, right?" Cimino's happy voice continued distantly behind the thoughts of both men, all the way back to base.

Another boy had died. The third in that ward in twenty-four hours. Of course they had all known he was going to die, but he had been sleeping quite peacefully half an hour previously. The next time the nurse looked, he was dead. He had served in the Army for four weeks when a bomb hit the camp. He was eighteen.

The nurse walked down the ward, drawing the curtains around each cubicle, then summoning an orderly with a hospital trolley. Her movements were carefully calm and unhurried, but the other patients knew the boy had died. By the time their curtains were pulled back again, his body would have gone and his bed been made up with a crisp efficiency to look as though he had never been there. No one would mention his name again.

Sitting in the tube on the way home, Margaret Sellinger felt drained. She had almost lost count of the number of soldiers she had watched die, yet she never grew accustomed to it. Each time was as painful and frustrating as the first. The past week of night duty had been a special strain, because humans, like all animals, preferred to die in the dark; and now, as she looked at each patient, she saw Halloran's face, and a new emotion—fear—was added to the burden of the rest.

Her head tilted to rest against the corner of the jolting carriage, and she closed her eyes, thankful to be arriving home too late to see Paul, who must have left already for the office. His searching eyes had often studied her, and she had sensed his anxiousness during the three weeks since that evening in Hanover Street, but she had been unable to meet his look.

It had never seemed possible to love two men at the same time, but now the woman discovered that it was. There was a sincerity and a vulnerability about her husband that was difficult to resist, and the only word to describe the quiet feeling she had for him was love—although completely different from the total commitment of her love for Halloran.

By the time the train stopped, her mind had wandered away from the pile-up of future problems and was dreaming of the next meeting with the American flier. She walked slowly up the garden-lined street and across the grass, without noticing either surroundings or neighbors until she reached the house.

The emptiness of it was like a physical slap. She faltered in the doorway before hurrying noisily to the kitchen to switch on the radio and clatter the dishes left from her husband's breakfast.

Ever since the train had taken their daughter, Sarah, to safety out of London two years ago, Margaret had lived stridently, in a hopeless attempt to overpower the childless silence. Even when the house was filled with friends, it still seemed empty.

There had been no hesitating over the decision to part with their only daughter. When the school had announced its intention of evacuating to a large house in Sussex, Margaret and Paul Sellinger had known, even without discussing it, that Sarah had to go, too. But not a day had passed since then without the memory of the little school party disappearing into the train packed with London's children, watched by crowds of smiling, waving, white-faced parents. A million children had left the city in three days, and although many had returned the following year, Margaret reminded herself as she went upstairs that there were still countless mothers living in empty houses just like hers.

The telephone rang.

"You weren't asleep, were you?" Paul's voice asked.

"No, just going to bed," she replied.

"How would you like to go to Sussex tomorrow?"

Her pulse skipped a beat.

"I've phoned the school," he was saying. "And we can take her out to tea."

"Oh, yes, Paul." She could feel her eyes smarting suddenly.

"There should be a train around nine," he went on. "So I'll meet you from the hospital."

The station was packed with men and women in uniforms of all ranks; units of soldiers carrying kit bags filing onto the troop trains; boisterous airmen in best blues hurtling from newly arrived trains, for a weekend's leave in the capital, a sprinkling of tall Americans and Canadians, mostly with good-looking girls on their arms; voluntary servicewomen in their severe felt hats, Wrens, smart in navy blue, and a few impeccable Polish officers. Uniforms outnumbered civilians by ten to one.

Paul bought newspapers and guided her through the crush to the platform. The train was only half an hour late, and as it drew in, he moved quickly ahead to secure a pair of corner seats. The rest of the compartment filled with soldiers and soon the corridors were packed with standing men, one or two still drunk from the night before.

"She said she wouldn't come without her friend. You know how it is," the cockney soldier next to Margaret was telling another.

"Yeah. Mine's got a sister that always tags along," replied his mate sympathetically. "So it was no go, then?"

"It was all go." The first winked back. "First I took 'em to the pictures, one on each side—to give me hands something to do. Then I took them to the pub, where they both got Mozart and Liszt on gin-and-limes. Bottle of Scotch on the way out, then home past the allotments, where, just by chance, it seemed a good idea to stop off in Uncle Alf's shed for a farewell snifter, and as I opened the door, both the little darlings just fell into me arms."

Margaret suppressed a smile and glanced over at her husband to see him doing the same. Their eyes met and her heart lurched painfully. He was an intelligent aristocratic-looking man, with light brown hair going slightly gray at the temples, the kind of Englishman who is always courteous and never raises his voice. People found that the more time spent in his company, the more attractive he became. Only a very mean-spirited man could have disliked Paul Sellinger.

The train stopped at all stations, and between them, chugged along at an unhurried speed, giving plenty of time to view the verdant April landscape, which reminded Margaret of Halloran and their day together in the country.

She and her husband spoke occasionally, politely passing over tea from the flask, and sandwiches and papers, and he inquiring if she would like the window open. Hating herself, Margaret was glad the compartment was full, with the active coming and going of servicemen covering the uneasy gaps between their words—although she could still sense his mind probing hers worriedly.

From Haslemere they took a local bus, which trundled through lanes turned into long green tunnels by overhanging branches and rhododendron bushes which brushed against the sides of the vehicle. An occasional break in the trees gave glimpses of the woods and downs of Sussex Weald, and once, a fallow deer started up from the bank to spring across their path and into the thicket at the other side.

Sarah was waiting at the end of the long school drive, and bundled onto the bus as it stopped, catapulting into her parents' arms with shrieks of excitement. Her mother hugged her hard, noticing with some sadness that, even in the few weeks since they had last seen her, the child had grown and looked a little older. The precious years of fun between the ages of six and ten, after babyhood and before rebellion, were being stolen from them. Sarah was eight years old, with pale blue eyes and straight blond hair bound in long pigtails, and the sophistication of a thirty-year-old. There was usually a fine line with little girls when you could not be sure whether they knew the effect they were having on you, Margaret thought to herself. But with her daughter there were no such doubts. Sarah knew the extent of her own impact exactly.

She established herself between them, still holding her mother's hand, and started the first of innumerable, excruciating jokes. Margaret watched her flirting with her father with happy amusement.

"What do you get when you cross a parrot with a tiger?"

"What do you get?" responded Paul.

"I don't know . . . but when he talks, you'd better listen."

The child was absolutely fractured with this, exploding into peals of laughter, which had the same infectious quality of her mother's and caused the busload of people to smile. Paul and Margaret groaned in unison.

"You think you're terribly funny, don't you?" Her father gave her a loving shake, and she nodded her head vigorously. "You're a wretched little girl."

She nodded again, still giggling. "If I am, it's your fault."

"Really?" He raised an eyebrow. "Why?"

"Mrs. Thomas said today that children are the reflection of their parents," she claimed, looking pleased with herself.

"Do you think that's true?" he asked.

"I don't know." Sarah looked thoughtful for a moment. "If it's true, why doesn't Dennis Caine have a mustache like his father?"

Dennis Caine was the swaggering ten-year-old who lived next door and upon whom Sarah had been fixated ever since he had pushed her off his bike during an Easter holiday.

"Maybe he's a reflection of his mother," Sellinger pointed out.

"She has a mustache, too," put in Margaret, and watched him cough in an unsuccessful struggle to maintain a dignified expression.

"Dennis calls his mother and father by their Christain names," Sarah was saying, looking from one to the other with calculating eyes. "I think that's a good idea."

"You do?" Her father looked down benignly, guessing what was coming.

"Yes," she said firmly. "I think I'm getting a little too old to keep calling you Mummy and Daddy."

"You don't call me Mummy and Daddy . . . you only call me Daddy," he retorted.

She took a swing at his arm with a small clenched fist. "I'm serious. I think that from now on I'll call you Paul."

"If that's what you would like," he replied tolerantly.

"Yes, Paul," she challenged with some daring. "That's what I would like." Then she turned to her mother. "And I think that from now on, I'll call you Margaret."

"I think I'll break your jaw," returned her mother evenly.

"I think I'll call you Mummy," Sarah backed down instantly.

Margaret cuddled her close, gave her a big kiss, and whispered, "For a short person, you're not bad at all."

The bus had stopped at last in the village. They piled out, chattering, into the high street, with its gabled Elizabethan houses, reminding Margaret of Halloran's fascination with the little Tudor inn. She tried continually to push the American flier from her mind, but he kept catching the unguarded moments, and only Sarah, swinging between them, was strong enough to replace him.

They crossed the market square to the hotel, going straight to the lounge with its chintz-covered armchairs and roaring fire. Two older girls in the school's distinctive brown Harris-tweed coats and velour hats were sitting at other tables with their parents, as this was one of the only two places to go during weekend visits.

The hotel somehow managed to retain a certain prewar flavor, with an elderly waitress in black dress and small white apron bringing fine china cups for tea. Through their regular visits over the past two years, she recognized the Sellingers and bent to whisper in Margaret's ear, "We've some Kunzle cakes, madam."

Sarah's sharp ears overheard, and she gave a great whoop. "Ooh Kunzle cakes! Yummee!"

The waitress looked slightly alarmed, and Margaret put a hand on the child's lips before nodding. "That would be lovely, thank you."

As they waited, Sarah drew lines with her finger in the deep brown wax of the coffee table and Margaret let herself sink back luxuriously into the deep chair.

"Judy Fox stole my key chain. You know, the one with the four-leaf clover on it?" the child was telling Paul.

"She stole it?" He gave her a searching look. "How do you know she stole it?"

"Well, I always carry it, and when I was changing after hockey, I couldn't find it," she explained. "Then, later, she had it."

Her father leaned forward to listen seriously, with a slightly baffled look on his face.

". . . And when I told her it was mine, she said she had always had it and that I wasn't the only one who had a four-leaf-clover key chain . . . and I know it's mine." His daughter was loudly peeved. "She's such a sneak. Everybody's supposed to be nice to her, just 'cause her father's died."

Margaret had been about to pour the tea, and paused, her eyes engaging Paul's for a fraction of a second. They had seen Bob Fox at the school Speech Day the previous summer. He had made an impressive-looking major, and his wife and young daughter had been so proud. Before the war he had been their lawyer.

"When did he die?" Sellinger asked his daughter.

"About two weeks ago. He was in Africa," Sarah replied briefly, before returning to the more important matter in her life. "She said it was her key chain, and it isn't."

It was good that she was too young to understand, Margaret thought, putting the special chocolate cake on her child's plate. But Sarah ignored it. She was looking at her father with the faintest shadow of uncertainty in her eyes.

"I'm glad you're intelligent," she said suddenly. "And you won't get killed."

"I'm in intelli*gence*. I'm not intelligent," Paul Sellinger smiled. "And you *should* be especially kind to Judy now."

His daughter jumped out of her chair and sat down on his lap, as Margaret watched her with growing apprehension.

"You won't die, will you, Daddy?"

"I thought you were going to call me Paul." He sidestepped lightly.

"Promise me," insisted the child.

So, she was not too young, after all. She really did know things no little girl should know. Margaret wanted to cry.

"I promise." Paul Sellinger gave the child a hug.

"And you will always love me," she insisted.

"I will always love you." He held up a hand as though taking an oath in the witness box.

"And you will always love Mummy."

"And I will always love Mummy." He looked toward Margaret, who dropped her eyes, holding her breath.

"Even when you're eighty," Sarah persisted.

He was still looking across. "I'll have to take my false teeth out of the glass and put them in to kiss you."

The fragile china cup slipped from Margaret's fingers and shattered on the polished wooden floor.

4

Thursday came and they were clinging together at last, kissing with a kind of desperation in the middle of the morning high tide of workers gushing along Oxford Street. The crowd pushed them to the wall, where they remained so fiercely locked together they were like one being. Halloran knew she could hardly breathe in his hold, but was incapable of releasing her, and he could feel her arms hard across his back as she pressed to him with all her strength.

For minutes they stood there, only conscious of having found each other again. Then gradually their limbs relaxed into indulgent playful movements and they were able to open their eyes and smile. There was a whole day ahead.

They strolled back to Hanover Square, arms still around each other like student lovers, and he lifted her easily into the jeep.

"Wouldn't you like to see London?" she wondered as they drove west from the city.

"This is Madison Avenue?" he queried sardonically, indicating the Victorian brownstones.

She laughed and curled up to his side. "I meant the sights of London. I thought all Americans wanted to see St. Paul's, Westminster Abbey, and Buckingham Palace."

Halloran, who had been in England for ten weeks without any feelings of deprivation at having missed

feeding the pigeons in Trafalgar Square, asked duti-
fully, "You want to show me around?"

"No," she admitted.

He put his foot down hard on the gas and the jeep
rattled from the bomb-cratered town.

At the outskirts, he slowed down to ask, "Where to,
Princess?"

"We could see the sea, if we go walking on the
Downs," she suggested.

The lieutenant skipped pointing out that he saw
the English Channel from his Mitchell at least three
times a week, and took the next main turning south.

After a few miles he drew into a lay-by to kiss her
softly and quickly, and then more slowly, keeping his
eyes open to watch emotion cross her face. When he
drew back a little, her mouth searched blindly for his,
and a moment of pure and loveless greed for her was
followed by instant protectiveness.

He kissed her forehead lightly and said, "It's your
turn to drive."

"I can't drive," she protested.

"If you can milk a cow, you can drive a jeep," he
insisted, vaulting over the side and bundling her, protesting, into the driver's seat.

For the next two hours they hiccuped in starts
and stops along the country roads and he watched
with teasing amusement as her expression changed
from terror into a self-congratulatory amazement as
their zigzagging progress mellowed into a compara-
tively smooth advance under her hands. They reached
a long, unbending stretch of asphalt. The wind was
coloring her skin and giving her hair a sinuous life of
its own.

"Right." Halloran shouted the challenge. "Faster."

She accelerated a little and grinned triumphantly.

"Go on! More!" he whooped. "Faster!"

That expression of bold defiance he knew so well
lit her eyes and she rammed her foot home. The jeep
gave a horselike leap forward and bucketed snorting

down the straight, not quite in control. Hedges un-
raveled from the small woodlands rolling across the
landscape, and a hill in the road sped toward them,
tossed them over its back, and was gone. She was
squealing, exhilarated by the speed, her knuckles
showing white against the steering wheel. Halloran
leaned back in his seat, full of mischievous enjoyment
at the discarding of all that English decorum.

A tractor appeared suddenly from a field gateway
ahead. The jeep wavered in its mad career and began to skid as the woman pulled wildly at the steering. A ditch as wide as the Erie Canal opened up before them. Halloran wrenched the wheel back. There
was a screech of metal, and he caught a glimpse of
the slack-mouthed country face on the tractor as they
eeled past in a cloud of burning rubber.

"Foot on the brake, honey," he instructed coolly.

"I don't know where it is." She had gone very
white.

"Middle pedal, baby."

The jeep jolted to a halt and stalled.

She took a deep breath, swallowed, released her
hands from the wheel and composed them on her lap,
then gave him a wide-eyed stare. Without a word
he climbed onto the road, walked around to open
the nearside door, lifted her out, carried her back
around the vehicle, and dumped her in the passenger
seat.

She maintained an air of ruffled dignity throughout. It was too much for Halloran, whose chuckles
exploded into yells of laughter, and, taking her in his
arms again, he felt her shaking with the same suppressed merriment.

It was raining when they reached the Downs, and
a brisk southerly wind was blowing off the sea, which
lay like a cold gray slab below. He raised a questioning eyebrow and glanced hopefully toward a coastal
village sheltered under the arm of the hills, but Margaret had already jumped onto the damp grass and

moved off, drawing the strong, fresh air in long sighs of relief at escaping from the city and the war.

He caught up, and their hands clasped. The Downs ahead were stark as moors, the sky turning turf and trees to a blue green which echoed back, so that they seemed to be moving in blue air. Lakes of mist filled the valleys below, the tops of clumps of trees showing through as islands.

Halloran and Margaret did not notice the rain as they walked, holding hands at first, then slowing to put arms around each other's waists and fitting their sides together with gentle pressure. He helped her over a wooden stile, and all at once, accepting an unspoken challenge, they began to race toward the copse ahead.

Halloran slipped on the wet ground and fell flat on his behind. The woman stood over him, gurgling with laughter as he glared up. He grabbed her ankle and pulled, and she pitched forward, grasping helplessly at the air for balance, to tumble onto him.

Their faces were wet and her scarf had slipped back so that soaked hair was streaked across her cheek. They kissed on the ground, rain falling on their lips. She licked the droplets of water from his face, and he raised himself on one elbow to curve her under him. Her breasts were firm under the cotton blouse, as she lay with one bare leg straight and the other drawn up against his thigh. He caressed her ankle and traced over the slim arch of her calf, and ice-cold darts of rain splashed the warm damp skin under his hand. His gaze scanned her face, and she stirred and searched his mouth hungrily, her eyes wide open and insistent. They made love like starving creatures.

There was an anguish about it, almost as though each was taking revenge against the bloody world by savaging the other's body, by raping each other, she as much as he. When it was over, she was sobbing.

For a long time they comforted each other, Halloran stroking her mud-streaked face and she touching the scratches on his forearm with faltering fingers. The rain had stopped, but water still dripped from the branches above, and the earth smelled tangy and clean. They knew it would never happen like that again. The diseased tissue of war had been cauterized.

Spring exploded over England like a fireworks display, with multicolored eruptions of flowers and blossoms and leaves destroying the muted green and brown winter camouflage, against all military orders.

Girls began to appear in bright prewar clothes, cleverly altered to the short-skirted, snappy style of the times, and with the arrival of the singing, nesting birds, the invasion was complete. Only one location remained impregnable. Spring did not get past the guards at the U.S. Army Air Force base in Hertfordshire. Even if it had, the acres of galvanized iron and newly laid concrete would have ensured it did not stay. There were no married quarters, with their accompanying pots of daffodils and geraniums, and the windowsills on the office building had been built on a slant to ensure that no female clerk put into practice any ideas about window boxes.

The sky was blue, the sun was shining, but the interior of the briefing hut was as chilled as it had been when they first arrived in midwinter. Halloran eyed the cold hot-water pipes bleakly. It was his conviction that Colonel Bart had chosen this hut specifically for its arctic temperature, in the misguided belief that sustained physical hardship produced ferocious fighting men.

Bart stood carefully within the circumference warmed by the small heater strategically kept on the platform. He surveyed the freezing air crews with obvious satisfaction.

Patsy, the office girl back home, had once taken a movie of him escorting the company president around the plant. The president had clapped him on the shoulder before departing. It had certainly been a milestone, and the colonel wished there were some way of having a movie made of himself addressing his men. The Army sometimes made educational films.

He drew up to full height, in case any hidden cameras were trained on the platform, and announced, "We're going back to Rouen today."

There was a mass groan from the men.

Cimino, looking even more debauched than usual, though no one could imagine how or why after a night out in Letworth, which was staunchly teetotal and refused to harbor a single bar, whispered to Halloran and the rest of the crew, "I think I'm going to be sick."

"We have reason to believe that the krauts are sending a trainload of ammunition from Rouen south," Bart was detailing, tracing the black railroad line across the map of France with his pointer. "Now, they're gonna be expecting us, so it's not going to be easy. We figure we're gonna get heavy flak."

"I'm definitely going to be sick." Cimino moaned, rolling his eyes.

The colonel wheeled around from the board and looked in their direction through slit eyes. "Halloran, you fly lead. Ritt, you fly second lead." He rocked back on his heels, causing a pronounced paunch to strain against the belt of his jacket, and inhaled. "Now, we got cloud cover from eight to ten thousand, scattered clouds from ten to fifteen thousand. You'll make the drop at six thousand. I know what it's gonna be like—so be careful."

"He knows what it's gonna be like." Halloran shot a glance heavenward and muttered hoarsely, "He flew a hundred missions over Lackland, Texas—and he knows what it's gonna be like."

There was a snickering among the men around him, and the colonel stiffened almost imperceptibly.

"We should have a five-to-ten-mile visibility below

eight thousand," he continued after a pause. "The approach should be from south to north."

"You gotta hand it to him," Halloran whispered *sotto voce*. "Nobody ever took Texas while he was there."

There was muffled laughter. Bart rubbed the side of his nose in a subconscious gesture which revealed his annoyance. The laughter had scuttled off like a rat, leaving only a few telltale imprints of smiles. Bart knew that Halloran was the cause of it, yet he could not catch him in the act. His face reddened.

"Takeoff is at 0830. Good luck, men." He spoke with mechanical rapidity. "I wish I could be going with you. Dismissed."

There was a loud scraping of chairs against the bare floor as the men stood up and began to troop out.

"Lieutenant Halloran . . ." Bart called. "I would like to speak to you for a moment."

Halloran stopped in the doorway, flanked by Hyer and Cimino, and deliberately kept his back to the colonel for a long moment.

"Take it easy with him," his blond copilot murmured nervously. "Don't say anything you'll regret later."

"Don't take it easy with him. Say something you'll regret later," was his bombardier's eager advice. "Maybe we'll get grounded."

The lieutenant turned and faced Bart, who was striding up the aisle between the chairs and stepped past without looking at them into the camp quadrangle, forcing Halloran to follow. They returned salutes to a group of rigidly marching other ranks headed by a drill sergeant.

The colonel's office was one of a row with windows overlooking the runway. It was a large, rather Spartan square with gray walls lit from overhead by two hanging white globes. Bart gave himself the protection of an oversized Army-issue brown wooden desk before gesturing to the pilot, still standing outside, and telling him to close the door.

Halloran did not quite lean against the wall, but waited in a lanky slouch that could not have been confused with standing to attention.

The colonel picked up a pencil and began toying with it thoughtfully before looking up and putting on a painfully friendly expression.

"Sit down, Halloran."

The lieutenant eyed the two dark green armchairs and then slumped onto the matching couch in obvious discomfort. There was a heavy silence before Bart cleared his throat and showed yellowed teeth in an attempted smile, which stopped before it reached the corners of his mouth.

He began with what he hoped was a penetrating and significant glance. "You know, in every group of men there is always one man the others look to for leadership . . ."

Straight from the textbook. Halloran studied the veins on the back of his hand.

The colonel persevered. "In this group, you happen to be that man. If you set a good example, others will follow."

Sounds of the mechanics making the last checks on the line of aircraft outside carried through the thin walls. The natural leader gazed studiously at the ceiling, shifting his feet, obviously uninspired. The colonel's breathing rate increased slightly and his head thrust forward, turning the glued-on grin into a threat, which belied the paternalism of his words.

"You have the makings of a fine officer. You could go far. Very far."

He paused expectantly, but on receiving no response, added with some edge, "It's your attitude that concerns me."

The flier had deliberately shifted his stare to a photograph of the colonel standing next to an airplane, and betrayed no sign of having heard a word.

"Do you understand what I am saying?" Bart grated aggressively.

"No, sir." The lieutenant remained indolent and expressionless.

Bart's control gave way with a snap, and he sprang to his feet and across the floor to bulge over Halloran. "I don't like you either, buster," he snarled through a mouth now twisted with hatred. "Just stop crapping around in the briefings. Understand?"

"No, sir," replied Halloran, eyes fixed lifelessly ahead.

"What do you mean 'no'?"

"I mean, sir, I don't understand, sir. What crapping around, sir?" the pilot responded flatly.

The colonel felt rage welling up like red ink behind his eyeballs. "You're a wise-ass. You even say 'sir' like a wise-ass," he spat.

"How should I say 'sir,' sir?" asked Halloran, deadpan.

"I'm gonna get you. That's what I'm gonna do," yelled the colonel, sending out spots of saliva. "You blink the wrong way, and I'm gonna nail you. Do you understand?"

"Yes, sir." Halloran's eyelids drooped. "You're gonna nail me."

"Get the hell out of here!"

Halloran climbed to his feet, stood at attention before the colonel, saluted, did an about-face, and left.

When he reached his aircraft, Hyer was standing under the wing with Cimino, who looked vaguely disappointed to see his pilot approaching without an escort of M.P.'s. It shattered his dream of the entire crew being implicated and shipped home to be court-martialed for insubordination—or even mutiny.

"You okay?" Hyer asked the lieutenant.

Halloran nodded and began to inspect the port landing gear.

"What did he say?" His copilot was curious.

"He said he didn't like my attitude," Halloran

summed up briefly, then crouched down and called over to Lucas, "Did you check this gear?"

"Sure, I checked it, sir," the sergeant responded, coming over to kneel beside him.

Halloran crawled under the belly of the aircraft and inspected the bomb bays and then the starboard gear. A puzzled look crossed Hyer's face. Halloran was growing more meticulous with every flight, and it made the second lieutenant nervous.

"I checked all of them—like I always do," Lucas was saying with a defensive note in his voice.

"Tire pressures?" Halloran queried.

"They're fine, sir. Is anything the matter?" Lucas scratched his ear and looked slightly irritated. "You've never done this before."

"Check them again," the pilot ordered, standing up to examine the nose gear.

Lucas' mouth tightened as he rummaged in his tool bag for a pressure gauge and knelt down by the tires again.

Halloran was aware of the crew watching him watching the sergeant. He was also aware that they were confused. He was confused, too, by subliminal images of wheels jamming and tires blowing and engines failing and propellers dropping off and the Mitchell spiraling to earth in flames, which left him edgy as a broken bottle.

He was tempted to return and double-check the bomb bay, but instead reached up to grip the floor of the aircraft, and effortlessly pulled himself through the belly hatch.

Hyer followed, and Lucas stared after them before raising surprised eyebrows at Cimino, wondering where the unshakable flier they all knew and loved had gone. But the bombardier was delighted.

"Boy, I really like his attitude. I really like it," he crowed, as he stretched into the belly hatch and took hold. "That's one fine attitude." He beamed down at Lucas. "Really fine."

Pulling himself up, he banged his shoulder against the opening again.

"Shit!" he swore loudly, wondering how the other guys always managed to hoist through without trouble.

Shared danger had developed an emotional shorthand in the air crew, which made certainty and boldness essential in their captain. Halloran's unexpected loss of both qualities left them all feeling uneasy.

On the other hand, the same reaction to their affair made Margaret Sellinger a better nurse. Both she and the American needed to defeat death, and she became even more painstaking and caring than before, with a tenderness toward every injured serviceman that stemmed directly from her love.

But her attempts to maintan normality at home were a complete failure. Paul Sellinger loved his wife and knew her every gesture and expression as well as he knew his own. They had always enjoyed a relaxed and happy relationship. Then, suddenly it had been like living with someone whose real presence was a thousand miles away. Although she went through all the motions and said the right things, he knew she had not been living with him for weeks.

Spring was overtaken by a glorious summer. Halloran and Margaret met every two weeks in Hanover Street and spent the day on a charmed, war-free island of picturesque villages and old-fashioned civility. They walked the soft hills of the Cotswolds and wandered through the New Forest, where the herds of small wild ponies still ran free. They visited ancient churches and glorious cathedrals and stately homes and ate in timber-framed restaurants full of polished brass and dark oak.

Halloran was entranced. He had never believed the publicity picture of Britain as a toy country full of quaint buildings and country folk smiling at garden gates, and arriving in London among people suffering the obscenities of war with such pigheaded endurance had confirmed that this was no picture-postcard place. But the Thursday road from Hanover Street led to another country, older and infinitely civilized. It was like making a time journey and discovering at the end of it his own roots in a place full of manners and customs outside his known experience, which, nevertheless, jogged his subconscious and seemed familiar.

The woman was so much a part of this other England, with a style unattainable elsewhere. Halloran got a real kick out of her natural courtesy, the unstudied elegance, and the way she fitted so perfectly with historic settings and country backgrounds. He even adored the extreme reserve in her which still kept her name a secret from him.

Yet there was a contrasting impulsiveness about her revealed in those occasional rebellious looks and when she made love. Sometimes she was like a kid accepting dares. Halloran would watch her drinking tea in that carefully controlled English way, and then she would laugh, suddenly, without restriction, lifting her shoulders, throwing back her head and showing her tongue between small, even white teeth. It was like loving two women, like being in love with England itself.

"I've arranged a surprise," she announced in that precise accent.

It was August and they were driving along the route they had taken on their very first outing to Kent. She was wearing sandals and a bright blue dress. His discarded jacket lay alongside hers on the back seat of the jeep. It was very hot.

All road signs had been removed in order to confuse invading troops or spies, and he ruffled her hair as she navigated. They got lost a couple of times, but eventually stopped at a small garage, where she had a hurried conversation with a boy of about twelve, who brought out a pair of rickety bicycles from a shed.

"That'll be two shillings each, sir," he said apologetically to Halloran.

The lieutenant peered across at the woman. "You expect us to ride these things?"

"No, they're just for pushing," she retorted, fixing a packed basket to one before mounting and circling the jeep.

Halloran, who believed pedal power was strictly for Fats Waller's large-footed broads, stumbled as he climbed down from the jeep.

"What's that?" Margaret swerved to a stop, staring.

"Flier's knee," he murmured. "Just happens in hot weather."

"Oh, too bad," she responded sweetly. "You obviously won't manage the jeep back, so I'll have to drive."

It was an unfair threat. Her driving had not improved. Halloran took over the second bike and swung onto its cracked leather saddle without a word. The boy backed behind a petrol pump as he wobbled across the forecourt and onto the road.

She had already made a kingfisher swoop down the lane and was disappearing around the first corner. Halloran labored after her, wondering how he had got into this. What had happened to that sophisticated New York world of cabs and subways? Of all women, why had he picked the one beautiful nut who insisted on frog-marching him through wind and rain, and driving like a Keystone cop, and who could imagine no better way of spending a summer afternoon than riding around on a bone-shaking deathtrap?

He rounded the corner, to be confronted by a hill. She was already at the top and had stopped to turn and gloat. The bike squealed in protest with every revolution. The sun blazed. A drop of sweat ran down his hairline and into his ear.

He pedaled furiously, skimmed over the top, and shot down the other side, with wild cowboy yodels, as he caught up with her and passed. The lane wound down through orchards already hung with red apples. Halloran lifted both feet off the pedals and swung his legs. He checked at the next corner. The bike went sailing on faster than before. Brakes had apparently not been included in the two-shilling hire fee. He took the next turning in racing style at an angle of sixty-five degrees. At the T junction ahead, there was little choice between the stone wall dead ahead and the sheet of water just to the right of it. Halloran chose the river.

The bike leapfrogged off the road, shied across the rough grass, kicked up its back wheel, and chucked him into the water.

When Margaret arrived, her face was shiny with tears. Halloran would have played half-drowned to extract maximum sympathy if the first glance had not shown she was crying with laughter. Throwing her bike down next to his, she collapsed on the grass, shrieking and tossing about helplessly. The bright blue skirt of her dress had ridden up the long brown legs. The American leaped out of the river and flung himself over her.

"Why didn't you just push me off Westminster Bridge—it would have saved the drive?" he yelled, shaking her.

She opened her eyes and caught a sight of his dripping face again. "You'd have missed the bike ride," she gasped, before twisting away with another ecstatic howl.

Halloran picked her up bodily and strode to the water's edge. She was still abandoned with hysterics, eyes closed and muscles limp. He crouched down on the bank, kissed her firmly, and dropped her in. She surfaced, gulping, with long green weeds trailing from her hair and down her arms, and still laughing.

"Help me!" she pleaded, choking, and he held out a hand.

She took it with both hers, gave a great wrench, and hauled him into the river with her, and slithered out of his grasp. By the time he shook the water out of his eyes, she had taken off the blue dress and thrown it onto the bank. Bra, panties, and sandals followed and she dived like a seal downstream to where the willows made a sheltering arch over the water.

Halloran had often wondered about lovemaking in the water. He stripped, too, and followed—and discovered it was easy.

Their clothes dried quickly as they ate the picnic she had packed in the basket, and afterward they dozed in each other's arms in the sun.

When the afternoon lengthened, they climbed onto the bikes again and followed the river path. It led back to their favorite Tudor inn, just in time for tea.

And then a plum-colored sunset was glowing through the lattice window and they were in bed with their faces touching. Smoke curled upward to the ceiling from the orange tip of Halloran's burning cigarette. They lay together silently for a long time.

"Halloran," she said at last.

"Yes."

"I love you." She paused, taking a long, slow breath. "My name is Margaret."

At last it was true. They were going back to the States for a lifetime of skinny-dipping, and lethal driving, and that incredible English accent. He took a long drag at the cigarette and said, "No kidding?"

"No kidding," she answered.

"You love me," he stated.

"I love you," she confirmed.

The name itself began to curl around his mind. "Your name is Margaret." He liked saying it aloud.

"My name is Margaret," she echoed.

He drew on the cigarette again, thinking about it, tying it to her.

"Maggie. I like the name Maggie," he said, half to himself, then turned his head. "I love you, Maggie."

She kissed him, drawing fingers through his hair.

"Did you ever notice how some names seem to doom certain people?" Names had developed an unexpected fascination.

She shook her head.

"Well, they do. I've never met a gorgeous Beulah in my life," he pointed out. "Maybe she was gorgeous until she found out her name was Beulah."

Margaret kissed him again and giggled as she pulled a leaf out of his still-damp hair.

"How many handsome Mertons have you ever met?" he was asking.

She had never met any Mertons, or even heard of the name Beulah. She bit his lip, and he caressed her absently.

"Little pink babies named Harry—it just never seems to fit," he went on, obviously intent on the theme.

Margaret nuzzled his neck, half-lying across his chest to burrow into his shoulder. As her hand ran over his flat, hard stomach, he smiled to himself, unseen, and continued talking deliberately.

"Now, you take Hubert. Do Huberts become Huberts because their parents named them that? Or do their parents look at them through the window in the hospital and somehow or other figure they have Huberts on their hands?"

She raised her head to kiss him full on the mouth.

"I love you, Maggie," he said against her lips.

"I love you, Halloran," she whispered back.

They kissed with passion now, forgetting all about Beulah and Merton and Harry and Hubert, aware only of Margaret and Halloran.

The wide staircase swept from the foyer, dividing about halfway up, its polished banisters and hand-turned supports curving in opposite directions. Paul Sellinger took the right-hand flight, which led to a deeply carpeted paneled corridor. He paused in front of one of the brass-handled mahogany doors before walking in.

The captain seated in a maroon leather armchair gave him a shrewd-eyed look of recognition. His chief, Major Trumbo, was swiveling in the chair behind a vast desk that must have been born in that office. Nobody could ever have carried it up the stairs.

He waved Sellinger to another prominently placed leather chair and said, "I believe you've met Captain Lester?"

Sellinger nodded toward Major Trumbo, "Yes, sir, I have."

Trumbo leaned back and lit his pipe, puffing a herbal-smelling haze into the air. He was a trim man in his late forties, with all the neatness and detachment of a bank's senior vice-president. He closed his eyes for a moment, concentrating on the cool smoke in his mouth.

"New tobacco," he commented, the pipe still clenched in his teeth. "You like it?"

"Yes, it seems quite pleasant," Sellinger responded easily.

"Aromatic," commented the major, almost to himself, his glance following the little puffs of smoke as they slowly rose above him like signals. He had that pinkish baby skin that makes some men look as though they never have to shave.

A comfortable silence filled the room, before he seemed to give himself a mental shake and visibly straightened his shoulders, frowning.

"Bad business . . . very bad."

"I beg your pardon?" Paul Sellinger looked disconcerted.

Major Trumbo nodded toward the other captain, who clicked open a leather briefcase, drew out a sheaf of papers, and began to explain. "As you know, two months ago, one of your agents—Reed—was dropped in Lyons. Two weeks later he was killed."

Sellinger nodded gravely. It had been a considerable loss to the department. One of their best men.

"A month ago, you sent another agent in," Harold Lester continued.

"Forbes," confirmed Sellinger. "A good man."

"Quite." Lester was brisk. "Yesterday, we received word that Forbes was found dead."

The lines around Sellinger's eyes deepened slightly and he cupped a hand thoughtfully over his chin. The implications of the news were devastatingly apparent.

The floor-length faded velvet curtains over the windows were partially drawn against the sun. The room was impressive, obviously the office of a man in authority. Its magnolia-papered walls supported an ornately molded high ceiling and dwarfed the three men. No one spoke for a while, until Trumbo's chair creaked as he leaned forward.

"What do you think?" he asked.

"I trained both of those men. I knew them well—very well," Paul Sellinger asserted earnestly. "They are . . . they were not the kind of men to make mistakes." The look he gave his colleagues was heavy with emphasis. "Especially mistakes so glaring that they would be found out in just two or three weeks."

Trumbo puffed on his pipe, listening intently.

"There's a leak. There must be a leak somewhere," Sellinger declared. "The identity of those men must have been known before they were dropped. It would have taken that long just to find them."

Harold Lester watched Sellinger without expression. He was a tall, inflexibly stiff man, with a thin military mustache, which stretched in a horizontal line over a mouth that never smiled or drooped.

"There's a double agent here—fairly high up, I'd say," Sellinger was insisting. "That's the only explanation I can think of."

"I agree," Lester put in.

Major Trumbo flipped through a tidy heap of files on one side of the desk and drew a paper from one.

"The last communication we received from Forbes was that Gestapo headquarters in Lyons has a list of double agents in London," he said. "He was going to try to get that list. That's the last we heard from him."

He drew on his pipe again and grimaced, taking it out of his mouth and glaring at it.

"This stuff is bloody awful. It may smell good, but it tastes like hell."

The offending pipe was tapped noisily on a solid pewter ashtray until it released its contents in a shower of sparks and Trumbo's attention turned back to the two captains.

"Well, it's obvious we're going to have to send somebody in to get that list."

Captain Sellinger raised his eyebrows. "From Gestapo headquarters in Lyons?"

"That's where the list is," the major pointed out in matter-of-fact tones. "That's where our man will have to go."

A sensation of depressed lethargy overtook Paul Sellinger. Forbes had been an articulate, almost dashing man, with more than enough guts and cunning to have kept him alive.

"He had three children," he murmured. "Forbes."

Trumbo opened a desk drawer, took out an old leather pouch of tobacco, and began to refill his pipe.

Memories of Bob Fox and Reed and Forbes and a dozen other friends, colleagues, and neighbors who had vanished from his life recently, crowded Sellinger's thoughts.

"It's obvious we're going to have to do this differently this time," Trumbo was saying. "No one—I mean no one outside this room—may know about it. That means no one in G-2. No one in OSS. No one."

"Our man must not even transmit the list back—once he gets it," emphasized Lester. "He must make a copy of it and bring it back, without the Germans knowing about it."

"Who do we have?" queried Trumbo.

Lester consulted his notes. "I've narrowed the list to two. McCallum and Wells."

Trumbo turned to Sellinger. "What do you think? They're both your men."

Sellinger folded his arms. The conversation had brought his attention sharply back to the problem, and he narrowed his eyes to think about the two named men. "McCallum is excellent," he confirmed, mentally running over the agent's experience and character. "Except he's just returned from four months in France. I don't know if he is emotionally fit to turn right around and go back."

"What about Wells?" asked the major.

"He's worked in Germany, so he speaks the language perfectly. His French may not be quite as good."

It would be an almost impossible mission, demanding an exceptional man. In fact, only Forbes would have thought of it in the first place and might even have brought it off. Wells was not Forbes.

"I'm not totally sure. He's a little below McCallum in proficiency. However, he's in better shape."

"Lester?" The major looked across for comments.

"Can you make him more proficient?" asked the other captain.

"How much time do I have?"

"Not too much," replied Trumbo.

Paul Sellinger steepled his fingers and admitted that he was not sure.

"We don't want a tired man," warned Lester. "I say Wells."

"Absolutely," the major agreed, and gave Sellinger a straight look. "You work with him."

"I'm not at all sure if he's ready." Paul Sellinger shook his head doubtfully.

"You'll make him ready." It was both an order and an expression of confidence.

The decision was made. Major Trumbo lit his second pipe and puffed contentedly. "That's much better. They can take that aromatic and put it in their noses."

5

It was the first raid over London for some weeks, and bombs fell on a church full of sleeping refugees.

Margaret and Caroline Welch, the eighteen-year-old daughter of family friends, had arrived at the hospital together for night duty when the alert sounded. The bells of the first rescue vehicles pulling out were already sounding, and Caroline, who had been driving one of the ambulances for most of that year, hurried off to the transport depot. Margaret went to prepare for the incoming wounded.

More bombs hit a block of flats, and it seemed only minutes before the nurse caught a glimpse of her friend's daughter helping to carry in the mutilated bodies on stretchers. Then the girl was gone again on another journey.

The lifts and passages filled with the drone of people in pain, punctuated by sudden screams as they were moved gently onto beds. Most were women, who called feebly for husbands and children. They were brought in, covered in dirt and debris, with bruised faces, torn clothes, and gashed limbs. Many were unconscious, but the eyes of those who were not were filled with the same glazed expression of terror.

Doctors moved among them, examining and injecting, while Margaret and other nurses worked with the patterned speed of long practice, refusing to hesitate over the disfigurements which met their eyes as

74

they cut away blood- and urine-soaked clothing and cleaned up excrement and bone-deep injuries.

Caroline Welch had returned several times with more patients, and now appeared again, struggling with another girl under the weight of a large woman, who was babbling deliriously. Every bed in the ward was full, and Margaret helped them place her on a nearby hospital trolley before they hurried away to another ambulance race through the night.

The newly arrived patient had lost consciousness as they lifted her. She was fat and middle-aged, with the haggard lines and reddened hands of a woman who had raised a large family in extreme poverty. Her coat had been loosened, and as the nurse pulled up the side of the blanket, a bloodstain was spreading rapidly through her skirt. Margaret undid the fastening and began to cut down the seam, then stopped, her eyes bulging in horror as a loop of intestine protruded through the opening. The woman had no abdominal wall left. Only the skirt was holding her body together.

She was recovering consciousness and murmuring, "Ivy. Where's Ivy?" Her eyelids lifted and she looked at Margaret through calm, beautiful eyes. "Have you seen Ivy?"

The nurse forced a smile and pulled the blanket back over the shattered body. "Ivy's coming, love. But the doctor must see you first."

The woman began to strain, as though trying to sit up. Margaret put a firm hand on her shoulder.

"Lie still, dear. You've been hurt," she said. "But it's going to be all right. The doctor's coming."

"Ivy . . ." the woman whispered before fainting again.

It was five A.M. Every ward in the hospital was crammed full, beds pushed together, leaving barely enough room for the nurses to squeeze between. There were beds in the corridors, and Casualty and the waiting rooms were crowded with those injured still able to stand. The raid had ended hours before, and now the stream of wounded slowed and the deep of the night was disturbed less and less by the harsh jangle of arriving and departing ambulances.

Caroline Welch stumbled in again, supporting an old man. Her eyes showed red-rimmed in grime-ingrained skin, and there was caked blood all over her dark blue uniform. She looked all-in.

Margaret helped her settle the old man in a chair before calling another nurse, taking the girl's arm and announcing decisively, "Time for tea."

"I can't," Caroline protested. "They're still digging them out of the rubble in Andrew Street. I've got to get back."

"Tea first," she insisted, pushing her into the staff room. "How many journeys have you made tonight?"

The girl shook her head uncertainly and muttered, "Not sure. Eighteen . . . perhaps twenty." Her hands were shaking and she moved clumsily from exhaustion.

The kettle was boiling in the small room, and three other nurses were already there. They were pale and dazed, and looked about fifteen. Margaret Sellinger was struck by a sudden image of her daughter, Sarah, and wondered if it would still be as bad for her in a few years' time. She sat Caroline on a tubular metal chair and put a cup in her hand.

They drank their tea without speaking, just grateful for a few minutes away from the carnage outside; color returned to their faces. Then Caroline Welch stood up.

"I've got to go. There's this bomb-disposal captain who keeps arranging these all-night sessions so we can meet in my ambulance." She grinned.

"Let me guess—his name's Adolf," suggested the short dark nurse.

"Nope! Wrong mustache."

"Why can't he ask you to meet him somewhere out of London—Berlin maybe—then we could all get some peace," put in one of the others.

"Too easy," she replied with a wink, and was gone.

At last it was seven o'clock and the day nurses took over. Margaret ached all over; even inside her head seemed tender, as though her brain was bruised by the anguish it had absorbed. For once, on reaching home she did not even notice the emptiness of the house, but just blundered up the stairs and fell, fully clothed, on the bed.

The telephone bell stabbed into the crowd of limbless, shrieking human bodies peopling her nightmare. She sat up, cold with sweat and trembling, disoriented for a moment, then reached for the receiver.

"Margaret," a girl's voice sobbed in her ear. "Margaret. They've all gone."

"Caroline?" she asked. "What is it? Where are you?"

"They've gone. Mum and Dad, Sue and the boys. The house was bombed. They're all dead."

It was an autumn offensive, the last effort of both sides to do as much damage to each other as possible before weather conditions slowed down the war in the air.

Missions from all British and Allied airfields increased. The number of wounded admitted to all hospitals increased, too: the one tide being closely related to the other.

Leaves changed color and fell from the trees. Winter began to close in again. Soon it became too cold for Halloran and Margaret to spend whole days in the country, and they began, like dormice, to look for warm, safe places in which to spend their time. They took to afternoon matinees, searching out light-hearted movies—*Chump at Oxford, Ziegfeld Girl, The Road to Zanzibar,* and even *Tarzan Finds the Sun,* through which they could cuddle and escape. They discovered tea dances and Glenn Miller, and silly songs like "Yes, We Have No Bananas" and "Run Rabbit Run."

Then the government was asking people not to travel, and Sarah came home on holiday. It was

Christmastime again, the fourth Christmas since the beginning of the war.

People wearing happy, furtive expressions began to crowd the shopping centers, scanning the department stores and planning surprises. The cold drizzle depressing the atmosphere did not matter. Starved of color and celebration, Londoners were taking to Christmas again like an alcoholic to five-star brandy.

Parcels full of tinned butter and clothes began to pour in from the States; savings were splurged; small luxuries, squirreled away long ago, were brought out of hiding and used. Carol singers visited the air-raid shelters each night, and pantomimes were advertised, and even the BBC became more cheerful.

The adults were still haunted by the brilliantly lit prewar Christmas city, but few children could remember that, and Harrods, with its garlanded columns and star-hung windows, thrilled Sarah out of her precocious composure. It was packed with shoppers gliding up and down the paneled escalators, crowding the aisles, and clutching packages—lacking traditional wrapping paper, but still exciting.

The child tugged at her mother's hand vigorously. "Mummy, hurry! Please hurry!"

Margaret, already laden with bulging shopping baskets and a dripping raincoat, gasped as a fragile-looking old lady rammed past with the aid of a dangerous umbrella.

"This may come as a shock to you," she pointed out to her daughter, "but I'm going as fast as I can."

Sarah jigged with impatience. "The third floor . . . it's on the third floor."

"What's on the third floor?"

"Something," the little girl called back over her shoulder, as, unable to contain herself any longer, she barged on up the escalator and crashed into a formidably aristocratic dowager.

The dowager gave Margaret Sellinger an affronted stare.

"Horrid little girl," said Sarah's mother sympathetically. "I wonder whose she is."

She sidestepped past and tore after the offending
juvenile, who had reached the second-floor landing
before she caught up.

"I don't understand why eight-year-old girls, who
don't really have much to do, have all that energy,"
Margaret complained in mock annoyance. "While
parents, who have small things like full-time jobs and
beastly eight-year-old girls to contend with, get the
short end of the energy stick."

Sarah stopped in her tracks and looked up with a
pair of obviously inherited challenging eyes. "If children have all the energy, why aren't we allowed to
stay up later than parents?"

She had a mind like a steel trap, and never missed
a trick. Margaret glowered.

"You're not a child. You're a forty-seven-year-old
midget."

The escalators had carried them to the third floor
at last. Sarah grinned and grabbed her mother's hand,
dragging her through the luggage compartment, like
a Great Dane taking its diminutive owner for a run.
They narrowly missed destroying the carefully bal-
anced display of leather suitcases, steamrollered over
an inoffensive assistant, and burst into the toy department.

Sarah came to a screeching halt and stood transfixed before a shelf of dolls. Margaret waited, using
pursed lips to hide a smile.

Her daughter walked slowly over to one of the
dolls with a transported look of total adoration on her
face.

The doll was an incredibly lifelike baby with a
china face, curly brown hair, china arms and legs,
and a soft material body. She was wearing a white
satin dress.

"Oh, Mummy, I think I'm going to die," mourned
Sarah, unable to take her eyes off it.

"Of what?" asked Margaret, unimpressed.

"Her eyes open and close. She's got real long eyelashes. Isn't she beautiful?" The child was near to tears with longing.

"Yes, she is." Margaret had to admit it, not daring to even peek at the price ticket.

"Isn't she the most beautiful thing you ever saw?" Sarah persisted, sensing victory.

"No," declared Margaret sturdily.

Her daughter turned a tragic face toward her and asked, "Who is more beautiful than she is?"

Margaret looked down and wrinkled her nose. "You are," she answered seriously.

Sarah hugged her impulsively, then snapped out of it, drawing back to look her up and down.

"You're not so bad yourself."

"Why, thank you very much." Margaret began to pick up her baskets again.

"Not at all," responded the child pertly before turning back to the wonder on the shelf. "Look! You can curl her hair. She can probably even cry."

"She can probably get pregnant," responded her mother caustically.

A huge red-coated figure with a detergent-white beard and rosy cheeks beneath yo-ho-ho blue eyes suddenly appeared at the far end of the department, and was instantly mobbed by a flock of squealing children, as dozens of well-bred youngsters broke from the restraining influence of nannies and mothers, Sarah among them, of course.

Father Christmas tramped toward his sugared palace, patted a couple of stuffed reindeer, and sat down on a great chair covered in polar-bear skins. The first child climbed on his knee and the rest were propelled into some kind of order. Sarah waited with rigid intensity, only her glance shifting every now and again from the jolly Santa to the white satin dream on the shelf, until it was her turn at last.

"And have you been a good girl?" Santa Claus asked after finding out her name.

She shot a slightly worried glance toward her mother before answering "Yes."

"Ha! Ha! Ha! I'm sure you have," boomed Santa reassuringly. "I like good little girls. Now, what would you like for Christmas?"

Sarah reached up and whispered in his ear. His eyes met Margaret's and he chuckled.

"Well, well. We'll have to see what we can do," he said, lifting her onto the floor again. It was as good as a promise.

Then they were off again, blazing a trail of disaster through the more sedate crowds, in search of a present for her father.

"I suppose there was no reason in particular you wanted me to see that doll," probed Margaret mischievously, as they stopped for breath on yet another escalator.

"No reason at all," vowed Sarah airily.

"Nothing to do with Christmas?" Margaret persisted as they stepped off into a jungle of brassieres and girdles.

"Of course not." She was quite indignant. "Mummy, when am I going to get breasts?"

"Next Tuesday. . . . Why?"

The child had stopped in front of an outsize plaster model, secured in an example of boned engineering that would have supported the pyramids, and replied thoughtfully, "I don't know. Sometimes I think they look silly."

"They look best with formal wear," agreed Margaret gravely.

They wended toward the rear of the ground floor, through scarves and artificial flowers and the handicraft section, to the men's department. It was like entering church. An air of hushed reverence surrounded the stiff, wax-faced mannequins in their dark, classic suits and frozen smiles. Solemn, elderly men in pinstripes with tape measures around their necks spoke obsequiously to impeccably dressed clients and looked around with some disapproval as the woman and small girl walked through this male domain. Margaret had the feeling that they would have been firmly escorted out, had it not been Christmastime, and she felt slightly self-conscious.

Sarah felt no such restraint and ran from displays of trilby hats to a glass case full of cuff links, twirling a small stand of cravats on the way. The atmosphere in the department deepened.

"What would Daddy like?" The child's voice rang irreverently.

A tall gray-haired man raised a frigid eyebrow in their direction.

"What about a false nose and a pair of scarlet briefs?" Margaret offered loudly.

The man's eyes jerked away.

"Be serious," Sarah admonished. "What do you think, really?"

"I think he'll like anything you give him."

"I want to get him something special."

They moved to the next counter to stare at white shirts and surprisingly colored braces and vests.

"What about a tie?" suggested Margaret.

"Nice," agreed Sarah, "but Daddy has lots of ties."

"Daddy has most of the things here," her mother pointed out.

"I want to get him something he doesn't have."

"Get him a dress," said her mother.

The child shrieked with laughter at this, and the male assistant crystallized. A handsome tweed-clad gentleman strode out looking thunderous.

"Just get him something from you, something you like," Margaret advised, smiling. "Daddy will love that, because it's from you, not because it's blue or red."

Sarah's attention wandered from the tray of handkerchiefs she had been examining, and there was a slight pause. Then she said unexpectedly, "Mummy, do you know any Germans?"

"Not too many."

"What are they like?" asked the girl.

"I don't really know," Margaret admitted. "Probably a lot like us."

"Do you think there are German children buying presents for their fathers, like I am?"

"Yes," answered her mother quietly. "I suppose there are."

Sarah had picked up a box of handkerchiefs and was gazing intently at them. They were white, with thin brown stripes around the edges.

"These!" she cried. "I love these."

Margaret wanted to kiss her, and it was just then that she had the idea. Why not move out of London after Christmas, down to Sussex? She could rent a cottage and work at the local hospital, and Sarah could stop being a boarder at school and live with her again. It would be a new start, away from London and Paul—and Halloran.

Blue eyes stared out from under blond eyebrows. The eyes were terror-struck and the man's face covered with perspiration. He could see nothing of the room to which they had brought him except the violent yellow-white light striking from the lamp angled full on him. All the rest was pitch black, like the cell where he had crouched for countless hours before.

"Once again! Your name?" the guttural voice rapped out in German from the darkness.

"Keller . . . Helmut Keller." The man in the chair cringed in desperation, his body beginning to shake. He had not eaten, nor been allowed to wash, since it began. He was not even sure if it was day or night. He was not sure of anything anymore, except the cramping pain in his belly and the endless questions.

"Where were you born?" the German interrogator demanded again.

"Essen."

The fierce beam from the lamp blazed down, casting dense black shadows like smudges on the prisoner's face, under the eyebrows, under the nose, and under the mouth, and making the beads of perspiration on his forehead glint. The interrogator sat behind the lamp, his face eclipsed. He, too, was sweating, his collar undone and damp skin on his neck just showing within the arc of light.

"When?" he grilled.

"Nineteen-eight."

"Rank?"

"Major."

The room began to revolve around the man under the glare. He could feel the chair shifting and put out a hand to steady himself. It met nothing. He squinted into the harsh light at the loosened braided collar as a trickle of moisture ran diagonally across his interrogator's jugular. The image of the other's omnipotence was destroyed. This was just a man, like himself. The prisoner jerked himself straight.

"Mother's name?"

"Ruth."

"Father's name?"

"Carl."

"What are you doing here?" The heavy German words sounded full of threat.

"I've told you time and time again," he returned in the same language.

"You will keep telling me," insisted the voice.

Again heat engulfed him in a sudden tide, causing blood to flush up behind his palid skin and perspiration to drip from his eyebrows into his eyes, stinging them with salt.

"I am here under the orders of General Wallheim." He was beginning to feel dangerously tired.

"What orders?"

His mind wanted to wander away to thoughts of Clare and the baby. He knew he had to concentrate.

"I've shown you the papers."

"Papers can be forged." The German voice was merciless.

He shook his head. "These are not."

"What are these orders?" the officer barked.

"I've told you." His hand ran unsteadily through his blond hair; then a sudden move from the interrogator in the dark jolted him back to attention. "General Wallheim asked that I give these papers to you. You are to deposit them in your safe and give me a receipt," he blurted fearfully. "That is all. There is nothing more."

There was the sound of a chair scraping on the wooden floor, a crisp rustling; then the voice snarled directly into his ear from behind.

"We know who you are."

The prisoner started, half-turning to reply, almost pleading, "I've told you who I am."

The interrogator's voice rose to a scream. "Do you think we are stupid?"

The movements in the dark were forceful and full of menace, and the prisoner raised an arm to ward off the blows he sensed about to strike.

"I've told you who I am," he repeated desperately. "Look at my papers, that's all—"

"And I told you!" ranted the officer. "We know who you are!"

The man lowered his arm, annoyed with himself for having made his fear so obvious. A spark of anger strengthened his tone.

"I don't understand why you are questioning me like this," he retorted resentfully. "My name is Helmut Keller. I am a major. I am here under orders from General Wallheim."

"Stop lying!" barked the interrogator.

The prisoner, clearly rattled, reached in his pocket and drew out a package of cigarettes with trembling hands.

"Please don't smoke," said the officer in English.

He put the cigarettes back in his pocket.

The light over his head was snapped off and the main lights in the room flooded on. The prisoner realized he had made a mistake, and looked deeply embarrassed. Sitting across the desk from him, the interrogator, Paul Sellinger, was rubbing his brow and looking at him with an expression of stern disappointment.

"Lieutenant Wells, English is a language you do not understand. You have never spoken a word of it in your life. They did not teach you English in Essen," he said slowly and precisely.

Wells slumped in the chair, feeling like an idiot. They were in a small whitewashed room, empty except for the desk, two chairs, and a wall clock. It must be somewhere in the basement of the ministry, he thought to himself. Both hands of the clock were at six. The interrogation had gone on for four hours.

"You are never to speak English, or respond to English, even around here," Sellinger was directing. "No matter who is talking to you, if it is in English you do not understand. I don't care if it is the P.M. himself who is talking to you. One slip like that and you are quite dead."

Wells looked sheepish and a little bewildered. He could never get used to the extraordinary suspension of time sense that happened during these sessions. The time locked in that claustrophobic black cell before interrogation was only hours but seemed like days. He knew the whole exercise had begun that morning, but his body believed at least a week had passed, and he was famished.

Sellinger stretched and stood up, looking drawn. "All right, lesson over." He nodded. "It's time we took a break."

He walked to the door, still preoccupied by Wells's mistake. The lieutenant remained seated, looking at him. He looked back and then smiled kindly.

"Don't be discouraged. You are really doing fine . . . just fine." Wells went on regarding him blankly.

"Come on," encouraged his senior officer. "I'll pay for the tea."

Still the man did not respond.

"Come on . . . it's all right." What on earth was

wrong with him? Sellinger began to feel awkward, and Wells gave him an odd, quizzical stare.

"Lieutenant Wells, class is over for the afternoon," he said firmly.

Wells still sat, staring, and all at once the captain understood.

"Let's go for tea," he said, in German this time.

Lieutenant Wells stood up and walked over. They looked at each other, and Sellinger was the first to smile.

Over tea they talked about the war in general. Wells was informed and intelligent and diligent, an officer who could be relied on always to do his best.

Writing up his report on the afternoon later in his own office, Paul Sellinger went over these qualities and rubbed a doubtful hand over his mouth and chin. Good qualities, but just not good enough. The man was unable to think on his feet, to improvise. Paul remembered Reed and Forbes and wondered whether quick wits could be taught. He knew they could not. The loss of another man, and one as utterly responsible as Wells, would weaken the department very seriously. As he dated the report, his fingers snapped in a sudden gesture of annoyance. It was Christmas Eve and he had intended to leave for home early to join Margaret and Sarah.

Reaching into the top drawer of the desk, he drew out a small square box carefully wrapped in white tissue paper and bound with red office tape, the most festive materials he could find in wartime for Margaret's present.

When he reached home, Sarah was already in her short white nightdress, and flung herself at him, bowling him onto the big velvet-covered sofa for an excited rough-and-tumble. He took a number of sturdy whacks in the solar plexus and had his nose pulled several times before bundling her under his arm, charging up the stairs deaf to her protesting shrieks, and dropping her onto her bed.

"Have you written to Santa Claus?" he asked as he tucked her under the eiderdown.

"Yes. Mummy and I sent the letter up the chimney just before you came home," she replied, reaching up to tug his ear with a giggle.

Margaret joined them, turning on the little amber night-light on the bedside table before switching off the main light, then going through the ritual of arranging the convention of stuffed animals around her daughter. Each one was checked and wished good night, and finally both parents sat on the edge of the child's bed and heard her prayers.

"Now, listen, you creature, it's late," Margaret said at last. "And if you want Christmas morning to come, you have to go to sleep."

Sarah drew Binkie Bear into her arms and declared in lively tones, "I can't sleep."

Her father stroked her head and smiled sympathetically. "I know it's difficult, but you must. Santa Claus won't bring you anything until you're asleep."

"Why?" asked the child, as she did every year.

"It's the rules." Margaret gave the same answer.

"I just want to say hello to him," the little girl explained persuasively.

"He's busy," said her mother. "It's his big night and he's got to see every child in the whole world."

Sarah snuggled down into the warmth from the feather-filled quilt and murmured in a worried voice. "Will the Germans shoot him down while he's flying?"

"No!" Sellinger exclaimed with unguarded force. "No, of course not."

She nodded, satisfied. "I don't really care what I get. I mean, anything will make me happy."

Her mother examined the blackout boards against the window for cracks through which chinks of light might show, then drew the flowered curtains across.

"Uh . . . it would be nice, though . . . if I had a little friend of my own . . ." Her daughter's voice was muffled by the bedclothes. "To play with."

"I'll have another baby," promised Margaret immediately.

Sarah laughed and sat up again. "You know what I mean, not a real person, just a . . . you know."

Margaret leaned over and gave her a kiss, pushing her gently back onto the pillow and asserting, "I haven't the faintest idea what you are talking about."

The child gave her a knowing smile and kissed her back enthusiastically, then turned to her father, who took her in his arms.

"Well, young lady, even if you're not tired, I am," he said, tucking her down at last.

"Wait till you see what I've got you," she whispered to him.

"If it's from you, I'll love it." He smiled back. Then they wished her sweet dreams and returned to the living room.

A coal fire was burning and sending flickering light across the large room to the little Christmas tree, which Margaret had bought in the street market and decorated with glass baubles carefully preserved since the late 1930's. Some paper chains, handmade by Sarah from strips of used envelopes painted different colors, looped across the ceiling, and large sprays of holly framed the window and the paintings on the walls. A sprig of mistletoe hung from the central light, and three woolen socks were pinned to the chimney piece and labeled "Daddy," "Mummy," and "Sarah."

Margaret took some notepaper, scissors, and a pen from the Georgian secretaire in the corner and sat on the sofa to write. Paul poured himself a sherry and settled to watch her fondly from the deep armchair opposite.

"Setting the trail?" he asked.

She nodded. It was the annual ritual that Father Christmas left a trail of clues in doggerel attached to a long string, which led all over the house from the child's bed to the hidden cache of presents.

Margaret began the first verse.

> Santa Claus has called tonight
> With toys and games for your delight.
> This long string will lead straight to
> The presents I have left for you.

She cut a strip of paper, printed the poem on it, wrapped it around a small bar of chocolate, and secured it to a huge ball of string made up of dozens of short lengths knotted together and saved throughout the year.

An hour went by during which she put together four more verses, before tiptoeing back to the child's room and tying one end of the string to the teddy bear's paw. Sarah was sleeping, her peachy face angelic and happy. Margaret's heart turned over.

"It's so strange. It's Christmas Eve and we're fighting a war," said Paul when she returned to the living room. "Fighting wars never seems to make much sense, and it makes even less sense on Christmas Eve."

His wife placed the huge open box containing the dream of Harrods under the Christmas tree, where the trail of string ended. The doll stared at her through gorgeous icy eyes.

"What is she going to do with another doll?" wondered Paul indulgently.

"God knows." Margaret grinned with a shrug, taking another box from a drawer of the antique bookcase and starting to fill the stockings with its contents. A precious orange in Sarah's, bits and bobs from Woolworth's, a pear each, and packs of cigarettes for herself and Paul.

"I'm off to bed." He yawned, coming over to kiss the top of her head. "What about you?"

"I've still a few things to do," she answered.

At last she was alone. Aircraft flew overhead, making the softly lit room vibrate slightly. She put some more coal on the fire, switched on the wireless to a program of carols, and leaned back against the cushions to gaze at the tree.

She sat for a long time, and then, just before going to bed, went out into the garden. It was a surprisingly warm evening, not at all wintry, with the moon as big as the sun. Above her, the barrage balloons sailed in a silver fleet across the sky, beautiful, and not at all warlike.

A sense of peace crept over her. All the anxieties evaporated and her mind emptied, leaving only a sense of being wrapped in warmth and love. It happened every year in this way at this time.

6

Cards and parcels from loving mothers and girl friends had swamped the camp, making everything worse rather than better. The men usually tried to keep their thoughts practical, but the recent daily mail delivery had made that impossible and everyone was invaded by nostalgia for the folks around the tree back home. Even the hard cases found wartime Christmas overseas an assault in the Adam's apple, and took to wild parties and benders with the intention of losing consciousness until the season of sentiment was over.

It was a plan which could have worked had it not been for Colonel Bart's fiendish program of bombing missions, which refused to make any allowance for Christmas and mercilessly forced hungover and sex-battered crews to fly impossible sorties over enemy territory. This caused regular reductions in the numbers of his own men, and Cimino had the theory that Bart was really an undercover Russian agent working for the downfall of Allies and krauts alike.

Halloran had ceased to care. The only mornings he woke to easily were those when he was to meet Margaret. On every other day, it took the combined effort of two alarm clocks, a basin of water, and Bob Azzurra's ham-sized fist to persuade him to acknowledge reveille. He was fed up with fighting. All he wanted was to stay alive and get the hell out of it with her.

Christmas Day was the worst. As soon as he opened his eyes, he knew it was breaking up. Something was wrong. She was farther away, closing herself off from him somehow. All at once Halloran realized that if the war did not end soon, she would slip out of his future and back into her protected English background. It was the first time he had felt any uncertainty.

He sat through the midday briefing without hearing a word, and in late afternoon trooped without speaking along the seemingly endless line of B-25's standing in the fog. Cimino had made one or two attempts to entice out of him some observation—the shortest optimistic comment on the flight ahead would have been enough—but even he had had to give up.

Fuel trucks were filling up the various tanks. Final armament loading was being completed, swarms of mechanics and pilots, climbing into and crawling from under the dark planes, like green ants. Halloran knew she was planning to leave him.

He and Hyer climbed into their seats, put on their earphones, and buckled themselves in before beginning the final checklist.

"Switches on," said Halloran automatically.

"Switches on," echoed the copilot.

"Starting port engine . . ." The routine began to penetrate through his absentmindedness. He stared through the window, beginning to register the opaque air outside for the first time.

"Starting port engine," obeyed Hyer.

The lieutenant leaned forward and pushed the starter button, and a cloud of black carbon spat out of the back of the engine on his side. The three-bladed propeller slowly began to rotate. He gazed at it blankly. One blade went by, then the second, and then the third. The engine coughed, like a heavy smoker waking up in the morning, and the black smoke from its lungs billowed under the wind. The propeller turned spastically, then caught and started to spin. Halloran was hypnotized. Soon he could not see the blades, just a blurred disk, and finally there was that strange optical illusion that made it look as if the propeller was spinning slowly backward.

Hyer was waiting, looking in his direction expectantly.

The pilot sighed. "Port engine on."

"Port engine on." The young second lieutenant could sense an unexplained tension. It made him feel awkward, and he looked beyond the captain at the engine, trying to think of something to say.

"I can never get over the way it looks like the propeller is spinning backward."

"Backward? The goddamn propeller is spinning backward?" Cimino's voice yelled from the nose cone.

"Forget it," grunted Halloran. But it was too late.

"Forget it?" Cimino's voice had taken off. "The propeller is going backward and I'm supposed to forget it?"

"It's an optical illusion . . ." Hyer faltered, the hesitancy in his voice making it sound like a lie. "I was just saying—"

"Forget it," Halloran snapped. "Starting starboard engine."

"Optical illusion my ass." Cimino was morosely skeptical. "How do you know forward from backward with a propeller?"

"When we take off heading for France, if we land in New York, the propellers are spinning backward," Halloran summed up briskly, pushing the starter switch.

"I hope they're spinning backward," the bombardier instantly wished in his ear.

The right engine reluctantly sputtered to life.

"Starboard engine on."

Hyer echoed it. Shudders began to run through the aircraft at regular intervals from the motor vibration. The fog had closed in, turning the neighboring Mitchells into remote shadows on either side. It was a crazy day to take off.

Halloran pushed forward on the throttles and spoke into his mouthpiece. "Tower. This is leader. Over."

"Leader, this is tower. Over."

"Starting to taxi. Over."

"Roger, leader. Over."

The plane inched forward. The spindly nose wheel turned and they taxied slowly toward the end of the runway. The second plane followed, and then the third, and on down the row, like a line of ducks waddling into muddy water.

"Just my luck, they're spinning forward," grumbled Cimino.

Behind them, the line of aircraft was growing longer, all in single file, with the mist completely obscuring the last in the line. Their wings wobbled slightly as they taxied down the bumpy runway, the clumsy movement making the engines appear too heavy for the bodies.

Halloran's eyes flickered over the dials and back to the opaque air outside, unaware that Hyer was watching him, as he had been watching for the past few weeks, and noting that the pilot did not seem to enjoy the airplane the way he used to. There had been a time when you knew, just by the way Halloran handled the controls, that he loved flying. Now it was different. The pilot's lips were tight and the muscles in his cheeks twitched slightly—just enough for Hyer to see.

"You want me to take it up?" the copilot asked unexpectedly.

"No."

The plane had reached the end of the runway, and turned, rolling to a stop. The others followed suit and began to rev up their engines, looking and sounding in the mist like a line of buzzing insects in a horror movie.

Halloran could feel pressure at the back of his neck as the apprehension built up, and his imagination rushed uncontrollably ahead across the submarine-filled Channel to France. He pushed forward on the throttles and began the final check. The engines strained and the body of the airplane began to tremble. His eyelids flicked as he stared out of the left-hand window at the air, now so thick it looked like a dust storm. He did not realize that his right hand had begun to shake, but Hyer saw it. An underlying sound was coming from the port engine, a hesitancy in its usual beat.

"Listen to number one," Halloran said to his copilot.

Hyer leaned forward and looked over Halloran's shoulder at the engine. The propeller was spinning. Nothing looked out of the ordinary.

"What's wrong?" he asked.

"I don't know," replied Halloran, frowning. "Something doesn't sound right."

It was coming very faintly, from deep in the heart of the machine, that almost indiscernible roughness, followed by a kind of stutter. Hyer must hear it, too.

"Leader, this is tower. Over." The voice sounded through the headphones.

"One second, tower. Over," Halloran responded, turning to Hyer to direct. "Check the RPM's."

The copilot glanced at the dial. "RPM's normal."

Halloran's mind rejected it. "Oil pressure," he snapped.

"Oil pressure normal."

"Leader, this is tower. Over."

The needling sound scratched under the voices of copilot and tower control insistently.

"Lucas . . ." Halloran called up the sergeant. "Are you listening to number one?"

"Yes, sir." Lucas, who had heard the exchange, had been straining to hear the engine since the captain's first words, but the vibration of the fuselage overlaid the turning motor with creaks and rattles of its own.

"Something doesn't sound right," Halloran was saying.

"I can't tell from here," the other admitted. "How are the gauges?"

"Gauges are okay."

"I can't tell from here," repeated Lucas.

"I hear something wrong," Cimino's voice yelled in panic from the nose bubble. "I hear everything wrong."

Outside, the fog was growing denser. The distant grating in the engine had become more pronounced. It might just be a loose pin. It could work its way out over the sea, or jam the controls when they were flying through flak. Halloran could not understand why the others did not hear it.

"Something's not right," he insisted. "Sometimes the gauges don't show it."

"Leader, this is tower. Please answer." Air-traffic control sounded impatient. "Over."

"Roger, tower . . . this is leader," Halloran answered. "Over."

"Begin takeoff," the order came back.

If they took off today, they would never come back. Halloran knew it and made the decision. "I've got a problem with my number one. I'm returning. Over."

Hyer stared at him, unable to believe it. The engine ran as smooth and regular as a healthy heartbeat as the plane veered off the runway.

"Roger, leader," tower had acknowledged, before instructing Patman, piloting the second aircraft, to take over as leader.

"Roger, tower," Halloran heard Patman's voice. "Over."

"Begin takeoff. Over," control ordered.

"Roger, tower," Patman answered again, and the engine of his plane revved as Halloran's aircraft began to head back.

The new leader started down the runway. The others closed ranks and began to follow. There was a slight lifting of the mist. Halloran's plane taxied in the opposite direction.

"Happy Christmas!" whooped Cimino, in ecstasy.

The dawning of Christmas morning was a noisy, breathless experience as Sarah leaped on their sleeping forms, shaking them awake and shrieking.

"He's been! Santa's been! And he's brought me *her*."

"That's tomorrow," groaned Margaret.

"It's today!" yelled her daughter, bouncing pitilessly. Paul had hauled the bedclothes over his head and turned into a moaning lump. Sarah stripped them back and howled down his sleeping ear. Her parents gave in and crawled into the day.

"It's only half-past five," wailed Paul, and the fire was still burning brightly to prove it.

"Happy Christmas, Daddy," sang his daughter. "Happy Christmas, Mummy."

"There's a lot to be said for communism, if they don't believe in all this," murmured Margaret.

"But everyone has Christmas!" exclaimed the child, shocked.

"Yes, they do, darling," she agreed, contrite and kissing her affectionately. "Happy Christmas, sweetheart."

"Can we open our presents now?" Sarah demanded.

"Not before coffee," she ruled, heading for the kitchen.

When she returned with the lifesaving tray, the dream doll was already locked in Sarah's arms, the contents of the child's stocking were scattered over the floor, and a first bite had been stolen from a red Canadian apple. The family sat in a circle and began to open parcels: a game of Monopoly, some books, and a dress which her mother had sewn during quiet nights on duty at the hospital for Sarah; a pocket-size chessboard and books for Paul.

"Fortnum and Mason's had this notice: 'No whiskey. No rum. No gin.' But it was beautifully painted!" Margaret explained the lack of Christmas spirits.

Paul produced a bottle from behind his back with a mock drumroll. Champagne.

Then Margaret opened her presents: a box of Charbonnel and Walker handmade chocolates from Sarah; silk stockings, books, face powder, and an exquisite Victorian pendant from Paul.

The gifts spread around them, and she felt a little tearful. Each one was an almost unobtainable luxury in 1942, and spoke much more of thought and time than money, days spent tracking down a shop with a supply of stockings, hours queuing for books, so scarce because of the shortage of paper, and the sacrifice of two months' sweet rations for the one-pound box of chocolates.

Sarah and the doll were lost in a private love affair. Margaret returned to the kitchen to baste the goose she had ordered six weeks before from the Soho butcher with invaluable Irish connections. At half-past ten they left the house.

It was strange not to be summoned there by bells, but the church had been bombed a few weeks before and the tower had collapsed. They entered the main door, to find a shell open to the sky and heaped with debris through which a pathway had been cleared to the altar. The chancel was still roofed, and a piano had been placed there to accompany the hymns. Holly and chrysanthemums decorated the windowsills and the cross. The congregation stood where it could, and the parson arrived chanting at the head of the procession of choirboys in white linen surplices, just as though nothing had happened to his church.

As the familiar service unfolded over her, Margaret thought of Halloran. The damp prayer books reminded her irresistibly of that day by the river, when he had dressed her in clothes not quite dried by the sun. It was the wrong place for such thoughts, but she did not feel guilty. She had not bought him a Christmas present, from a semiconscious superstition that, if she left him out of this most intimate of festivals, he might somehow cease to exist along with her own guilt. Now she regretted that, knowing he would be alone and lonely, while she was cocooned in the security of family and tradition. As the chords crashed tunelessly from the old piano again, she realized she had not heard a word of the sermon.

The rest of the day was perfect; the goose tasted as though it had been roasted in honey, and the extraordinary Christmas pudding, made from the dried-fruit ration, with curious additions of carrots, chopped prunes, and gravy powder, looked as dark and rich as a prewar brandy-soaked version, and was remarkably edible.

They walked in the park and played Monopoly and sang some carols around the tree, and then Sarah and the Harrods doll closed their eyes in unison.

"Sarah's hands are so small. During the day, when she's running around like a maniac, she doesn't seem so small," Margaret remarked to Paul later that evening after they had looked in on the child on their way to bed. "When she's in her bed, and she's sleeping, I think she shrinks."

"I know what you mean," her husband replied through his toothbrush from the bathroom.

Margaret climbed into bed and switched off the light on her side, leaving his lamp on as he returned to the room.

"I wonder what the other side is thinking right now," he remarked as he got under the covers. Margaret closed her eyes tightly.

He moved closer to her, but she did not stir. He looked at the long muffled shape of her under the eiderdown and lightly touched her hair as he lay down. His hand moved down to her bare shoulder and then around her, drawing her closer to him.

"Good night, darling," he said.

" 'Night," she answered sleepily.

He switched out the light on his side, leaned over, and kissed her cheek.

"I love you," he murmured in a low voice.

"Love you," she muttered, sounding almost asleep.

He lay back and remained motionless, listening to her steady breathing, feeling the covers gently rise and fall with each breath. His eyes were open and he made no attempt to go to sleep, not trying to hide the hurt, knowing how terribly wrong it all was.

Margaret kept her breath even. Her eyes had opened to the protection of the dark. A tear ran down her cheek, past the corner of her mouth, and fell, making a small wet spot on the pillowcase. She could not see her husband's face, that he was not sleeping, that his eyes, too, were open. She did not have to see. She knew.

The officers' club was like a West End nightclub, all low lights and smooth music. It had been lavishly decorated for Christmas and was packed with fliers trying desperately to be festive. A haze of purple smoke from their American cigarettes hung like a blanket under a net of balloons.

It was that time of night when the best dress uniforms had begun to crumple and most men were drinking rather than dancing. A few figures were already starting to slump across tables, or girls, and the smoke and heat had created a thirst five deep around the bar. A sudden hunger caused a run on the hamburgers, and a few wised-up women were beginning to think about cups of coffee.

Only the Glenn Miller Orchestra on the stage retained any semblance of smart turnout, performing a swaying, uniform parade of trumpeters blowing in one direction and trombones the other, and saxophones weaving in unison through syrupy-sweet arrangements of "Moonlight Serenade," "String of Pearls," and "Serenade in Blue."

The entertainments committee had had quite a skirmish with a west-of-England camp for the band's Christmas services and had resorted to using the per-

sonal interest of a three-star general for some ulti-
mate rank pulling. The general looked in on the evening with satisfaction. The rows of bandsmen, almost
lined up by height, would have gladdened the heart
of the most homicidal drill sergeant.

It had been the duty of every officer for weeks
past to ensure a generous supply of females for the
Christmas-night party, and none had been more con-
scientious than Cimino. He had devoted every free
hour to the task, with the result that, when the coach-
loads arrived from London and all towns within a
twenty-mile radius, four of the girls expected to
spend the evening with him. It had been a very
charged half-hour, even for the son of a Chicago
bartender.

He had met the first and avoided the second in the
crowd. The third had stalked off in a righteous wrath,
and the fourth had agreed to share him with the first.
As neither of these women was less than stacked,
the bombardier was torn by fantasies of lust and
trepidation for the first half of the night, until number one jitterbugged off with a normally withdrawn
captain who had unexpectedly emerged from a bottle of tequila and a salt cellar as the extrovert of the
year. Cimino, unscathed, was grateful they had all
been English girls. A quartet of Americans would
probably have left him scratched to ribbons.

Colonel Bart, gimlet-eyed, appeared, progressing
around the crowded floor like a snow plow cutting
through a twenty-foot drift. A short, ugly woman,
clinging nervously to him, was abandoned as he
caught sight of two lieutenants beginning to wave
their fists in a drunken argument.

"Break it up. Break it up here!" he roared, threat-
ening them with his stomach.

They backed away with raised hands, one of them
tripping into the lap of a pretty girl and the other
forgetting whom he had last been talking to. Bart
turned back, triumphant, to find that the little ugly

woman had not waited. He felt tired and filled with an unfamiliar longing for his wife, Wilma.

"Harriet, you have a beautiful throat. Do you know that?" Cimino's eyes were not focused on the neck of number four.

"My name's Phyllis," she corrected, swaying impossibly toward him, so that he felt in danger of dying a magnificent death from suffocation.

"Of course it is," he agreed, unblinkingly fixed on the voluptuous mounds. "You have a beautiful throat too."

It was a good line, original, he remembered, and had once worked very well on a Canadian girl. Cimino was smashed.

"Do you want to dance?" Phyllis was asking.

Why did broads always want him to fling himself around dance floors? He glared sourly at the crazy apes boogying in the center of the room, jackets discarded and showers of sweat spraying their partners. Uncivilized.

Phyllis was tugging at his sleeve, and he turned to her solemnly.

"Susan, my darling, normally that would be a wonderful suggestion." His finger ran down the side of her neck and began journeying toward her cleavage. "Under certain conditions, I am your actual Fred Astaire. However, since the injury . . ."

Temptation moved out of reach, but stayed in mind.

"What injury?"

Cimino took a gulp of Scotch and shook his head sorrowfully. "Oh, I don't like to talk about it." His eyes became distant, with what he hoped was an expression of nobility and courage.

"I didn't know you were wounded." Phyllis sounded suspicious.

"Just a little shrapnel," he responded airily.

"Why weren't you sent home, if you were wounded?" she asked sharply.

"They wanted to . . . I wouldn't go." His chin jutted with fierce determination and he swung his head to stare darkly at her. "Nothing will keep me from flying."

"Lieutenant . . ." Phyllis was touched. "That's . . . that's really very . . ."

"Paula, my sweet, it's nothing to make a fuss about," Cimino read the signs and snaked an arm around her, while gazing deep into her eyes. "Sometimes the pain . . . What's life without pain, I always say. How about another drinky?"

There was a collection of empty glasses in front of them, for which he was mainly responsible, although he had managed to ply four of them into her.

They had met in the milk bar in bone-dry Letchworth, an unlikely venue which Cimino had risked his reputation by entering, only in order to discover the time of the next bus out of town. The immediately apparent attributes of Phyllis behind the counter had reminded him that there was more to life than alcohol, and he had bought a milk shake, and missed the bus.

The band stopped without warning and the lights went up unkindly. Everyone blinked and looked annoyed. An officer seized the microphone to announce that the last buses were now leaving the camp for the towns. There was a universal groan, and one attractive but determined-looking brunette left the room.

Tremendous noise rolled over the club again in a raucous medley of braying brass and shouting voices. A passing figure lurched unsteadily and threw Phyllis and Cimino against each other. It was an omen, he decided, drowning in heavy scent and gin fumes.

"It's Christmas night. We gotta look at the moon," he ruled, grabbing her hand and heading for the exit.

The freezing air slapped him and hurled Phyllis into his arms. He maneuvered around the side of the building, not losing his grip for an instant. The Letchworth milkmaid squeaked and shivered and then became happily energetic, whether from passion or through trying to get warm, Cimino did not stop to ask.

He was just beginning to work out the shortest route from the officers' club to his quarters when a clatter of running steel-tipped soles resounded on the concrete path and a group of soldiers stormed around the corner, shouting. Phyllis squawked, jumped back from him, and straightened her skirt. A riot of fists and boots broke over them.

Within seconds the girl was swept away, her hen-like alarm sounding shrilly above the uproar. A number of artificial stars were added to Cimino's moonlit mood of romance, when a gigantic figure with a demolition ball for a head butted him against the wall.

"Can't we settle this over a Coke, or in church, maybe?" pleaded the bombardier as the demented guy kept ramming him in the dark.

The night began to sing with the tinkle of breaking bottles and bones. Bodies took off like Batman and, after short flights, splatted to the ground like overripe tomatoes. Finally, after a long and painful interlude, disembodied white belts and puttees and a lot of truncheon waving signaled the arrival of the M.P.'s, one of whom picked up the bombardier by the lapels, registered his second-lieutenant bars, and dropped him with a disapproving grunt. Cimino remained in a supine slump until the battered soldiers were loaded into the jeep and driven off to cooler accommodation, and Phyllis appeared again, clucking in agitation.

"Time for another drink, honey." He struggled to his feet and propelled her back to the security of the bar.

Hyer, not quite his impeccable self, possibly even a little frayed, came over with his arm around a sleepy-looking matching blond. Another girl was with them.

"Hey, Cimino, I need some help," Hyer said out of the side of his mouth.

"Hyer . . . Hello, Hyer!" Cimino slapped him violently on the back, while waving his other arm at the bartender.

"Scotch, bourbon, and gin—gin, gin-and-lime," he ordered, indicating a girl for each gin, then turning his attention back to the copilot. "Have you met Barbara?"

"Phyllis," corrected the milkmaid, without rancor.

"Have you ever seen such a throat?" He surveyed her with hot eyes.

Hyer leaned close to his ear and whispered urgently, "Cimino, listen. I got this one all primed—except she won't leave her friend alone, and . . ."

Cimino looked blearily from one girl to the next and then at Hyer. "I've always harbored a suspicion that blue eyes don't see good—too much inbreeding," he accused. "Have you taken a good look at Dorothy?"

"Phyllis," pointed out Hyer automatically, and the milkmaid gave him a grateful smile.

"Right." The bombardier nodded. "That happens to be an architectural marvel right there."

His hand strayed around her back and under her arm, and she giggled obligingly.

"What am I going to do?" Hyer sounded hoarse.

Cimino considered the problem and surveyed the crowded room. A familiar uniformed figure sitting in glum solitude at the far end caught his eye.

"What about Halloran?" he said. "Give one to Halloran."

Hyer followed his glance and seemed doubtful. "I don't know . . ."

But Cimino had already sprung up from the barstool, fired by his own idea, and grabbed Phyllis' hand.

"Come on, Rita. We'll all go over and be with Halloran."

He stumbled through the crowd, crashing through

pair of dancers and feinting between the tables
packed around the polished wooden central square.

"Hey!" cried Phyllis. "I thought you had an injured leg."

Cimino stopped dead and cast his eyes to heaven.
"My God!" he whooped. "I can walk again!"

7

The air grew thicker with steam and noise as the officers' Christmas party crescendoed into a chain-smoking racket of slurred, raised voices and blasting musicians. Only the invisible but powerful barricade erected by Halloran's brooding scowl had protected him from invasion by revelers. Hunched over a half-empty bottle of beer, with a cigarette dangling from his mouth, he seemed oblivious to the chaos around him and did not even look up as Cimino led the charge to his table.

After abandoning his aircraft, he had spent the first part of the evening stretched on his bunk, until his own company became intolerable and he had drifted over to the officers' club. The celebrations came as a surprise. He had forgotten it was Christmas Day, but he had taken the empty corner and, apart from a tentative approach by a girl with an aggressively Joan Crawford mouth, he had been left alone.

Cimino, however, was too plowed to be sensitive to the lack of welcoming atmosphere and shoved the others into chairs, forcing the extra girl to sit next to him.

"Ladies, this is our leader." He gestured expansively. "Leader, these are our ladies."

"This is Elizabeth." Hyer pushed the extra girl nearer. "Elizabeth, meet Halloran."

"Hi," said Elizabeth in an incongruously English voice.

Halloran came back from a long distance and focused on her without smiling. "Hello."

"And this is Audrey," yelled Cimino joyously.

"Phyllis." The milkmaid sounded tired.

Halloran nodded and looked beyond them and around the room. For hours his mind had been full of questions, switching from the canceled mission to Margaret and back, wondering about the sounds he had heard from the faulty engine, about her plans for the future, and how the bombing operation had gone for the rest of the flight.

It was obvious he was not in a gregarious mood—obvious to anyone except the people at the table, where the girl, Elizabeth, had decided he was very attractive.

"I'm from the village quite near here," she said. "Where are you from?"

"New York."

Family Christmas. He knew nothing about Margaret's family, not even whether she had children—only that she had a husband. He remembered boyhood Christmases, indulgent and protected, full of surprises. Mom and Dad close and whispering together for days beforehand, then happily loving after all the parcels had been opened. Family Christmas was dangerously powerful. He could feel vibrations from her rejecting him.

"Elizabeth worked on the decorations," Hyer was saying encouragingly.

"They're very nice," he responded flatly.

"Nice!" The copilot sounded indignant. "Why, Elizabeth and some local nurses took a plain old officers' club, and with the simple use of crepe paper and some cardboard reindeer, they transformed it into an officers' club with a lot of crepe paper and cardboard reindeer."

Halloran did not hear a word. His attention had

shifted to the entrance door, as if he were waiting for someone to come through.

Cimino, who was now so drunk he could hardly talk, swayed over and tried to communicate.

"Have you ever seen a throat like Hillary's?" He let a clumsy hand fall on his partner's piled-up hair. "Teresa, my darling, let's go someplace where we can be alone."

"I want to stay here." Phyllis shook him off plaintively. Cimino had lost most of his appeal at the same time as he lost his shrapnel-embedded leg, and anyway, she was beginning to feel sick.

"It's Christmas." He rubbed her neck with a vigorous caress and peered at her from under heavy lids. "And I am your actual serviceman alone overseas."

She turned her head away a little sulkily. "I want to stay here."

The cigarette in Halloran's mouth had turned into a drooping roll of ash and his bottle of beer remained untouched. It was the only one he had bought since arriving. He was still staring at the door.

"Have you ever been to Chicago?" Elizabeth was gushing, wide-eyed. "It must be very exciting there with all the gangsters. My brother told me all about Al Capone and the jazz musicians in the nightclubs. He plays trumpet, you see."

"No . . . no, I've never been to Chicago." Halloran could not take his eyes off the door.

"He's told me about the gang wars and that mayor who is almost as bad as the criminals." She had a breathless little-girl voice that could have pierced a chess grand master's concentration. "You'd think everyone in America would go to have a look at Chicago, really. I mean, it's like living here and never going to London."

"Not quite, honey." Hyer looked up from a whispered conversation with the sleepy blond. "America's a big place."

Elizabeth, whose travel experience extended to a

maximum radius of fifty miles, looked confused.

"Where is your patriotism?" Cimino was pleading with sad spaniel's eyes riveted on Phyllis. "The Allied morale is at stake here."

She gazed back at him and explained carefully, "I think I'm a little tipsy. I want to stay here."

The bombardier drew himself up and squinted. "Marion . . . perhaps you're a spy."

"Are you feeling all right?" Elizabeth touched Halloran's arm.

"Yes," he snarled, and she flinched back, as though burned.

"Let me put it another way." Cimino drew his girl friend close. "Let's fool around."

"Okay." She beamed back at him and stood up.

"There is a God." Cimino renewed his faith and tried to stand too.

The dancers on the floor had begun to conga around the room, reeling between the tables, picking up befuddled couples as they went. A few chairs crashed as the tail of the conga whipped around. Cimino, who had been failing in his attempt to stand up, was, fortunately, knocked back into his. The train of people zigzagged faster and faster, like a gigantic millipede scurrying away from a garden spade. It wound itself into ever-decreasing circles, until the head collided with the stragglers and the long procession collapsed, covering the floor with shouting, laughing bodies. The Glenn Miller Orchestra played on, unsullied by a single spot of perspiration or a loosened tie.

A group of officers appeared in the entrance and grinned over the scene. Halloran's face stiffened and he scanned each one as they made their boisterous entrance.

"They're back," murmured Hyer superfluously.

Between twenty to thirty men drifted in over the next quarter of an hour, distinguished from the others in the club by being freshly bathed and shaved and by the fact that they were all sober. Each time a new face appeared, Halloran strained forward in his seat.

"Where's Patman?" he asked at last.

Hyer, whose attention had been distracted from the blond by the obvious tension, said soothingly, "He'll be here in a minute, don't worry."

"Who's Patman?" demanded Phyllis, who had also sat down again.

Cimino's hand traveled up the outside of her thigh. "Patman, my luscious Linda, is the brave soul who flew lead instead of us this fine day, because of a port engine with a holiday spirit. Let's drink to Patman."

He raised his glass in a jaunty gesture, before emptying its contents in one, then propelled himself to his feet, swept up the girl's glass, and headed back to the bar.

Phyllis watched his reeling advance, gurgled, and leaned over to whisper to Elizabeth, who had slid her chair back from the table and was looking neglected. Hyer's girl was dozing on his shoulder.

"I don't see him." Halloran craned his neck.

"He'll be here . . . in a minute." Hyer, too, was stretching to see each new entry through the door.

The pilot caught sight of a massive figure resolutely crossing the far end of the room toward the bar. He paused long enough to excuse himself politely to Elizabeth before moving swiftly onto the dance floor.

The band was playing "Pennsylvania 6-5000" and the crowd was growing collectively drunker. Without really noticing, Halloran bumped into four or five couples shuffling around, buried in each other's shoulders for support. The huge second lieutenant with the crew cut had just collected his beer from the bartender when he caught up.

"Hey, Beef . . ." Halloran greeted him.

"How you doing, Halloran?" The big man nodded amiably.

"How did it go today?" Halloran tried to make it sound casual.

"Not so good." Beef tipped the bottle up and took a long, saturating draft. "We lost three."

He finished his bottle and looked down on the lieutenant's six-foot-one height through lazy eyes and nodded. "You are one lucky son of a bitch, let me tell you."

Halloran felt his guts jolt and he stared at the other's face. "Where's Patman?"

"One lucky son of a bitch," repeated Beef, banging a demanding fist on the bar and seizing the second bottle, which appeared instantly.

The uproar in the club had cut out. Halloran felt suddenly unable to breathe. It was as though he and Beef were the only two there.

"Where's Patman?" he repeated.

"I never saw an airplane break up into so many little pieces," observed the giant second lieutenant, gulping the beer as though the English barman was about to call "Time" any minute.

"What are you talking about?" Halloran forced his attention.

"He took a direct hit," replied Beef laconically. "Must have been in the bomb bay with a full load."

A fearful desperation took hold of Halloran. He had known it all night. He had known it from the moment Patman's airplane, going in the opposite direction toward take off, had passed his.

"He could have bailed out. Maybe he bailed out."

"Not a chance." Beef shrugged. "I never saw so many little pieces."

He thumped the second bottle down in exchange for a third, then swiveled his eyes over its upturned bottom.

"Where's Cimino? I'm gonna tell him," he announced. "If it wasn't for that engine of yours, it would have been you instead of Patman. I'm gonna tell Cimino to go kiss that engine."

Halloran turned away, the color sucked from his face. He was going to throw up. Glazed, he started toward the john, oblivious of everything around him. Everybody was shouting "Pennsylvania 6-5000" each time the band reached that part of the chorus. In a trance, the lieutenant blundered past his own table.

Hyer reached out. "Hey, what's the matter?"

Halloran turned his sick eyes on him and begged hoarsely, "You heard it, didn't you? On the port side —something wrong—you heard it?"

"Sure, sure," Hyer lied clumsily, startled by his captain's appearance. Halloran looked insane, eyes bulging and skin damp and transparent. "Sit down, take it easy."

Halloran wheeled to Cimino, who was blissfully sprawled over a triple Scotch, and grabbed his arm.

"You heard it. You heard something wrong, didn't you?" he insisted.

The bombardier looked up, purblind and crowing. "Every time an engine starts up, I hear something wrong," he replied merrily.

Halloran hated him and glared at the three girls blinking stupidly up at him. He could hear that deep grating in the engine as clearly as if he was still sitting in the cockpit.

"There was something. There was . . ." He twisted around, bolted from the table and out the door, almost knocking someone down on the way. Hyer took off after him.

Cimino perked up at the action, and thinking it was all in fun, clambered to his feet and set off with doglike enthusiasm, shouting, "Ladies, let's follow the leader! Come on, Francine."

Halloran had burst from the building, running like a wild man. The yellow light from the doorway splashed onto the cold ground and then was wiped away as the door swung closed again. For a moment the only sounds were his gasping breath and running feet. Then the yellow light and the sounds of "Chattanooga Choo-Choo" spilled out again, as Hyer tore after him.

"Halloran!" he yelled. "What happened?"

Halloran kept on running. It had begun to rain and the wind was against him, driving the heavy drops into the crevices of his face. Steam was coming out of his mouth, and when he reached the field the ground was already stickily wet under his feet.

Cimino and the girls had careered through the door, giggling and far behind, imagining this was all part of the festivities. Elizabeth had already tripped and muddied her dress. The others hauled her up and on, colliding with each other and shrieking, toward the airstrip.

The sounds of the officers' club grew fainter in the blue-black of the night, and Halloran reached the long line of parked B-25's. They looked eerie under the moon, bulging with hostility and threat; efficient, adaptable killers. He had once reveled in the design and handling of them, had almost found them beautiful. Now they looked like a line of bodies in a huge open-air morgue, all undergoing autopsies, as crews of mechanics worked on them, each under a bare white light.

The port-engine cowling had been removed from his plane and a mechanic in Brooklyn Dodgers baseball cap was inspecting the insides of the engine with a flashlight.

Halloran accelerated through the mud and gripped him by the arm, glowering down at him with steely eyes.

The man looked startled. "Lieutenant?"

"You found it . . . didn't you?" Halloran challenged frenziedly.

The man's glance jerked away, and he tried to release his arm. "I . . . I . . . don't know yet . . ."

The pilot shook him and clenched a fist in his face. "You found it. Goddamn you, you found it. Right?"

He pushed him against the airplane, holding him by the shirt. The sharp ring of metal on metal sounded from the neighboring aircraft as its landing gear was checked. The mechanic was looking at Halloran like he was face to face with a mugger in a dark alley. "Lieutenant . . . please . . ." he pleaded.

Halloran, with murder in his face, thumped him against the fuselage and shouted, "Tell me you found it!"

Hyer, who had seen the two lock from halfway across the field, rocketed up and flung himself on the pilot's back, heaving him off.

"Take it easy! Take it . . ."

Halloran, berserk, shook loose and went after the mechanic again. The man had dived behind a wing for shelter, but the lieutenant's furious clutch found him again and dragged him back.

"The port engine! The port engine!"

"Please . . . I . . ." The mechanic had gone white and he rolled his eyes toward Hyer for help.

The copilot plunged in again, grabbing Halloran, who was now furiously convinced there was a conspiracy between them, and fought back, screaming, "Tell me you found it! Tell me!"

Cimino, arriving with the girls, viewed the struggle among the three with interest.

"Hey! I wanna play too." He bounded toward the arena. "Excuse me, Flo, I'm gonna play, don't go away."

Hyer was once again wrestling with his captain, and the mechanic was cowering between the wheels as the drunk bombardier stumbled up and seized Halloran in a bearlike hug, overbalanced and pulled him to the ground.

Hyer sprang forward and pinned him there, bawling, "Everything's okay. Don't worry . . ."

Halloran struggled viciously, lashing out with legs and knuckles, but the combined weight of the two second lieutenants was too much for him.

"Let's do two out of three falls," whooped Cimino, rolling in the dirt like a lunatic dalmatian.

Halloran's head had fallen back in agony. He was

almost sobbing. "I heard it! I heard it! Patman, I swear to you, I heard it!"

Water dripped off the nose cone of the Mitchell and into his eyes, so that it was impossible to tell whether there were tears there as well. His features were distorted with frustration and guilt.

"Easy. It's all right." Hyer waited for him to calm down while keeping a cautious hold on both his arms.

Halloran was still staring up at the cloud-cluttered sky and screaming, "Believe me, Patman!"

The girls thought the whole scene very funny and were snickering as Hyer and Cimino lifted him to his feet. He held on to them weakly, utterly destroyed, and they began to drag him away. The mechanic cringed, transfixed against the airplane, watching this apparition in disbelief. None of the rest working on the other B-25's had noticed the incident, and the clanks and crashes of their tools resounded in the dark.

The three fliers floundered across the rough grass toward the buildings, Hyer being the only one relatively capable, and buckling under the weight of the other two.

Cimino, who had enjoyed the romp, was eager for another and kept pulling at his arm and asking, "Where we going? We gonna wrestle again?"

Halloran was muttering and groaning to Patman.

Hyer led him farther away, talking gently. "Just rest . . . don't worry . . ."

Behind them, the mechanic bent down and picked up his flashlight. It was broken. He straightened his Dodgers baseball cap and stared after the receding figures of the air crew followed by the three girls, and Halloran's raging voice carried clearly back to him.

"Goddamn you! Goddamn you, Patman!"

Before the war Paul Sellinger had been a stock-broker, showing flair as well as acuteness. He was

successful. Men playing the market trusted and liked
him. They shared the same tastes and knew each
other's families and came from the same conventional
background of prep school, public school, and Ox-
bridge. It was a time when the strength of the old
school tie was at its most powerful.

Operating, for Sellinger, provided excitement. He
made few inspired guesses, but enjoyed taking cal-
culated risks, and saw his career as a serious game, to
be played with humor and a certain style. But this
speculative side of his character did not show in his
private life. At home he was a steady, charming pro-
vider, witty and considerate, the almost-too-perfect
husband.

It was only when the war came that he began to
suspect his life had, in fact, been remarkably sheltered. He had never moved out of his circle, made
any unorthodox decision, or questioned the establish-
ment in any way.

After call-up, he had been stationed near London
for normal military training. Margaret had begun
nursing, and soon her letters and conversation were
full of extraordinary experience, stories of despair
and courage. When he had been attached to intelligence, his first reaction had been one of extreme disappointment. To his surprise, he realized he had been
looking forward to action.

Intelligence was full of oddballs with agile minds,
and led into strange and previously unsuspected
areas. Sellinger found himself working with psychia-
trists, writers, actors, small businessmen, and even
criminals, all with wits for use against the enemy. He
learned how to train men to withstand types of tor-
ture and abuse he had never before imagined possible. The years before the war had been innocent
times for him.

Forbes, the agent recently killed in France, had
joined the service a few weeks after Paul himself and
was a very different man. Flamboyant and extro-
verted, he seemed an open book superficially. Yet

although they became friends and regularly took a drink together at the end of each day before going home, Paul Sellinger discovered very little about the other's life. On file he was married with a family and had been an "entrepreneur," which could mean anything. Beneath the exhibitionist show, he gave nothing away and occasionally displayed almost alarming perception.

"You're a gambler," he had said unexpectedly not long after they met. "I want you to meet someone."

Sellinger, already aware of Forbes's weakness for the tables, grinned. "Not one of your poker school?"

The agent had tried before to draw him into that, but now shook his head. "No. Though he's not unconnected. It's someone who wants a favor and who can do you and the department favors."

They took the subway to Plaistow. Paul Sellinger had never been to the East End of London before. The devastation was appalling; acres and acres of rubble-strewn land pitted with craters where only a few weeks before, thousands of people had lived. The buildings still standing were mainly slums, small back-to-back hovels, or tenements crammed with poverty-scarred women whose children had all been evacuated and whose men were now soldiers.

The occasional gaunt church rose out of the devastation, usually partly ruined, but with the notices of the coming Sunday's weddings pinned to its doors.

Forbes led the way down claustrophobic alleys, where the remaining dilapidated houses leaned perilously against each other for support, wide cracks gaping in their walls, slates missing from their roofs, and broken glass still jagged in the window frames.

"Where the hell are we going?" demanded Sellinger at last.

"Almost there." Forbes pointed to a dingy pub a few hundred yards ahead.

The interior was stark, dark, and dirty. A collection of broken noses and football-sized fists was arranged around its tables, and the hard-eyed woman behind the bar gave them an unfriendly stare, until Forbes leaned over and said a name softly to her. Sellinger hoped he had not heard correctly.

Without a word, the woman half-opened a door behind her and gestured them through.

The man was waiting in a deep armchair in the expensively furnished room beyond. He stood up and cuffed Forbes on the shoulder in friendly greeting. Sellinger was filled with sudden anger. He had heard correctly—the name of the biggest villain in the city.

The man surveyed him through old, cold eyes, then offered a drink.

"No, thank you," the intelligence captain responded icily.

"Not keen on the company?" The man chuckled.

"We'll both have brandy, thanks," Forbes put in quickly, maneuvering his colleague into a seat.

"I'll tell you what I can offer first. Then I'll tell you what I want." The man went straight to the point.

"I'm quite sure there is nothing that I or my department can do for you," Paul Sellinger stated firmly. "Nor anything you can offer us."

"Touchy, isn't he?" The man raised an eyebrow and looked over at Forbes.

He was burly and middle-aged, with thick, curly gray hair and the relaxed confidence of a winner. Only a certain immobility of facial muscle and the low blink rate betrayed total ruthlessness. The man would kill without qualm, but had no need to anymore. Others did it for him.

"Your reputation's beaten you to it." Forbes explained Sellinger's hostile reaction.

"Yeah." He guffawed genially, not taking his eyes off the captain, then began, like a father, "Now, son. You know who I am. I'm the boss. Nothing goes on in this town without me knowing. And that's what I can offer you. Knowledge—who really arrives among the refugees from Belgium, Holland, and France who's up to funny business, earwigging where they shouldn't and indulging in a bit of two-way radio chat with Uncle Goebbels perhaps. Selling info, maybe. My boys know things Old Bill never finds out. We'll turn these Jerry finks over to you."

Sellinger returned his scrutiny calmly and said, "You would do that anyway."

The man roared with laughter, thumping the arm of the chair. "Right. Dead right. No kraut spy would stand a chance with my lads. Only, we wouldn't hand him over. We'd give him concrete socks and drop him in the Thames."

Sellinger stood up, preparing to leave.

"Sit down. I haven't finished," the man said. "My boys are the best in the country. We got skills your department needs—if you want to go creeping all over the continent without getting nicked by the Gestapo, that is."

"What skills?" asked Sellinger skeptically.

"Breaking and entering, mate, escaping, thieving, lock-picking. You name it. My top men could teach your top men plenty."

Sellinger stayed wary. "And what do you want?"

"It's a family matter." The man looked unexpectedly sheepish. "I got a nephew. My sister's boy. He's been a spoiled little bugger and now he's got himself into real bother. I'd let him take what's coming to him. But my sister's just lost her old man."

"What has he done?" Paul asked, carefully noncommittal.

"He's deserted."

"Then I can't help him. There's nothing I can do for a deserter."

"Yes, there is," insisted the man. "He's not been AWOL long. He got compassionate leave, see, when his dad died. Then he met this silly young chick and run off with her. Now, the lads have tracked him down and I've got him, but I want him returned to the Army with no trouble. Because of me sister."

"And how do you think I could do that?" asked Sellinger.

"Easy, mate. It's all figured out," replied the man.

"All you got to do is say intelligence picked him up 'cos he had connections and that you've been using him for information over the past couple of weeks."

Sellinger felt annoyed. The man was right. The techniques he offered could be invaluable to their agents, but doing business this way went against his instincts. He glared at Forbes.

The man caught the look and grinned. "It's almost true," he pointed out persuasively. "After all, he has got connections—me and my boys." He held out a hand. "Is it a deal?"

Paul Sellinger frowned, hesitated, and then took it.

"It's a deal," he confirmed.

Later, he felt oddly pleased with himself for having gone ahead. For some reason, he would have liked to tell his wife, but all aspects of the job were top secret, and in any case, he had never discussed his civilian work with her.

The deal worked. Even after Forbes was lost in France, the man kept his promise, which was why, not long after Christmas, Sellinger and Lieutenant Wells made their way south of the river, out of uniform and by bus, to the block of Victorian warehouses to meet Harry Pike.

Harry Pike was obviously a mistake. He was supposed to have been born a ferret. Instead he turned out as a person. Two coal-black berries for eyes flanked a thin nose that always looked like it was sniffing out info and intrigue. He was a thin, bent little man, and twitchy.

They found him waiting for them in the basement, in a large, bleak room with small barred windows at ceiling height. A pile of slatted wooden crates furnished one end, and a row of different types of safes was lined up at the other, near the work light. The place looked like an off-Broadway stage during rehearsal.

The safecracker formally introduced himself and

shook hands with them as they walked in, then apologized for not having provided refreshments. He was too nervous to inspire confidence, and a flicker of doubt disturbed Wells's face.

The diminutive man cracked his knuckles and wondered if they had come far, flushed, and corrected himself, "Sorry about that. Forget I asked. Mustn't ask you gents anything, the man said."

He glanced restlessly up at the windows, as though expecting to see a platoon of boys in blue looking down on him. The gray afternoon was broken up as it passed through the bars and painted a pattern of heavy stripes and thin checks on the wooden floor and the safes.

Wells shifted impatiently, and Harry Pike threw him a startled look, then approached the line of heavy metal boxes gingerly.

"Now, you 'ave your basic types wiv which you could be confronted," he began, putting a bony hand on the first and patting it, with an unexpected little smile. "It is important to remember that anyfink what was made to be locked can be unlocked."

He looked up, nearly grinning, black eyes restored from death by a glint of fanaticism. "You got your two main types—your combination and your key lock. Your combination works on a series of what's called tumblers. Now, you 'ave to first sus out if it's a three- or four-number combination, and then if you first go right or left."

He caressed the safe, running a nicotine-stained finger along its corners and talking to it, as though he had half-forgotten Wells and Sellinger.

"Then you have your key lock, which is simply a matter of finding the proper key." He had become remarkably perky. "In the absence of a key—a problem which has confronted a lot of different geezers— there are certain rather delicate instruments which will do a right proper job. Then it's a matter of learning how to use them." He paused and eyed the two intelligence officers with a Chaplinesque lift of the eyebrows. "Mind you, my personal preference is to blow the bleedin' things up."

Sellinger, who was seated on a crate, leaned forward to comment, straight-faced, "We want to look at something inside the safe, without the people who own it knowing anything about it. Don't you think that blowing it up might arouse some suspicion?"

"You got a point there," agreed Pike.

"How long will it take to learn how to open one?" asked Sellinger.

The safecracker straightened and rubbed his chin, weighing them up very doubtfully. The neurotic had been replaced by the master, and it was the frown of any craftsman on being confronted with two geezers who expected to learn his skills in five minutes.

"Well, now, you 'ave to understand openin' these things ain't the sort of thing any old bloke can do." He swayed back on his heels and tucked his thumbs into the sleeves of his vest. "It's what you might call a gift—if I do say so meself."

"Let us assume Lieutenant Wells is gifted," encouraged Sellinger.

Pike turned back to the row of safes and admitted, "If it's your key locks—a couple of days." Then he pointed to two in the center and shook his head. "If it's your combination, I'd say about six months."

Sellinger took a slip of paper from his pocket and glanced at it. "The safe we're interested in is a . . . 'Kohner 335.'"

"That's a Jerry safe," observed Pike instantly.

"Yes, Harry," agreed Sellinger patiently. "You may have noticed we happen to be at war with them."

"You got a point there." Harry looked philosophical.

Wells had gone over to crouch in front of the first safe to examine it curiously.

"Which is it?" asked Sellinger.

"You 'appen to be in luck," said Pike. "It's a key lock. Any schoolkid could crack it. As a matter of fact, I cracked one just like it when *I* was a schoolkid."

He reached into the pocket of his badly fitting jacket and took out a small leather case, unbuttoned it, and revealed a set of metal picks shining like surgical instruments. "Never travel without them," he declared jauntily. "I mean, you never know when the missus might lock you out, or somefink."

Footsteps clanked over the grating in the pavement above, and he hesitated instinctively before selecting a medium-sized pick and pointing to it with the forefinger of his left hand. "Now, 'ere you 'ave before your very eyes your pick."

He leaned down to one of the safes and continued, "'Ere you 'ave your safe, which is almost exactly like a Kohner 335."

Inserting the pick in the lock, he carried on the lecture to the accompaniment of the faint scraping and scratching of the demonstration.

"You insert your pick in your Kohner 335. You feel your way through the elements. For your personal information, there 'appen to be four. . . ." His face grew remote and he bent his ear close to the iron door. "You feel . . . one . . . two . . . three . . ."

There was a soft click.

". . . four," said Harry Pike, looking up with a beatific smile and pulling down the brass handle. The door sprang open. He waved an expansive arm at it, like a circus performer waiting for applause.

"Apple pie, I tell you." He smirked. "Bloomin' apple pie."

8

In the days following the blowing up of Patman's air-craft and the Christmas-night party, Halloran stayed on his own, rejecting ordinary contact with other fliers and all Hyer's attempts to draw him out. Wherever he went, he carried in his head the sound of Patman acknowledging the tower's instructions to take over as leader in his place, and he read a contempt in the eyes of the other officers that was not, in fact, there.

The weather had deteriorated, stopping all flying during those few days. He spent most of the time lying on his bunk, mentally going over and over that final check on the B-25, hearing echoes of the curious grating in the engine again and blaming himself harshly for having dropped out of the mission.

He remembered the first operations Cimino, Hyer, Lucas, Giles, and he had flown after arriving in England, the bombardier's plaintive monologue ever in their ears. The gut-twisting moments of terror had somehow added to the edge of them. There had been a real kick in dodging the flak and scoring, and on the way back to base, they had bawled silly songs.

> We're making a beeline for Berlin,
> Blindfolded we'll soon find the way.
> We're making a beeline for Berlin,
> Though no one will ask us to stay.
> It's true that we've not been invited . . .
> We just want to spring a surprise.

We bet poor old Fritz
Will have forty fits
When we start laying eggs in the sky,
When we start laying eggs in the sky.

Outmaneuvering enemy warning systems and anti-aircraft fire had held the same highs as any more old-fashioned daredevil challenge, like mountaineering, riding motorbikes through flaming hoops, and exploring. Halloran had come back from those bombing flights feeling good—but not anymore.

When he could leave camp, he headed for an unattractive pub in Stevenage unfrequented by air-base personnel. There he got drunk. On restricted nights, he hunched on the end of the officers' club bar and got drunk.

He knew what had happened to him, but could not understand why. Meeting Margaret had changed his whole outlook. In peacetime, such a change would have been for the better, giving him depth, making him more caring and careful. In war, it was disastrous. He knew. And he knew what he had to do.

All flight crews had an extra day's leave for New Year's. Halloran's fell on the Tuesday. He did not even try to secure the jeep, but took the early-morning train to London, going over what he would say when they met. He was sure she wanted it that way. Since before Christmas he had sensed her thoughts veering away and resenting him.

They met in Hanover Street and exchanged strained smiles. It was a dank, inhospitable day with chilling winds funneling through the narrow Mayfair streets and stirring up bits of dirty paper and refuse. They walked without speaking, and every now and then she glanced at his set features, then looked away.

A bus was passing, and on impulse Halloran grabbed her arm and ran for it, leaping onto the platform just as it pulled away. It was an instinctive action, connecting them with their first meeting—

only, this time they had caught the bus together. As they sat down, she quietly put her hand in his. He gave her an unhappy glance and drew her roughly against his shoulder.

The bus took them to Holland Park, and they walked to the little empty orangery to sit in the shelter of its warm glass. There, Halloran told her about Patman, brusquely, almost as though it did not matter, but she knew, and reached over, putting both arms around him and kissing a long, anxious kiss, pressing to him, as though trying to absorb the hurt, asking wordlessly to be used for comfort. Gently he returned the kiss, cradling her against him, letting her unlock his numbed emotions once more.

They found a hotel a short walk away. The second-floor bedroom overlooked a small walled garden, paved except for a bed of hard-pruned rosebushes and a plot containing an unidentifiable tree, a bare branch of which scratched against the closed window in the winter winds.

Afterward he held her close and lit a cigarette, just as always.

"When we're together . . . sometimes . . . sometimes I feel so close, I don't know where I end and you begin," she murmured, gazing almost sadly at the leafless branch outside. "I never knew it could be like that . . . I never knew."

The end of the cigarette glowed electrically as he inhaled smoke and stroked her sleek dark hair.

"I never felt anything was missing before. I was happy before I met you. I was." She was whispering now, in a troubled way, as though bewildered. "I never felt I lacked anything, I just . . . I just wasn't sure if this was it . . . if this was everything. Maybe that's why I went with you that first day at the bus stop."

She half-raised herself on an elbow to study him, her eyes distressed. "It's so damned unfair. I try so hard to forget you. I try so hard." She looked away, her voice dropping, talking to herself. "I end up spending all my time trying to forget you, which is the same thing as thinking of you all the time. It's so damned unfair."

Her head fell back on the pillow, which puffed up around it like a wide-brimmed bonnet. She was so little, he always felt a sense of shock at the sight of her lying beside him: small, adolescent breasts under his hands, hips like a boy's. He gathered her into the crook of his arm again and listened.

"I don't want to hurt anybody . . . I don't want to do anything wrong . . . I don't want to hate myself."

He knew how that felt. There was a long silence between them, disturbed only by the persistent tapping of the tree against the glass, wanting to break in on them, just like the rest of the world.

At last she whispered again, turning away slightly, "Sometimes I sit across the dinner table from him. I watch him. I want so desperately for him to do something, or say something, or be something I can hate."

She had never talked about her husband before. Halloran stubbed out the half-finished cigarette and lit another, his face blank.

"And he never does. God, I've hurt him so much. Sometimes I look up, and he just turns away—quickly, as if he didn't want to be caught looking."

She moved uncomfortably at his side, ashamed, and plucked at the quilt with long, nervous fingers.

"Sometimes I hate myself, and I wish I'd never met you." She paused. "Then I'm with you and it's so strong . . . and I don't ever want to let go. I hold you . . . so closely . . . and I shut my eyes. And I don't know what is me and what is you."

She had stirred back to curl against him, warm and needing, her arm stretching across his chest to his shoulder, her lips moving against his neck as she wondered, "Why doesn't it work out the way it's supposed to?"

He rubbed the back of his hand against her face and laid the burning cigarette in the ashtray on the bedside table. For a long time he did not talk.

"I don't know. I don't know how it's supposed to work," he admitted at last. "I never cared too much about anything—so I never had anything to lose."

He was not accustomed to talking about himself much, and the words came hesitantly, with long breaks between the phrases.

"I don't even know anymore what I heard in that engine. A few months ago, the whole propeller could have fallen off and I wouldn't have turned back."

The discarded cigarette was still smoldering in the ashtray, but he lit another, taking time over placing it between his lips and letting the lighter flame for seconds before touching the tip.

"It's so damn easy to be brave, when you don't have anything to lose."

Footsteps sounded softly along the carpeted corridor outside and stopped at the door. The handle turned with a rattle, which contrasted noisily with their quiet murmurs. When the door remained locked, the chambermaid moved on to the next room and they heard her humming as she bustled around it.

"I'm scared now. I don't want to die and not see you anymore," Halloran said. "Nothing makes any sense until I'm with you—and then everything makes sense. I don't want to let go of you. I just want to be with you all the time."

There was an expression of such naked humiliation on his face that Margaret could not bear it.

"You'd be disappointed." She put on a deliberately playful smile.

He matched it with a rueful grin. "Maybe you would be."

"I don't know . . ." She pretended to size him up. "You'd fall out of love with me if you saw me with curlers on my head."

He gazed back seriously, deep into her silvery blue eyes. The grin had gone.

"I don't know anything except that I want to see you with curlers on your head. I want to be with you when you have a cold. I don't want to wake up in the morning and not be sure if I'm going to see you in the evening." The words were coming in a rush now, and he had tightened both arms around her. "I'm tired of missing you . . . and I don't even know your last name."

It did not matter about her name. Nothing mattered, except their being together. She did not have to be beautiful, or well-groomed, or even good company. She just had to be there.

"I'm all in pieces," he said against her forehead. "And I want you to put me back together."

She kissed him savagely. The tree rapped on the window. The voice of the maid in the next room rose. Margaret was almost afraid. "Hold me now and make everything outside go away," she pleaded.

Their lips parted against each other. She twined her legs around his and he held her body across his in a strong, sure embrace.

"On the way in to see you," he began, moving his face over hers, "I was trying to find a way to tell you we shouldn't see each other anymore."

She nuzzled at him and admitted in a low voice, "I did the same thing."

They lingered on each other, longer this time, closing their eyes, drawing to each other with leisurely, certain movements, searching for and finding all the reasons and all the answers as they started to make love.

On the way back to the base, Halloran thought about their relationship, going over in his mind the places they had been, the experiences they had shared, and the way they were together. There was no question now of ending it. They were bonded for life as surely as a pair of wild greylag geese. Somehow he had to get through the war to reach her at the end.

There were other men who did it, quiet and unobtrusive men, each getting on with his personal mili-

tary action as best he could, though hating every minute of it: men living for the time when they could
close once more with adored wives and sweethearts
back home and never leave again. Halloran had always considered them dull, but by the time the
train arrived at his destination, he had made resolu-
tions to carry through the rest of his service in the
same way without any chickening out. He and Margaret could only be sure of making it together if he
played the war game straight.

The afternoon with her had left him feeling healed.
Brooding over the future, the meaning of life, or personal philosophies had never taken up Halloran's time,
but now he realized wryly that he believed in destiny.
It had been inevitable that he and Margaret should
meet. He returned to the camp convinced that he
was bulletproof. Nothing would kill him before their
ordained cycle of love was complete.

Cimino was scuttling across the camp central
square as he made for his quarters. Unlike the lieutenant, the bombardier spent a great deal of time pes-
simistically brooding over the future and working out
ways to avoid it. He had this notion that the more
activities you crammed between the bombing missions, the longer the time span between them and the
more chance they would be canceled. So he scuttled.

On this occasion he was scuttling away from a
heated meeting of the entertainment-organizing committee, on which Cimino was honorary disorganizer.
This time they had rejected several of his brainwaves,
including the suggested opening of an official bor-
dello in Letchworth, to make up for the lack of
alcohol there, and the waiving of all liquor charges
to officers by incorporating the club bar account
into the camp fuel account, for payment by the U.S.
government. He had continued protesting and invok-
ing disaster on the other recalcitrant members of the
committee between mouthfuls of a snatched meal and

was now scuttling toward a date with the thinnest girl within a ten-mile radius. Basically, his taste was for females of Mae West proportions, but Ida Lupino in *Moontide* had made him consider there might be more to less.

Cimino's was a world filled with overpowering lusts and fears and impulses, plots and conspiracies, morbid mournings and manic celebrations, all aggravated rather than eased by prayers and superstitions and faith in curious gods.

"Hi, Halloran," he shouted, screeching to a halt. "Listen, we gotta get old George Berman off the entertainment committee. He keeps pushing for visits by opera singers and ballet dancers. I mean, who wants it?"

"George Berman wants it," Halloran pointed out.

"Yeah, well, I got this idea for a substitute for George Berman," announced the bombardier. "You."

"Oh, no," replied Halloran promptly. "Committees are strictly vendettas, and entertainment committees are mob vendettas."

"But I got these great plans." Cimino was eagerly persuasive. "Do you realize we need never pay for another drink in the club again? You think about that, Halloran. Just by a simple shifting of the account from one column to another in the base ledger, free booze forever. I mean, who knows one row of figures from another? They're all numbers. One little airplane would burn a whole year's intake of alcohol on a single flight to Rouen. All we gotta do is say it did, but old George Berman keeps scaring the others off by going on about auditors and court-martials and dishonorable discharges—and he doesn't even drink. In fact, that's what's wrong with him. And that's why we need you, *I* need you, Halloran."

Halloran grinned and shook his head. "I guess the idea of being court-martialed for not paying for a bourbon kind of puts me off, too, Cimino."

"You'll regret it. A chance like this doesn't come often," warned Cimino, beginning to jog, in anticipation of moving on. "By the way, the Texas Ranger wants you."

"Bart?" queried Halloran. "What's that about?"

Cimino shrugged and remarked, "He looked sort of smug, that's all I know."

It had to be connected with the missed bombing mission. Bart had been waiting too long to pass up such a peach of an opportunity for bringing him down. Halloran went to his room to wash up and shave, then he dressed with unusual care, unaware that even the way he wore his clothes gave the colonel hate fantasies.

A short while later, gazing down at the tubby senior officer, whose eyes were narrowed into glittering slits of victory, he wondered vaguely how he managed to generate such venom. It did not seem possible that only his own feeling of mild scorn for the man could have inspired such a vitriolic reaction. Halloran could not know that Bart saw in his tall, lanky, casual self-assurance the supersuccessful male, the American dream of manhood he himself had no hope of being. Bart imagined Halloran with a permanent succession of ravishing women panting after him, Halloran returning home a decorated war hero, Halloran strolling up through the boardrooms of multinational companies to the presidency and riches and distinguished middle age, just because the son of a bitch looked good and fitted in without effort with all the other smart-pants.

A sheet of paper with a few terse typed paragraphs, the engineer's report on the engine of the lieutenant's B-25, lay on the desk in front of him. Halloran's failure. He would make damn sure the jumped-up New Yorker never got decorated or promoted after this. He waved the pilot to a seat and waited, gloating, letting the bastard sweat. Then he gave a wolfish leer and began quite honestly, "Nice to see you, Lieutenant Halloran."

"Nice to see you, sir," Halloran responded warily.

Bart stretched back in his chair in enjoyment. "I . . . ah . . . have a little problem."

A mischievous guess flitted uncontrollably through Halloran's mind. But no, not Bart. The corners of his mouth twitched involuntarily. "Yes, sir?"

Bart saw it and his nostrils spread as he drew in air and rasped, "It's a mission . . ." He released the air slowly, watching the lieutenant reveal sudden stress by attacking a spot on the armrest of the green chair. "A special mission. The . . . ah . . . group sent word they needed a volunteer."

There was no need to allow the bastard to get under his skin when he had him fixed. The colonel savored his own comfort as much as he savored the flier's discomfort.

"It's . . . ah . . . considered to be a bit risky, so they wanted it put on a voluntary basis. It's for tomorrow night."

Halloran's eyes had hooded and his face masked into a soldier's professional lack of expression.

Bart contemplated him for a moment, then stuck in the knife. "About the other day, Lieutenant. I checked with the mechanic. Strange . . . he couldn't find anything wrong with your port engine."

He rustled the short report unnecessarily between his fingers and watched Halloran's knuckles whiten as he rubbed that spot on the armrest.

"If you felt something was wrong . . . then I'm sure there was something. If you heard it . . . I mean, a mechanic isn't a pilot . . . right?" Every pause was exquisitely timed to mean the opposite of the spoken phrase before. "I never pay any attention to rumors. . . . Never. Of course, there has been some talk around. You know how a base is. You can't pay any attention to that kind of talk. . . . I don't believe for a moment you made the whole thing up about that engine. . . ." He saw the hate come up in Halloran's eyes and sipped every second, like it was vintage wine. There would not be any clever remarks from this quarter during his briefings in future. This was one big-time boy who would not be swaggering around for a long time.

"Where was I? Oh, yes . . . about the mission tomorrow night. I knew you would want to volunteer for it." He stretched his mouth in a repelling smirk over the oily tone. "Not that you have anything to prove, mind you . . . it's just that I knew you would want to go."

Halloran's body was still in the position of relaxed sprawling on the chair, but every muscle was rigid. He wanted to dive screaming over the desk and smash Bart's sneer through the back of his bald skull.

The colonel sensed it all and leaned forward with fake avuncularity to conclude. "I told operations to have the engines double-checked in the morning . . . so I'm quite sure you won't be disappointed again, and have to cancel the flight."

Halloran was staring at the mark he had made in the armrest. He looked up at Bart, who smiled benignly at him.

The park was just opposite the rear entrance to Whitehall. Major Trumbo made a habit of taking a brisk walk around it daily, preferably immediately after luncheon at his club. It was a healthy way to aid the digestion and air the mind, he felt. By that hour, the gardens were becoming less crowded as workers drifted back to their offices. A few old ladies might emerge from nearby flats to walk small dogs, and occasionally a pair of young lovers—the boy in uniform—could be seen gazing at each other through rapidly darkening eyes as their pupils expanded with signals of desire.

Trumbo enjoyed seeing them and he enjoyed stopping to feed the ducks on the lake. Every day he took a bread roll from the basket in the dining room and put it in his briefcase for them. Such a pastime in such a place gave at least the illusion of peace.

On this day he was accompanied by Paul Sellinger, but still stopped as usual at the water's edge and began breaking the roll into small pieces. It was cold, and both men wore heavy overcoats. Sellinger had thrust his hands into his pockets to keep warm and was thinking with some longing of the warm office. He wondered why his chief always chose to hold outdoor conferences in inclement conditions. Wind whipped ridges on the water, which rippled to the bank in irregular flurries. The ducks quacked and splashed greedily at their feet.

"Is he ready?" asked Trumbo.

"I think he's as ready as he's ever going to be," Sellinger replied.

"What do you mean by that?" probed the major.

"I can't be too specific." Sellinger sighed lightly. "There is nothing wrong with Wells. He does everything the way he is supposed to. I would simply prefer him to be a bit more spontaneous."

"Spontaneous," echoed Trumbo, as though considering the word itself.

The captain expanded the report. "Once you teach him something, he learns it. However, I'm not totally sure how he will react if something occurs that he isn't prepared for."

"Well, then, let's hope you have prepared him for everything," commented the major calmly.

"That would be nice." Sellinger was too polite to indulge in real sarcasm.

The fastest duck snatched the last lump of bread as a pair of elegant swans floated up. That was what he disliked about birds, Paul realized suddenly. Their eyes indicated no feeling. They were just bright glass beads pinned in by a toy manufacturer, giving no hint of pleasure or rage. Did birds enjoy themselves? The fact that their songs and flight seemed so attractive to humans did not signify much, he thought to himself. The swans arched their necks and raised their wings and hissed. No mistaking that. The two men retreated to sit on a bench, in view but out of reach.

Major Trumbo automatically took out his tobacco pouch and started to fill his pipe. A very old man shuffled by behind them, tapping a walking stick loudly and muttering to himself. There were no children; there never were these days, and the lack of them always made Paul feel melancholy, reminding him of Sarah.

"New stuff, this," the major was mumbling as he lit the pipe. "Supposed to be a cooler smoke."

A homely-smelling fog half-obscured his face for a moment or two, and he announced from behind it, "We're not going to send Wells on a regular flight. I'm afraid we have to be a bit paranoid about the leak in intelligence. We're going to drop him in a totally different way."

Trumbo stopped and stared aggressively into space, concentrating on the experiment in his mouth; then he shook his head and tutted impatiently.

"If this stuff is cool, I'd hate to see what they call hot."

The pipe was removed decisively and tapped against his heel so that it spat out the contents of its bowl in a heavy gob.

"We're not going to use intelligence personnel for the flight. Chaps don't even know about it," Trumbo continued. "We're not even going to use a transport aircraft. As a matter of fact, we're not even going to use a British aircraft."

He stuck the empty pipe back into his mouth and sat full of sphinxlike mystery, waiting for the captain to ask for more details. It was an old habit. Paul Sellinger smiled to himself and did not oblige.

After a few minutes Trumbo shot him a disappointed glance and stood up, turning to walk rapidly toward one of the park exits. Sellinger paced along beside and waited, but the major did not oblige either. No further information was offered.

They reached the pavement and he turned. "I say,

Sellinger, do you mind coming with me across the street? There's a tobacconist over there."

Half an hour and two satisfactory pipes later, the plan to use an American bomber for the drop into France was revealed. Sellinger returned thankfully to his small cluttered office.

It was a comfortable place and the clutter was not from sloppiness. It came from his habit of collecting all kinds of little things and not wanting to part from them. Old books of poetry, photographs of school and university cricket teams, one or two Japanese net-sukes, a charming, cliché paperweight richly encrusted with tiny, brilliantly colored flowers under its icy dome, a small collection of snuffboxes. Paul Sellinger was an incurable frequenter of junk shops.

The afternoon trolley drew up at his door, clanking with cups, and the fat lady in the floral apron brought in his tea. Usually she was jolly to the point of suffocation, but today she was oddly quiet and there were dark red smudges around her eyes.

"Something wrong, Mrs. Clarke?" asked Sellinger.

"It's my son, Bobby, sir," she replied, her face beginning to crumple. "He's reported missing in North Africa, sir."

"I am so sorry, Mrs. Clarke," he said, real concern in his voice. "Would you perhaps like to go home?"

"No, thank you, sir," she answered. "It's best I keep working."

After she had gone, he gazed for a long time at the silver-framed photograph of Margaret smiling from his desk. Thoughts of Forbes and Mrs. Clarke's son and his family preoccupied him, juxtaposed in his mind, as though all were connected. Margaret's face finally dominated and he found himself concentrating on his marriage, trying to see himself through her eyes.

The city was full of servicemen on leave and in transit, handsome in their dress uniforms and full of extraordinary stories of adventure and escape, living each day with furious verve in defiance of the risks ahead. They were gallant and undeniably attractive. Even ordinary old friends returned from action with that potent gloss of experience.

And there were the others, the men she saw every day, shattered and mutilated, courageous and infinitely enduring. They, too, were touched by the magic of heroism. Sellinger found himself wanting.

He was a quiet man by nature, kind, courteous, considerate, and clever; his acute brain was his principal asset and of far more use to the war effort than the offering of his body as cannon fodder. He was profoundly patriotic. The taproot of his existence reached deep into the heart of England, and he worked, always to the point of exhaustion, for her. It was not enough.

He reached into his breast pocket and took out the handkerchief with the thin brown stripes that Sarah had given him for Christmas. It was still pressed in its original folds, unused. He looked from it to the photograph of his wife. His head gave an almost imperceptible movement of purpose and he reached for the telephone.

The hospital was an old building, built one hundred years before, to house lunatics. Various wings had been added later, connected to each other by drafty covered ways. Its corridors were narrow and dingy, its elevators antiquated and unreliable, its wards big as airplane hangars, but still grossly overcrowded. It was cold and inefficient and almost impossible to maintain at a properly hygienic level. Nurses and doctors alike cursed its inadequacies daily and its sludge-brown and bilious-green paintwork did nothing to aid the recovery of their patients.

The beginning of the year had brought a flu epidemic which cut the staff by fifty percent and coincided with yet another increase in the number of wounded admitted. The beds had to be squeezed together so tightly that a sick soldier in one could reach and touch the man in the bed next to him.

Margaret's night duties had stretched into day, and for several days she had snatched what sleep she could at the nearby flat of another nurse, rather than making the journey back to Hampstead. Like all her colleagues, she was working in a tired trance and had reached the stage of having to double-check all the drug and dressing rounds to make sure no one was overlooked.

The nurses grew short-tempered with each other and with some of the recovering but demanding men. Bed-making and bedpans, thermometers and meal-serving, sluicing and pulse-counting merged into a timeless, endless routine, which they carried out with mechanical expertise born of long practice.

A group of doctors was making the rounds of the ward, picking up the metal chart at the end of each bed and cracking vain jokes to the men who waited so hopefully.

"How's my leg, doctor?"

"Nothing like a shot of shrapnel to make you immune to cannonballs, Sergeant Barting."

"What about my kidneys, doc?"

"Who needs two kidneys inside, soldier, when you can keep one in a glass jar on the mantelpiece to show your friends?"

"I want to go home. When can I go home?"

"You wouldn't deprive our young medical students of the chance to study that rib cage of yours, would you, Mr. Tucker? We can't let you go yet. You're needed here in the interests of science."

Margaret carried in two small trays of food, placing one on the bedstand of a man with bandages over one eye and around his head.

"Hello, love," she greeted him.

"What is it today?" he asked suspiciously.

"Smoked salmon, spring lamb and asparagus, followed by a selection of cheeses."

"Oh, bleeding bully beef and spuds again," he grumbled, lifting the metal lid up and peering at the corned beef.

She turned to the next bed and joked, "Dinner is served, m'lord."

The occupant grinned back. "I'll take it in the study, thank you."

The soldier next to him was unconscious, being fed clear liquid through an intravenous drip. She caught sight of his face as she passed, and her heart turned. He looked about sixteen.

"Phone call for you," a hospital orderly told her as she hurried down the ward. "In the nurses' station."

That was the small room where she and Caroline had rested on the night the local area around the hospital had been so badly blitzed. Records of patients were kept there in filing cabinets, which had overflowed from the overcrowded office.

Margaret picked up the receiver and heard a distant murmur at the other end. The noise from the ward merged with the clatter and chatter of nurses and doctors taking and returning the documents, and made it almost impossible to hear.

"Hello? Hello?" she said. "I can't hear you . . . it's madness here."

She paused, and a man's voice sounded faintly.

"Is that you, Paul?" she asked.

Sitting at his desk, Paul Sellinger cradled his telephone receiver against his shoulder and contemplated the photograph of Margaret in his hands.

"Yes . . . yes . . . can you hear me now?" he answered.

"Yes. You have to speak up."

He could hear the noisy activity behind her and raised his voice. "Is that all right?"

"Yes . . . fine. Is anything the matter?" She sounded puzzled. He had never rung her at the hospital before.

"No. Nothing. I had no special reason for calling. I'm sorry if I've disturbed you." He tried to sound reassuring, but the hands holding the silver frame were shaking and his eyes looked strained. "I just wanted to hear your voice, that's all."

The color drained from Margaret's cheeks. She hunched toward the phone, holding the receiver in both hands and trying to block out the bustle around her. All her senses told her something was wrong.

"Don't be silly, you haven't disturbed me," she said quickly. "I'm glad to hear your voice, too."

There was a hesitation, and then he said steadily, "I love you, Margaret."

Her eyes widened with something like panic. "I . . . I love you, too," she murmured.

"I know I'm not that special," his voice said in her ear.

She was wrung with sudden anguish, wanting to reach out to him, but her voice sounded remote, almost sharp. "What are you talking about? Of course you're special."

"No, I'm not, and we both know it." It was a statement made without rancor, but with regret. "It's just my curse to be so damned ordinary."

"Paul . . ." she began, shocked by this out-of-character conversation.

"I do so want to be dashing. It's not that I don't want to be," he was saying earnestly. "I can't blame you for finding me unexciting."

He sounded touchingly sad. Margaret shook her head helplessly, and held on to the table for support, knowing she herself had caused his distress.

"Oh, Paul . . . I don't know why you are saying this." The love developed through their years together welled up. "You're very special . . . and very dashing . . ."

She wanted to take him in her arms and ban Halloran from her life forever.

Above her head the loudspeaker suddenly blared. "Nurse Sellinger. Ward four, please."

Its resonance must have carried along the wires, because Paul said again, "I didn't mean to disturb you."

"Paul . . . please . . ." She spoke urgently. "I'm so glad you called."

"Nurse Sellinger. Ward four, please." The disembodied voice in the speaker sounded impatient. Margaret glanced up at it, torn between the summons and Paul's need of her.

"Paul . . . I'm sorry . . . they're calling me."

"I understand, darling." His voice was warm and gentle. "I'll talk to you later. I love you."

"Paul!" she called desperately.

There was a click at the other end of the line and the dial tone burred loudly. Margaret Sellinger stared at the dead telephone, stunned.

In his office Paul Sellinger hesitated for only a moment after replacing the receiver; then he took a piece of headed paper, wrote a quick note, and slid it into a white envelope. He moved Margaret's photograph nearer, so that she smiled straight up at him, and he sealed the envelope and put it in his pocket.

Leaning across the desk, he pushed a button on his intercom.

"Yes, Captain Sellinger?" the secretary's voice answered.

"Get me Lieutenant Wells on the line, please," he directed.

9

Colonel Bart apparently used a sickly after-shave lotion which made the overheated air smell sweetly, like a nursery or a morgue. Stepping out of his office was better than being released from chains.

Halloran sloped unhurriedly toward his quarters. The night was agreeably harsh, rubbing against his skin like an abrasive pumice. He deliberately turned his face to it, siphoning its icy breath into his lungs. His knotted muscles loosened and the incoherent raging in his head was swept away. If he had not spent those hours with Margaret that day, he knew he would have choked Bart's taunts out of him.

At the entrance to the billet he turned and looked up at the blue sky, scattered with flashing and sightless eyes, its unimaginable enormity reducing a man to less than a microdot. Halloran grimaced over the futility of his own preoccupations and went indoors.

Sitting on the edge of his bunk, he lit the inevitable cigarette and let its weaving snake of smoke hypnotize him into emptiness. For a long time he sat quite vacantly. The cigarette burned down unsmoked and finally fell from his relaxed fingers. He was unaware of his foot automatically crushing its stub. A short while later he was unaware of reaching out and lighting another and allowing that, too, to burn away.

Fragmented thoughts floated back gradually, disconnected images of the airplane and Margaret . . . a

snatch of conversation overheard in the mess . . . the
memory of an unknown face on the London subway
. . . Bart's habit of hooking his thumb in his belt
while talking . . . Margaret . . . nurses . . . that nurse
who had brought him ice cream after they'd removed
his tonsils when he was eight . . . Margaret.

Gradually he realized that he was relieved, almost
glad Bart had forced the next night's mission onto
him. Since seeing her again that afternoon, he almost
believed he was immortal.

Cimino and Hyer greeted the news over breakfast
with querulous protest.

"Wouldn't you know it," griped the bombardier.
"Just when I've discovered Letchworth's answer to
Olive Oyl and I was gonna play Popeye."

"Litvinov and Baker took twenty dollars off me last
night and I was going to get it back tonight," Hyer
joined in. "And I woke up this morning feeling real
lucky."

"I know how you mean," Cimino sympathized.
"When you feel lucky they send you on a mission.
When you feel unlucky, they send you on a mission.
You could bet on it—and win. No wonder you feel
lucky."

It was dark by the time they met again on the airfield under the bulk of the B-25. The night was clear
and cold, no moon, but no cloud either, a good night
for flying to enemy territory. Halloran ran his hand
over the metal skin of his Mitchell before climbing in
through its belly. As he settled comfortably into the
pilot's seat, it was like returning to a familiar place
after a long time away. He felt easy and certain.

The cockpit dials lit up red for night flying and
reflected against his face, making it glow as he and
Hyer went through their preflight check busily. His
mind had switched to automatic just as it used to before each operation. He felt that keen sense of anticipation, verging on excitement.

"Hey! It's dark out!" Cimino's aggrieved voice carried through the headset.

"No kidding!" Halloran responded sarcastically.

"Really. I wouldn't fool you." The bombardier played it straight back.

"How come we're the only plane taking off?" asked Hyer, staring through the glass into darkness.

"This is a special mission," explained Halloran.

"Lucky us," commented the copilot. "Didn't I say this was our lucky day?"

"Hey, listen." Cimino's familiar alarm was sounding again. "When it's dark out, you can bump into things."

Halloran promised faithfully to be careful.

Hyer was still looking bewildered, his head turning to examine the interior of the aircraft behind them as he pondered the idea of a special mission.

"Where are the bombs? We have no bombs on board," he wondered at last, his tone shaded by some anxiety. "We're a bomber. We're supposed to drop bombs. Where are the bombs?"

"No bombs. I like that." Cimino applauded. "You know bombs are dangerous, on account of the fact that they can blow up."

Halloran was trying to make final checks and calculations, interrupted by their voices through his earphones. Hyer was getting as bad as Cimino, he thought to himself, and aloud demanded, "Both of you, shut up, please. We're waiting for an English guy named Wells. You're going to drop him, instead of bombs."

"I like that, dropping a person instead of a bomb." Cimino, in the nose bubble, was even happier. "On account of the fact that people don't blow up, like bombs do."

"Starting port engine," announced Halloran firmly.

On the grass outside the airplane, the mechanic with the Dodgers baseball cap was keeping a wary distance as he watched the propeller start to turn on the port engine. Colonel Bart had ordered him to be present in case of last-minute hitches, but as that crazy guy Halloran had approached with his crew, the man had ducked out of sight around the front of the Mitchell and emerged only after the pilot was safely on board.

The starboard engine started, and both began to rev up. Halloran watched from his window, noticed the mechanic lurking on the rim of the pool of light, and grinned sheepishly, raising a friendly hand in his direction. To the man on the ground it looked like a threat, and he backed hastily out of sight.

"How do they sound, sir?" Giles was asking from the ventral turret.

"They sound fine. Even if they don't sound fine, they sound fine," the lieutenant replied instantly, ready to start taxiing to the runway, keen to be off. "Where the hell is that English guy?"

"It's dark out," Cimino reminded him, still sounding surprised at this nightly phenomenon. "Maybe he's not so stupid."

But Hyer, who had been looking out his side, still brooding over his lost twenty dollars, said, "Over there . . ."

The dipped lights of an approaching vehicle spotted the field faintly. Halloran swung from his seat, hunched into the well of the plane, and dropped out through the hatch, crawling under the nose to avoid the spinning propellers. The wind created by them kicked up a dust storm, and the noise was deafening.

A gray Army sedan pulled up nearby. The driver, a corporal, climbed out and opened the door for Colonel Bart and a man wearing the uniform of a German SS officer.

Halloran gave Bart a casual salute. It was returned peremptorily.

"Hi, Colonel. Is this Wells?" the pilot asked, the lazy contempt in his eyes matching his drawl.

Bart's rotund figure stiffened as he sensed his dignity being affronted yet again.

"No. There's been a change of some kind," he snapped. "This is Captain Sellinger. Captain . . . this is Lieutenant Halloran."

The two men shook hands and Sellinger gave his warm and eager smile. Halloran liked him at once and grinned back.

Her husband's extraordinary telephone call left Margaret Sellinger in a state of anxious bewilderment. He was a naturally reserved person and came from a background in which the control of emotions was considered to be a duty. He rarely if ever admitted to depression or stress, and any worries he may have had during their ten years of marriage had been kept to himself. They discussed problems relating to Sarah's upbringing and shared most domestic and social decisions, and he did not hide the fact that he loved Margaret dearly, but he had never spoken to her as he had during the call to the hospital that day.

She knew it had to do with her affair with Halloran. There was no doubt that Paul sensed the growing distance between them she had been unable to disguise, and somehow it had made him feel less of a man. Margaret thought over their years together, during which he had unfailingly provided for herself and the child, cushioning her life with affection, loyalty, and security, and dealing with every financial demand. He was an exemplary husband and father. She felt sick with herself for having caused him to doubt himself and to expose this despair so openly.

During the next few hours the staff nurse reproached her twice for leaving tasks half-finished, and after several patients requiring blanket baths had been overlooked, the ward sister called her to the office.

"How many hours' duty have you done, Nurse Sellinger?" she asked.

Margaret, barely aware of what day it was, took some time to work out the answer. "Twenty, sister."

"And yesterday?" she queried.

"I really can't remember." Margaret looked blank and exhausted.

"How long did you work over last weekend?" probed the senior nurse.

"Two days, I think," she replied.

"Well, it's time you went home for at least forty-eight hours," the sister stated.

"There are only two other nurses on the ward," Margaret protested.

"Yes, but they came on duty this morning, so they're quite fresh—and I'm here," pointed out the other woman. "Overtired nurses are dangerous nurses, and I think you have done all you could be expected to do, so I don't want to see you for the rest of the week."

Margaret dozed on the subway home, dreaming troubled, disoriented dreams which left a nervous residue, but no memories, when she awoke with a start at her station. She was too tired to notice the biting cold, and the walk down the short, expensive street to her house seemed to take a very long time in the early darkness of the winter afternoon.

She was only vaguely surprised to find the hall light burning as she opened the front door, and she absently thought Paul must have left it on by mistake that morning. She put her umbrella in the small corner stand, then wheeled toward the soft scuffle behind her.

Sarah, barefoot and in a pink quilted robe, had appeared and was running down the stairs.

"Mummy! Mummy!" She jumped into her mother's arms.

Margaret Sellinger was suddenly suffused with pleasure and hugged and kissed the child adoringly.

"Isn't this a lovely surprise," Sarah was shouting. "Daddy wanted it to be a lovely surprise."

"Oh, it is, darling," replied her mother, happily picking her up and swinging her around in a wide arc.

"He phoned Miss Rogers this morning, and I think he told a bit of a fib to get me home," the little girl told her. "But it worked, 'cause they put me on the train at Haslemere straightaway, and here I am."

They wandered, with their arms around each other, into the living room, where a coal fire was blazing, and they sank onto the sofa beside it. Margaret kissed her again.

"Mmm. Your hair smells good."

"Mrs. Carlin washed it and got soap in my eyes."

"Did you cry?" asked her mother.

"Wouldn't you cry if Mrs. Carlin got soap in your eyes?" the child retorted.

"Yes, I expect I would." Margaret nodded, and then glanced behind her through the open door into the hallway. "So where's Daddy?"

"He came to meet me and brought me home, and then went out," said Sarah. "Mrs. Carlin gave me lunch and was going to have me all dressed and ready for when you came home, but you're early."

Margaret felt suddenly and inexplicably frightened, and asked, "Did Daddy say where he was going?"

Sarah bounced on the springy seat beside her. "He left a note on the pillow. I think that's romantic."

The sense of fear clutched her more tightly. She stood up and hurried into the bedroom, switching on its light, although the blackout screens were not yet in place over the windows. The sealed envelope was on the clean white pillowcase on her side of the bed.

Margaret picked it up and turned it over once or twice before sitting down on the edge of the bed slowly, afraid to open it. All her instincts told her something was very wrong.

Sarah galloped through the door and jumped on her lap. "What does Daddy say?"

Margaret slit the envelope very carefully, as though intending to reuse it. She drew out the folded paper and stared at it.

"What does he say? Go on, read it!" Sarah ordered urgently.

Her mother's eyes scanned the writing and widened. It was a short note, but she was trembling by the time she reached his signature.

"Is it mushy?" Sarah wanted to know hopefully.

Margaret caught sight of herself in the dressing-table mirror opposite; her eyes were huge, and heavy shadows dappled her drawn face around them and in the tired hollows of her cheeks.

"Daddy . . . Daddy has to go away." She tried to sound normal. "On a little trip."

"When will he be back?" Sarah asked with interest.

"Soon. Soon."

"Will he bring me something?" the little girl wondered, and then drew back from her mother. "You're all wet."

Margaret realized for the first time that it must have been raining outside and she had forgotten to take off her coat. Her hands ran absently over the damp lapel, as Sarah jumped off her knee and rattled on, "I did a painting of a *Tyrannosaurus rex*—in orange. Have you ever seen an orange *Tyrannosaurus rex?*"

She had reached the doorway and turned. "Come on, Mummy. Look at it."

Margaret did not really hear her, and kept looking down at those few words on the headed paper. She wanted to pick up the phone on the bedside table and talk to him, and reassure him. But it was too late. There were no details, but she knew he had gone on some wild, treacherous mission, and might even be killed, unnecessarily, just because of her. Her face stared back at her from the mirror like a death head, and she felt panic-stricken. She moved toward the door as in a slow-motion movie.

"Mummy! Come on!" Sarah's imperious voice carried up the stairs. "Come on!"

The plane rumbled over the English coastline to the Channel, and soon only the muscles of the sea were flexing beneath it. Halloran could see them in the starlight, sleek and black and deceptively solid. Some miles to the west a flight of aircraft was droning back from France, a squadron of British Lancaster bombers, probably.

The B-25 ducked into an air pocket and bounced out again like a kangaroo. Cimino yelped, and Halloran grinned. It was almost like taking a joyride, and he was tempted to do a roll just for fun, to give the bombardier something to pray about.

Hyer was watching the lieutenant fly, intrigued by the change. Halloran was more like his old self, relaxed and genuinely enjoying the machine in his control. The copilot stretched in his seat and whistled softly to himself, tilting back his head. Above the glazed fairing the stars slid smoothly across the sky, making it seem as though the aircraft was suspended motionless over the water.

In the nose cone Cimino had been wrestling with the problem since they left base, and not being good at keeping such worries to himself, finally came out with it.

"I don't mean to be pushy," he began, "but that Englishman we've got on board . . . he isn't an Englishman. He's your actual kraut. You can tell by the little lightning bolts on his collar."

"Yeah. I forgot to let you know. We've decided that the Germans can't lose," replied Halloran. "So we're going to join their side."

"Oh, goody. I just love the uniforms," rejoiced Cimino. "Not to mention all those big blond Fräuleins. When do we start?"

Halloran, who had forgotten his passenger until the interruption, inquired through his microphone, "Captain Sellinger . . . you okay?"

"Quite well, thank you," the Englishman's voice carried back.

He was sitting quietly in the belly of the plane, adjusting the string of his parachute and thinking with calm curiosity about the days ahead. Margaret would be home by now and would have read his note. He hoped she understood and that the presence

of the child would counteract any alarm she might
feel, but the journey to the American air base and
this flight from England made her seem very far
away. He was surprised to find the pain of their
estrangement receding with her. The future held his
attention and already seemed more real.

"We're over the French coast," Halloran's voice was
informing him. "We'll steer clear of any German positions."

"I'm beginning to think this is not such a crazy mission," Cimino put in.

"When the time comes, we'll remove the belly
hatch, Captain. That's where you'll drop through,"
the lieutenant went on. "Remember, keep your arms
in tight to your body until you're clear of the props."

Sellinger felt his pulse lurch slightly, but not un-
pleasantly.

"I shall remember. Thank you," he answered com-
posedly.

The matt land below was a vague mass of shadow,
not a single light betraying town or village, just soft,
deep charcoal gray, like a raincloud. Hyer closed his
eyes, tired after yesterday's all-night poker session. A
voice from above and behind announced that Sergeant Lucas was singing.

> Oh, the colonel kicks the major,
> And the major has a go.
> He kicks the poor old captain,
> Who then kicks the NCO.
> And as the kicks get harder,
> They are passed on down to me.
> And I am kicked to bleeding hell
> To save democracy.

Cimino clapped loudly and shouted, "Where'd you
get that, Lucas?"

"Off this English Wren I met," he answered.

"You sure she wasn't a sailor in drag?" goaded Halloran.

"No, sirree. She was a genu-ine all-female female,"
came the stout reply.

Paul Sellinger smiled quietly to himself. All those
reports of the casual ease between ranks in the U.S.
forces were obviously true. It would be hard to imagine such an exchange between a British officer and
enlisted man. Crouched in the airplane, surrounded
by the relaxed and good-natured crew, he felt supported and protected, and wondered how it was going to be, alone out there in the night.

Halloran was humming "Macnamara's Band" in
echo of Lucas' song. They could all hear him through
their headsets, and he gazed idly through the window at the stars, feeling more content than he had
for months.

Suddenly the sky lit up yellow-white. Halloran's
face reflected the flash, and the sky went black again.
There was another streak followed by the sound of
shell explosion. The airplane shuddered violently in
the flak.

One by one, searchlight beams pierced upward
like lances from the ground, swinging through the
air until their points of steel light quivered on the
big bomber, which was shaking like a toy in the hand
of a child throwing a tantrum.

"Oh . . . Jesus Christ!" Cimino's voice sounded
strangled.

The violent balls of incandescence were shattering
all around them, turning Halloran's face from the
deep red of the gauge lights on the control panel to
neon yellow-white. His lips had tightened as he
fought to gain control of the machine. Beside him,
Hyer had woken up with a start and was checking
the dials, with shock still in his eyes.

Sellinger, who had been flung across the belly compartment by the first explosion, was trying to crawl
on hands and knees toward the ribbing for something
to hang on to, but kept being bounced away.

Halloran had been momentarily paralyzed by the
first eruption of antiaircraft fire, but then a familiar,

cold clarity took over and all his wiles and skills as a
flier surfaced again. Now he was flying in a kind of
grim exultation, twisting and banking and diving in
an attempt to dodge the searchlights.

Flak detonated to the left, and he veered sharply
away. There was a head-splitting sound and a flare
whiter than anything imaginable as the plane took a
direct hit on the right. It dropped as if there was a
hole in the night. Halloran pulled back on the wheel
with his whole weight. The aircraft found support-
able air at last and staggered forward.

"How bad is it?" he shouted to Hyer.

The plane twitched upward again, impelled by another hit, bucking through the dark.

"Oh . . . Jesus." Cimino's voice was a mumbled
groan beneath the racket.

Wind was shrieking in the cockpit.

"How bad is it?" Halloran yelled again, and then
looked over.

Hyer was strapped in the copilot's seat. His mouth
was open, blood gushing from it. The windows on his
side of the cockpit were fragmented, the shredded
metal of the wall flapping in the gale. Hyer's chest
was clawed open. His neck was at an angle it should
not have been.

Halloran's eyes remained riveted on him. "No! It's
a mistake. It's all a mistake." He refused to believe it,
the pointlessness of it, and searched stupidly for a
reason. "Maybe because we're flying at night . . . it's
too dark."

"Dear Jesus." There were bubbles in Cimino's voice,
as though he was talking through a glass of water.

Halloran reached out and touched the second lieutenant's dead hand. Rich, blond, handsome, young
Hyer, their mascot, the charmed force in the shelter
of which they should all have been safe.

"You're not supposed to die . . . not you. Don't you
understand?" He pulled at the cold fingers. "It's all a
mistake."

Hyer's body was flapping as the airplane shook, his

head bobbing up and down, his right hand, palm up, waving on his knee. It could not be possible to rip up such a life at random. Surely it was not possible. Halloran looked frantically around and howled at the night.

"Stop it! Stop it! It's a mistake! I keep telling you it's all a mistake!"

A thin moan sounded through his headset. "Oh . . . Jesus . . ." Cimino in the nose cone.

"Lieutenant Halloran! Lieutenant Halloran!" an unrecognized English voice called. "Are you all right?"

Who the hell was it? The pilot snapped back into awareness, and remembered.

"Sellinger! We're hit up here," he shouted back. "It's bad. I don't know if I can keep it flying."

The plane was staggering down the sky.

"I'm afraid we've been hit back here," Sellinger reported.

"How bad?"

"Rather bad." It was a typical English understatement.

"Lucas! Giles!" Halloran called his sergeant and corporal, but there was no answer.

"I think they're dead," said Sellinger.

The bombardment of flak stopped as the searchlights lost them, and the sound void was filled only by rushing air and the single lame engine stuttering and coughing. Something was missing. There was a voicelessness.

"Cimino! Cimino!" Halloran yelled.

The plane jerked sideways. There was no answer. He flipped the automatic-pilot switch, unstrapped himself, and climbed out of his seat, giving Hyer a last horrified stare before leaving the cockpit. Plunging into the passageway, he crawled down to the entrance to the glass nose. Wind was blowing through to the interior. The antiaircraft fire started up again, its flashes illuminating the sky, its explosions combining with the gale into a pandemonium of noise.

The front of the nose had been blown away. Cimino was slammed back against the entrance. Fighting against the air current, Halloran reached him and turned him over.

A scream was torn from the pilot. "Don't . . . don't do this . . . please . . . don't . . ."

His hand had jerked instinctively to his face, fingers spread protectively in front of his eyes, his guts heaving up to his throat in revulsion at the sight.

Sellinger squeezed through the entrance behind him and looked down at the body. "My God . . ."

Halloran had dragged his hand down again and was gaping, hypnotized by what was left of his friend.

"He has no face," he said dully at last.

"The two men back there. They are both dead." Sellinger was shaking, but forced the words out steadily, fighting for self-control.

"He has no face," Halloran repeated wonderingly, lips drawn back with instinctive disgust and misery.

Cimino's leg was resting against his foot, and as Halloran moved back, blood pumped through the bombardier's pants.

The stark truth of their situation slapped Halloran, and he twisted away, pushing Sellinger through the passageway to the body of the plane. They had to get out. He tore at the belly hatch and finally hauled it up. A gust of wind screeched through. Pulling at the captain, he guided him forward.

"Keep your arms close. Don't pull the ring until you're clear." His instructions were almost lost in the uproar as he shoved the Englishman through.

Seconds later, he, too, was tumbling through space, headfirst in an endless drop. Insanely, he remembered a boyhood wish to drop a nickel from the top of the Empire State Building to see if it really would make a hole right through someone on the sidewalk below.

The darkness below looked deceptively fleecy, offering for an instant an invitation, escape from all the horrors and turmoil of his life, everlasting oblivion. A shell whizzed past, with a whine so close that his body faltered in its plunge. Rage filled Halloran, and he pulled the ring.

His chute opened and he was jolted upward, then settled to a slow, floating fall. Looking around, he could see Sellinger's chute open to the left, and looking up, he saw fire licking through the midsection of the plane where Giles and Lucas were. Sadness engulfed him. Cimino, Hyer, Giles, Lucas, and himself—war had made them closer than a mere team working together. They had each become part of the others. He touched his face, and it was wet for Cimino's lost features, and there was a hard band of pain in his chest where Hyer's heart had been torn out. It was like they had slaughtered half of himself. He felt bloody and bitter at the futility of it.

The searchlights were racing back and forth. The pilot knew that if he and the English captain were spotted they would have a lot of fun picking them off. A beam fixed on the shimmer of Sellinger's parachute and held, highlighting the ballooning silk for the antiaircraft gunners below. They must have seen him. Halloran waited for the line of flak, but the searchlight moved on in a slow arc, screen-wiping the night. Then his own face became bright, and he held his breath as it shaved him and kept on going by.

In the sky above, there was a sudden gigantic explosion. The pilot stared up at the orange sun of light that used to be his aircraft. Then his eyes swiveled away and down, in time to see the ground rush up. He forced his body to stay loose and roll with the impact. Then he felt the jab of a bundle of twigs in his back and sat up.

Sellinger was already on the ground, pulling in his chute, which lay like a giant mushroom behind him on the field. Halloran began to gather his, too.

The outline of a copse emerged from the night murk; a few more feet to the right and they would both have been hung up in its trees. They bundled up the parachutes as small as possible and hid them in some bushes, then stumbled quickly through the wood until they came to a dense thicket. Forcing a gap, they crawled to its center and slumped against the bark of a gnarled tree, trying to catch their breath. Sellinger was gasping too loudly. Halloran stared up through the bare branches above. The searchlights had gone out. The stars were winking cheerfully back at him. There was not a trace of what had happened a few moments before.

"It's all gone. It's like someone took a vacuum cleaner and straightened out the mess," he said to himself. "That's not right. They should have left a mark."

He felt an old-fashioned shock at such insensitivity, such lack of respect, that life could really be so cheap. The stars seemed to shine brighter and mock him. The earth beneath smelled of damp and rotting vegetation, smelled of death. Halloran wanted to get the hell out. His angry eyes unintentionally marked down Sellinger, whose heavy breathing faltered as he attempted to smile.

"Do you know where we are?" he asked.

Halloran's mind uncannily conjured up a clear picture of the dials on the control panel, just as they had been before the aircraft blew up. "I'd say about twenty miles south of Lyons," he answered.

Sellinger began to clamber stiffly to his feet. "Well, that's where I have to go."

"I'm going to try to make my way back to the Channel," Halloran decided. "That's in the other direction."

The resistance would see him onto a fishing boat, if Jerry did not find him first. A number of men at the base had returned that way after bailing out in France. Halloran knew he was not going to die, just as he had known it when they took off; the only difference was that now the certainty of it made him feel sick.

As he stood up, Sellinger walked over holding out his hand and sympathizing. "I'm really sorry. I know how you must feel, and I'm sorry that I caused all of this."

Halloran wrenched his eyes back from the sky and looked at the hand and then at the man. He had such an open face, and the eager smile of their initial meeting had been replaced by a sincere expression of involvement. It was impossible not to like him.

"No. It's not your fault." The American lieutenant shook the hand, and added, meaning it, "Good luck."

"Thank you. Thank you for everything," stressed Sellinger, meeting his eyes.

They crawled from the thicket to the edge of the wood, where Halloran checked the sky and turned to go. He had gone only a few steps when the captain's hoarse whisper made him stop.

"I beg your pardon, Lieutenant. Lyons is north of here, you say?"

Halloran turned and confirmed it, slightly puzzled. The Englishman's stance in the shadows seemed unsure, and Halloran could sense embarrassment.

"I hate to impose on you . . ." Sellinger ventured softly after a hesitation. "However, do you happen to know which way is north?"

Halloran glanced up at the north star, brilliant over all in the sky, then looked at the English spy in the SS uniform.

"Sure," he replied, and pointed toward the farthest edge of the field. "That way."

"Thank you again," said Sellinger courteously, waved, and started walking.

Halloran shook his head and felt a grin twitch at the corners of his mouth as he set off again. He had gone about twenty yards when a yelp sounded behind him, loud as a summons to all sorts of undesirable ears. He stopped.

"I say . . . Lieutenant Halloran . . ." Sellinger's English voice carried across the silent night like a clarion

call. "I really am sorry to be such a burden on you
. . . except I wonder if you wouldn't mind giving me
a hand."

Halloran waited for a platoon of krauts to come
charging through the trees accompanied by a regiment of tanks and Luftwaffe air cover. He ran over
before Sellinger could send out more international
cries for help and found him lying on the ground, his
ankle caught in a rabbit hole and twisted. Freeing
it, he examined it gently. The captain was in obvious
pain, and the ankle was already badly swollen.

"I don't think it's broken—but probably sprained,"
Halloran told him. "It's going to be sore for a while."
He paused and looked down at the other man
thoughtfully, then continued, "Do you mind if I ask
you a question?"

"Not at all." Paul Sellinger waited quietly.

"I was wondering," began Halloran, rubbing his
chin. "Considering the fact that you don't know
north from south . . . and you can't take ten steps
without falling on your ass . . . I was wondering if you
have ever done anything like this before."

"Ah, now that you mention it . . ." The Englishman
gave that wide smile of his. "No."

"Wonderful." Halloran's eyes shot heavenward in
unspoken prayer. Then he stretched out a hand and
heaved the man up. Hauling the Englishman's arm
over his shoulders, he gripped him firmly and they
both started off together, heading north.

The pilot philosophically searched for some com-
pensatory observation, but could only conjure up:
"Well, you look very spiffing in your uniform."

They limped on together in silence. The ground
was uneven, and at one point he felt his left foot sink
into marsh. Water oozed over the top of his flying
boots and squelched down to his toes. The philosophical approach vanished, and he began fruitlessly to
query what he was doing in such a godforsaken place
in such inept company. The Englishman was very
heavy.

"I don't want to go with you, you know . . . not one bit," said Halloran. "You don't know what the hell you're doing—and I sure don't know what the hell I'm doing."

Sellinger hobbled along, leaning on him and listening without comment. The wood where they had rested slid farther away into the darkness, and another yawned like a black cave ahead.

"Here I am . . . while we speak . . . going with you," Halloran was muttering, no longer quite so certain of immortality, but unexpectedly wishing for it. "We're going to get our asses shot off."

He hoisted the injured man higher onto his shoulder.

"I'm really grateful to you. I really am," Sellinger offered earnestly, as though Halloran was giving him a lift by car from London to Brighton.

"That's just swell," commented the American flier sardonically.

10

An unnatural stillness descended on the rest of the wood as the two men crashed through it, and eyes watched them, unseen, from boughs and holes as its occupants halted the night-long hunt for victims and food. The trees were dense, and spurred branches kept hitting them, and once an owl skimmed huge and silent past Sellinger's head, making him grunt with fright.

He was in worse pain and overloading Halloran's arm. They had found a stout stick, which he tried to use as a crutch, but it was not much use. They blundered on for the next hour without speaking, and without progressing really very far. The wood seemed endless. Halloran tried to picture the ordnance survey maps of the area he had studied back at the base, to figure out exactly where they were, but he could not remember noticing a sizable forest on any of them.

He tripped over a tree stump and cursed. A pair of headlights shone straight in his eyes, and he hit the ground, pulling Sellinger with him. They were on the edge of a road. A German patrol rumbled past, its trucks brushing streaks of light across the trees. Halloran was sure they had been seen, and waited for the vehicles to stop, but they roared on. He waited until the noise of their engines grew very faint, then hoisted the Englishman up and hurried across the road to the continuation of trees at the other side.

"How far do you think we've gone?" asked Sellinger.

"How should I know?" Halloran was irritated. "You're the goddamn spy, not me. Don't you guys have some kind of magic manual that teaches you all that stuff?"

"Yes . . . yes, we do," the other admitted slowly.

"Didn't you ever read it?" challenged Halloran.

"I helped write it." Sellinger sounded awkward.

"Well, what did it say about measuring distances?" the American grilled.

There was a silence, and they continued along for a few minutes. Then Sellinger mumbled, "I can't remember."

"We're going to get our asses shot off," Halloran confirmed dolefully.

They seemed to have been going for hours. Halloran could not understand why they had seen no houses or buildings, or why the goddamned woodland seemed so endless. How in the hell had the jungle got planted in France? Perhaps they weren't in France at all. It felt more like Brazil. Were there Germans in Brazil? Why not? There were Japs in the Pacific. Perhaps the patrol had not been German at all, but an English unit on an exercise in the New Forest. Perhaps they had never left Britain, but had been shot down by their own men.

There was a snarl, followed by shrill barking as they came to an unexpected cottage in a clearing guarded by an hysterical dog. Lights went on in an upstairs window, which was flung open. Halloran and the Englishman shrank back behind a tree. A figure appeared, silhouetted against the light, with a chamber pot in its hand. There was a solid splash of water. The dog howled and scuttled off. The window slammed down and the light snapped off. The two men crept away.

They were exhausted. Sellinger was almost asleep on his feet, and Halloran was aching all over. A thin sliver of silver light was beginning to rim the hills. In another half hour the sun would be up. Halloran knew they had to find shelter and scanned the unfolding landscape. Some distance to the left, he spotted a small farmhouse surrounded by buildings, a cowshed on the edge of the cluster. He practically dragged the English captain across the last field to it.

A pair of skinny tethered cows lumbered to their feet and looked alarmed as the fugitives entered the barn and made their way up to the loft. It was stacked with sheaves of hay and smelled sweet as summer. Paul Sellinger dropped down, asleep before he landed, and Halloran covered him completely with the hay, then covered himself, hearing the reassuring sound of the animals munching below before he, too, collapsed.

The telephone rang shrilly in the dark, and the woman in the bed started awake, reaching for the light switch and the receiver in the same dazed gesture. The lamp clicked on and the scream of the bell was silenced.

She mumbled, "Hello?"

"Mrs. Sellinger?" It was an impersonal, official voice. She blinked in sleepy apprehension. "Yes."

"This is Major Trumbo."

For most of the night she had been unable to sleep, worrying about Paul and blaming herself for his wild decision. Finally an almost alcoholic stupor had overtaken her, and now wads of cotton plugged her brain as she tried to gather her senses again.

"What time is it?" she asked.

"It's about five-thirty," replied Trumbo. "I'm sorry to call you at this ungodly hour . . . however, I'm afraid I've got a bit of bad news."

Terror gripped her. "Paul! It's Paul! Is he all right?"

Major Trumbo said it bluntly. "The plane he was on was shot down."

Margaret's hand flew to her mouth, clamping in

the cry. Her muscles turned to water. She tried to speak, but no words came.

"I have no more information than that at this time," the major was saying. "It's quite possible that he bailed out and he's absolutely fine. I just don't know now."

He waited for a response. Margaret's mouth tried to release sound, but she could only rock in silent agony.

"Mrs. Sellinger. Are you there?"

"Yes . . . yes . . ."

"As soon as I learn anything more, I will be sure to call you. Your husband is a good man—intelligent —I'm certain he's all right."

The brisk optimism of his tone carried to her, but the words did not make sense. He paused, still waiting for her to respond, then went on in a slightly baffled way, "I just can't understand why he went in place of Wells. Don't understand it at all. Not like him to be so impulsive."

Margaret knew why, and the knowledge made her feel dizzy with self-loathing. The room blurred in front of her eyes, and her body swayed. She clutched at the side of the bed.

"I will call you as soon as I hear anything," Trumbo was saying again. "I'm sure he's fine."

"Thank you . . ." choked Margaret at last. "Thank you for calling."

She hung up the phone in slow motion and sat transfixed, her hand still stretched before it, for a long time. Grief and guilt blanked out all thought. Her pulse slowed to a rudimentary fitfulness and her breath became so shallow that her lungs seemed lifeless. It was as though her own existence paused. Then incoherent feelings scrambled back, and she felt chilled, her body shaking under the thin nightdress and her teeth beginning to chatter slightly. She got out of bed painfully and reached for her robe, not really aware of what she was doing. Her bare feet made no sound along the carpeted landing, and she hesitated outside Sarah's bedroom before opening the door silently. The child was asleep, her arms around the Harrods Christmas doll. Margaret stood there in the doorway, and two great tears rolled down her cheeks.

The pile of yellow-green hay was striped with the first gold of the morning sun slanting through the slats of the wooden cowshed walls, and countless particles of dust danced in the columns of light. The farm cockerel had already crowed, but the other stock were still lethargic from the night, the cows in the shed below lying lazily on their steaming straw beds and the farm collie comatose in his kennel.

In their hollowed-out cave under the sheaves, Halloran and Sellinger were sound asleep and quite invisible from above. Even in his exhaustion, the American had taken time to construct the hideout with care. Their faces were puckered with lines of tiredness and smeared with mud, and Halloran had a red weal across one cheek, where a branch had sprung back to hit him in the dark.

Suddenly his eyes jerked open and all his senses alerted. The hatch in the floor scraped, and a heavy boot stamped down on the hay, inches from his hand. The second boot stepped across him, to be followed by the smaller feet of a young woman. Sellinger started to stir out of his sleep, and Halloran's hand moved swiftly to stop the movement. They looked at each other in abject horror as a German voice spoke guttural French almost over their heads.

It was answered softly by the French girl, with a giggle in her voice. Even to Halloran, who spoke nothing but English, it was obvious they were flirting. There was a lot of rustling in the hay and then a feminine squeal. The girl skipped away, and the soldier ran after her. Halloran craned his neck to see through a gap in the sheaves as he caught her and began tickling. She rolled on the hay, laughing and kicking long brown bare legs in the air. The German tumbled on top, shouting happily, his weight pushing them both out of sight. The American and the spy could hear her urging him to be quieter in case her father heard. There was a lot of whispering, and little explosions of muffled laughter, and then the sound of clothing being taken off. The soldier's jacket was thrown away, to fall right on top of Halloran.

They could hear the lovers move, the rustling of the hay growing less, until it was as though only a mouse was trotting through it. The soldier was murmuring love talk in atrocious French, his voice growing lower and quieter. The girl had stopped laughing, and her breath was coming faster. Halloran and Sellinger could hear them gasping rhythmically and in unison. They exchanged trapped glances. The German was grunting loudly and the girl began to moan, as though hurt, as though sick. Then they heard the shot.

Halloran twisted around to peer through the veil of hay. The girl, half-undressed, was standing over the dead soldier, a revolver dangling from her hand. As he watched, she spat on the body, pulled on her panties, and tugged at her blouse, then turned to pick up the uniform jacket.

As she moved, she stepped on Sellinger's bad leg. He let out a yell of pain, and she whirled around, pointing the gun at the hay. The Englishman uncovered himself and stared at her in terror.

"*Je suis anglais*," he said in perfect French.

Her face remained stony. She was very young, about seventeen, and pretty, with a cap of short dark hair and a saucy face and brilliant, mischievous eyes, resistible only to priests—and Sellinger, on whose gray SS uniform they were hooked with unmistakable menace.

"*Levez vos mains*," she ordered, the weapon twitching in her hand.

Sellinger eyed the body on the floor behind her and raised his hands above his head instantly. Halloran kept his head down and listened to the repeated, "*Je suis anglais. C'est vrai.*"

There was the ominous click of the pistol being cocked. Sellinger flinched. It seemed a ludicrous way to die, with a sprained ankle in a French barn, being mistaken for a German officer, and having achieved nothing. But the girl was certainly homicidal. She glared down at the mound of hay covering the American.

"Do you think you could give me a hand here?" he asked rather plaintively. "She's going to kill me. She thinks I'm a German."

Halloran heaved out of the dried grass, grinning at the girl and murmuring, "I wonder why she would think you're a German."

The Englishman threw him an impolite look, and the girl, who had stepped back, now pointed the gun at him. Unconcerned, he brushed the dust and strands of hay from his flying jacket, opened it, and pointed to the American uniform beneath. She looked from it to Sellinger and back.

Halloran kept grinning. "Betty Grable . . . Hershey bars . . . Yankee Stadium . . . Hello, Joe . . ." he introduced himself persuasively.

She gave a sudden delicious smile and lowered the gun.

As the American flier stripped the uniform from the dead soldier and put it on, Sellinger told the farmer's daughter how they had come to be hiding under the hay in her cowshed. If Halloran had understood, he would have approved of the terse description. Sellinger made the destruction of the B-25 and their escape through the night sound like a Sunday-afternoon stroll. When he had finished, the girl muttered something and disappeared.

"She could mean big trouble," warned Halloran, getting ready to make a fast exit.

"Not with our friend lying about there," the Englishman pointed out, gesturing at the nude, dead German.

"What a way to go." Halloran shook his head.

Minutes later, she returned with a bag, and laying a checked cloth on the floor, as though preparing a picnic, drew out bread, cheese, some garlic sausage, and a bottle.

"Wine! But it can't be eight A.M. yet." Sellinger sounded genuinely shocked.

Halloran gave him a disbelieving look and instructed, "Take it, and eat as much as you can. We don't know when we'll find food again." Nothing would have made him admit that he, too, would have preferred coffee, though he might have drawn the line at tea.

He remembered it was Thursday, the day for meeting Margaret. He wondered what she would do, what she would think. They had never discussed the possibility of his not being there every second week, waiting in Hanover Street. He was not even sure whether she knew the name of his camp, where she could get news, though maybe it was better she did not. He felt angry with himself for not having made some plan.

Beside him, Sellinger chewed stoically through the breakfast, like he was carrying out orders, and the girl sat on the hay, her skirt spread out around her, watching them both with an expression of innocent pleasure at their appetites. The killer light had faded from her eyes. She looked enchanting in the filtered sunlight, and it was impossible to believe that only half an hour before, she had seduced the German boy to this place and shot him dead while he was actually making love to her.

She read Halloran's perplexed glance and began to talk in a low voice to Sellinger, faltering at first and then growing more fluent, her hands beginning to gesticulate, the words spilling over themselves, expressions of pain and rage and contempt and loathing and a terrible power closing in successive masks over

the young, almost childlike face. Halloran thought
you could guess the whole story without understanding a word, just by watching that face.

Sellinger made sympathetic noises and then interpreted at last. "She said she had a brother who was
killed by the Germans. Her father refused to do anything about it. He's a collaborator—out of fear more
than anything else, I should imagine. She says she is
doing what her father should be doing."

The farmer's daughter had stood up and was beck-
oning them toward the trapdoor and the wooden
stairs leading down to the cowshed. Sellinger limped
down last.

She led the way through a door at one end of the
shed to a dairy, where cream was sitting in large,
shallow enamel bowls and the previous evening's milk
from the two bony cows was still in the churn. Halloran touched her arm and stopped beside it. She took
a liter measure from the shelf and dipped it in. It
was rich and creamy, and the men drank about a pint
each.

Beyond the dairy was a tractor shed, and parked
behind the tractor was an open German staff car.

The girl jerked an unrepentant thumb toward the
loft, where the dead man lay, and said, "*Son auto.
Prenez. . . .*"

"It's his car and she says we're to take it," Sellinger
translated, then turned and kissed her hand. She
stared down at it and then at him. Halloran crossed
and kissed her cheek. Tears gathered behind her
smile, but did not leave her eyes as she waved good-
bye.

They headed southeast, with Halloran at the wheel,
along a straight road lined with poplars. In the distance they could see the peaks of the Alps. Already
the land was bulging with hummocks and hills, although the Rhone Valley would slice them in half
and there were still more than one hundred miles to
go to reach the Matterhorn. It was a clear, blue day,
hopeful with sun. If they had not been haunted by

the horrific essence of the last twenty-four hours,
they might have taken a boyish delight in pursuing
the adventure. But neither man spoke, and Halloran
decided to head for Switzerland.

They had traveled several uneventful miles when
Sellinger suddenly commented, "This is going to work
out rather well."

"I'm thrilled," he responded flatly.

"As an SS officer, I'm entitled to an aide. You're
wearing the uniform of a sergeant," the other explained. "It won't look at all out of place."

"Where won't it look out of place?" queried Halloran
with caution.

"At Gestapo headquarters in Lyons," replied the
man from British intelligence.

Halloran jammed on the brakes, and the car
screeched to a halt as he swung in his seat to growl,
"Listen, friend. You have a perfect right to get killed,
if that's what you want. But I've got a right to stay
alive."

Sellinger nodded sympathetically. "I fully appreci-
ate the position I've placed you in, Lieutenant." He
gave a concerned sigh. "However, I don't think I can
do this thing alone, because my leg is hurt. And this
job has to be done. It is vitally important."

Halloran shook his head. There was no doubt the
limeys were nuts. They got involved in a war in
which all their original allies were defeated within
the first five minutes, they rescued their entire army
off the French beaches in dinghies and fishing boats,
and they sent out spies like Sellinger who could not
walk straight, tell north from south, or what day it was,
but still expected results.

Halloran knew when he was beat, but made a last
try. "I don't speak German, in case you haven't noticed. How am I going to fool anyone if I can't
speak German?"

"If you don't speak to anyone, no one will know
you don't speak German." The answer was cool.
"That makes sense, doesn't it?"

The lieutenant scowled. That was another thing. How come they always made him feel like he was back at school? He crashed the car into gear and scorched off, still wondering how the Stan Laurel beside him had got him into this mess.

He brooded over it for several minutes as they hurtled along, then half-stood from his seat and yelled, "Shit!"

After Trumbo's call, Margaret Sellinger had made no attempt to return to bed. She had looked in on Sarah and then gone to the kitchen and automatically put on the kettle. Sitting at the table, ashen-faced, she had drunk cup after cup of strong, sweet tea until dawn, wondering whether her husband was captured, injured, or dead. How would she find out? Perhaps they would send a telegram. She began to dread, yet need, the arrival of the postman. Not knowing was worse than the truth.

There was to have been a concert next week, a rare performance of Bartok, and he had secured tickets. He had a certain wistful way of listening to music which she always found appealing. It was one of his frustrated wishes to be creative, but he had had to settle for being appreciative instead. She remembered the times they had queued all night for standing room at packed performances when they were first married, and when he had bought their first wireless, and spent night after night glued to the program in a kind of wonder that such music should come so easily and in such abundance to their living room. Margaret Sellinger was filled with longing for the ordinary, unappreciated times they had spent together.

"Mummy! What are you doing up so early?" Sarah appeared unexpectedly beside her. "I looked in your room and you weren't there."

Margaret ruffled her hair and tried to smile, standing up to open the larder door busily and bring margarine and milk from its cold slate shelves for breakfast.

She would take the child to the zoo for the day, or to the cartoon cinema, if it was very cold. Then she remembered it was Thursday. Halloran's day. She had to see him. He would know what she should do. The child grumbled with justification at being left with Mrs. Carlin, and Margaret did not reach the subway until nearly lunchtime.

Arriving in Hanover Street so much later than usual, she hurried to the doorway in which the American had hidden her that first night, and where they always met. He was not there. She checked her watch, her face tight with the tension of the past hours. Wind was blowing from the square again, and she put her hands in her pockets. It was such a cold little street.

He must have grown cold, too, and gone for a coffee, or a beer. Once or twice she began to walk around the gardens, but only reached halfway before returning quickly to the doorway, in case he had returned and found her still missing. By late afternoon she was crouched on its steps, hugging her legs. The sky was growing darker; she looked at her watch again, and then up and down the street in a reflex, without hope. Halloran would have come if he could. Something terrible must have happened. She had lost them both. She rested her head on her knees and wept silently.

The soft pack of Camels was tapped against the dashboard and a tobacco-filled cylinder slid invitingly out. Halloran put it in his mouth and flamed the lighter.

"You'd better get rid of those cigarettes," Sellinger advised.

"What?"

"And that lighter," the English captain continued. "They're American."

A lorry full of Germans roared by, like an omen, its driver saluting the uniformed spy. Halloran had cupped the smoke in his hand as they passed, and then chucked the packet and lighter into the ditch at the side of the country road. He did not suppose they were going to be able to stop off to buy kraut cigarettes. It was obviously going to continue to be an expedition full of frustrations. He gave the Britisher a sidelong glance.

The man was sitting, apparently quite relaxed, looking at the passing countryside. It was a clever face, but sort of naive, the face of a man who should be writing a thesis in a university somewhere, or playing about with test tubes in some laboratory, but not belting toward the enemy and odds on death. Halloran was younger than Sellinger, but he felt much older.

"Mind if I ask you something?" he said.

"Not at all." Sellinger gave his open smile.

"Why are you doing this? Why did you go instead of that guy Wells?"

They drove on for a while. The English captain was still looking at the fields and rolling landscape.

Eventually he murmured with diffidence, "'It's rather complicated. I don't know how to answer that."

"Try," encouraged Halloran, feeling a real curiosity.

"All my life, no matter what I did . . . I've always been the same thing . . . pleasant. I'm pleasant. I was on the stock exchange . . . a pleasant profession. . . . I'm rather pleasant-looking, if I do say so myself. . . . If anyone were asked to describe me, they would say I was pleasant." He paused and looked embarrassed.

Halloran felt puzzled. True, the guy was pleasant, but so what? What did the spying business have to do with being pleasant? Maybe he was weird, as well as pleasant.

"I never minded it that much before . . ." Sellinger was trying to explain. "Except now it is beginning to hurt . . . more than I ever thought anything could hurt."

The American shrugged. "I don't know what you mean."

"Take a look at yourself," urged the other.

"I can't . . . I'm driving."

"I'm serious." Sellinger's voice was low. "You take a good look at yourself. You will see a hero."

Halloran gave a shout of laughter. "That's a lot of crap. I'm not a hero—and I don't want to be."

"Even if you don't want to be one, you are. You can't help it," Sellinger insisted. "You're the one who is ice skating on the lake when the little boy falls in the freezing water . . . and you save him. I'm the one who gives you my coat to wrap him in. When it's all over, you're on the front page of the newspaper, telling everybody it really was nothing . . . and I have a wet coat."

"You're nuts!" It was true, he was nuts. They were all nuts. Halloran chuckled over it.

But Sellinger's next question came as a surprise. "Have you ever been in love . . . truly in love?"

Margaret instantaneously filled his mind, so completely that he could smell her clean skin and see her honey-brown hair streaming in the breeze beside him. The car skidded slightly on the road.

"Yes," said Halloran.

"I'm in love," Paul Sellinger affirmed. "I married a woman who is my morning . . . my afternoon . . . and my evening. She loves me, too—in her fashion. It's just that she looks at me sometimes . . . and she wants me to be more than I am."

He paused and gazed through the window, lost for a long moment, then added softly, "And she's right."

The car sped on along the straight, empty road to Lyons, and Halloran studied Sellinger through the rearview mirror.

The building was a huge block of marble and granite with a series of steep steps that led up to a gargoyled entrance. It looked as though it had once been a courthouse, but now a monstrously large red flag with a black swastika was billowing from a brass pole over the entrance. The Gestapo headquarters at Lyons.

Halloran drove up to it and stopped. What looked

like the entire German Army was driving by in jeeps and armored cars, and walking on the street.

"You've got to be kidding," he said to himself, immobile with apprehension.

Sellinger leaned forward and whispered to him, "You're supposed to get out and open the door for me."

The American jumped, as though a mailed kraut hand had tapped him on the shoulder, shot out of the car, and opened the rear door. Sellinger led the way up the marble steps and under the heavy shadow of the flag. Halloran opened the glass-and-wood main door for him, and he marched stiffly through.

Their footsteps echoed on the inlaid marble floor of the large foyer, and Sellinger strode unhesitatingly to the imposing staircase. His injured ankle still gave him a slight limp, which could have been a war wound, and a group of passing soldiers saluted him. He returned the gesture curtly. Halloran could hardly stop himself gaping.

The stairs led to a long hall with civilians and uniformed men moving busily across it between rooms. Sellinger indicated with his eyes a set of double doors at the far end, and Halloran hurried ahead to open them. They marched through into a large square of a room, and some of the soldiers who had been lounging there sprang to attention at the German SS officer's presence.

A clerk behind a desk straightened his collar and queried, "Yes, Colonel?"

"These are from General Wallheim. Put them in your safe. They will be picked up at a later date," Paul Sellinger barked in German.

"Yes, Colonel." The clerk stood up quickly to obey the order.

Halloran was impressed. The limey captain might not know how to walk straight on a dark night, but he certainly seemed to know how to negotiate this death trap, which was just as well, because Halloran felt like a setup for enemy target practice. His pulse was rac-

ing and he tried to avoid meeting the eyes of the other
soldiers in case one should speak to him.

"I want a receipt," Sellinger was saying.

"Yes, Colonel," agreed the clerk.

"What are you waiting for?" snapped the "colonel."

The man jumped, taking the papers hastily and
turning to an alcove at the back of the room. The Englishman watched him carefully. There was a metal
cage in the alcove, and inside that was the safe. The
man turned the lock forward, then backward twice
and forward again before the door swung open and he
deposited the papers in it.

It all seemed to be taking a suicidally long time.
Halloran remained rigidly at attention, trying to become invisible and waiting for the doors behind to be
flung open by a complete military unit headed by
the Führer himself.

The clerk scribbled at the desk and handed over the
receipt with a salute. Sellinger clicked his heels and
wheeled around, then waited, poker-faced. The American realized he had forgotten to open the door and
rushed to it with an apologetic grimace as the English
spy marched past. They paced the length of the hall,
returning salutes, and down the stairs, Sellinger holding tightly to the wooden banister to take the weight
off his ankle.

A pouter-chested sergeant was blocking the way
across the foyer. Light coming through the high windows reflected off the polished floor behind him, making him look massive. This was it. Halloran's mouth
went dry and he licked his lips, his mind careering on
through the doors to the waiting car, his body priming
to hurtle past, hopefully dragging Sellinger along and
subduing the giant with a well-placed chop or two en
route.

As they closed in, the German sergeant suddenly
leaped to twanging attention, eyes front and right arm
outstretched like a semaphore signal. They swept past,
Halloran flinging back the doors, accelerating down
the steps, and wrenching open the car for Sellinger,

before running around to the driver's side, diving in, and starting the engine.

He could feel a glaze of perspiration breaking out all over him. A convoy of trucks stamped with swastikas was grinding past, forcing him to wait before driving off. He met Sellinger's eyes in the driving mirror.

"They've changed it," the English captain said. "They've put in a new safe. It's a combination safe, and I haven't the foggiest notion of how to open it."

Halloran put the car into gear.

"I love it," he said.

11

The clocks had not yet been put back for spring, and so the nights closed in early. The homeward-bound crowds were hurrying past Margaret, sitting waiting on the steps in Hanover Street, when she raised her tearstained face at last. She had no idea how long she had been sobbing there, but although one or two passersby glanced at her, no one stopped. Londoners were not easily moved or perturbed, and most had shed plenty of tears over the past few years. They did not believe in interfering with others, and there was nowhere else in the world where you could preserve such personal privacy—or be so alone. The high rate of suicide in the city's bed-sitting rooms was not surprising, although, ironically, that was one statistic which had dropped since war began.

Margaret thought of Sarah and Mrs. Carlin, but could not bear to return to the too bright, warm home. She wandered down Regent Street to Piccadilly Circus, past Eros, symbolically imprisoned in protective boarding. She drifted into the large, impersonal Lyons Corner House. It was full of tired and disgruntled-looking customers eating fried Spam and sausages made of bread crumbs, and drinking a kind of tea which seemed to be made from iron filings.

Margaret stirred her cup and stared into space in abject misery, unable fully to understand her own isolation, conscious only of shattering loss. By the time she took a sip, the liquid was cold and a thin brown scum had formed on it.

"Hi, honey," a deep American voice said behind her.

Halloran! She whirled around, her eyes alight, her face transformed, to stare into the face of an unknown G.I.

"Now, that's the kind of hello I like." The soldier grinned, promptly sitting down beside her. "Lead on, baby, and I'll follow."

Margaret flinched as though he had hit her. She was reeling with shock and fumbled on the bench for her handbag.

"I'm sorry . . ." She faltered. ". . . a mistake."

"Aw. Don't be like that." The G.I. grabbed her hand as she tried to edge into the aisle between the tables. Near to hysteria, she jerked it away, knocking her cup over. The cold dark liquid spilled over his uniform.

"You bitch!" he shouted.

She turned and fled.

She knew her eyes were still swollen when she reached her local subway station, and realized she could not be seen yet by the child. Walking slowly up the hill, past the pond to the heath, she passed the pub on the corner. The sight of it added to her distress as a reminder of evenings spent there with Paul and friends—so sure the love and fun and friendships would last forever that she had forgotten to value them, before the war, before Hanover Street.

The grass was springy as a Wilton beneath her feet. The new moon had risen early. She had noticed it low in the afternoon sky while waiting for Halloran. Now it was at its height, slim as a fillet of platinum, surrounded by cold stars. There was a purity about the night in its winter frost that touched and calmed her, slowing down the reaction of panic she had felt ever since Major Trumbo's telephone call. She sat on the grass and let the icy air drive against her. It was like plunging into the sea. Her thoughts became more coherent. Her scattered emotions concentrated into a sense of quiet grief.

By the time she reached home, Margaret Sellinger was in control of herself once more. She put on her glasses before opening the front door into the well-lit hall.

Sarah met her in a flying tackle of affection and then observed, "Your eye's all bloodshot, Mummy. Have you been crying?"

"No, silly." Margaret smiled and tugged one of the child's pigtails lightly. "I got something in it today and the wind has probably made it look worse."

She managed to appear only a little more restrained than usual during the next two hours before her daughter went to bed. Then she sat before the fire in the living room and opened Paul's note again.

It contained no information about the mission. She did not even know where the plane had been shot down. She tried to believe he was safe, and she tried not to think of Halloran.

Margaret left early the next morning and arrived at the imposing Whitehall building not long after the porter had opened its heavy doors. It was a place not unlike the Gestapo headquarters in Lyons, with a pillared entrance hall and wide, polished oak staircase. She followed directions to Trumbo's office, knocked once, and walked in.

He was already at his desk, and stood up, slightly startled by her unexpected appearance. They had met once or twice socially, and he came quickly around the desk, hand outstretched toward her.

"Why, Mrs. Sellinger. What a pleasant surprise."

"I'm sorry to barge in on you like this, Major Trumbo," she began. "It's just that I haven't heard anything since we spoke last, and I've been beside myself. I was hoping that you had learned something new."

Trumbo touched one of the armchairs in a courteous invitation to her to sit down, then sat in the one opposite.

"Would you like some tea or coffee?" he asked.

"No, thank you," she replied.

He lifted a carved box from his desk and opened it. "Cigarette?"

Margaret shook her head and challenged impatiently, "Major, what on earth happened?"

He gave her a reproving look, as though she had broken some rule, then admitted slowly, "We don't know. The plane is missing. Not a trace. Not a word. Nothing." He shook his head, frowning. "I still can't understand why Paul acted so impulsively."

"I can," Margaret murmured to herself.

"Really? Why?" queried her husband's commanding officer with curiosity.

"It's not something I can explain," she said lamely.

Trumbo felt uncomfortable, afraid that the woman would break down and cry, wishing she would go away and let him get on. Women did not fit in with situations like this.

"Mrs. Sellinger, I assure you I will contact you the moment I hear anything." He tried to sound sympathetic and reassuring. "I've spoken to the American colonel—Bart, I believe his name is—and they are waiting for some word themselves."

"Who is Colonel Bart?" she wanted to know.

"Paul was in an American plane from the Eighth Air Force. This man Bart is the wing commander." Trumbo determined to give no more details. Sellinger could be all right, and their plan might be in operation. He could not risk security.

Margaret asked at once where she could find Colonel Bart.

"At Letchworth," the major replied reluctantly.

To his relief, she stood up and went to the door, turning before leaving to thank him and apologize for being a nuisance.

"Mrs. Sellinger, seeing Colonel Bart won't accomplish anything," he cautioned. "He knows no more than I do."

"I'm sure you're right," she agreed politely. "Thank you again."

She left without waiting for a response.

After leaving the SS headquarters, Halloran and Sellinger cruised around Lyons to pass the time. It was an unprepossessing town, and the fact that they were both hungry and under strain did not increase its attraction.

Sellinger outlined his plan for gaining access to the German safe, and the American shrugged. He had given up trying to apply normal standards of reasonable behavior to his English partner, and besides, he was so relieved at getting out of the marble mausoleum without a kraut bayonet in his gut that he could not begin to imagine ever returning there.

"Pull over," the English captain directed, indicating a small café fronted by empty tables.

"Food?" queried Halloran.

"Hopefully," the other replied.

The flier jumped out to open the rear door and prepared to follow.

"Not you!" Sellinger fixed him with a glare. "Wait till I get back."

He marched off, leaving the American standing at attention on the pavement by the open car, feeling stupid. Sellinger seemed to stay in the bistro for a long time, and outside, in the cold, Halloran could picture him eating a huge hot plateful of food—the best, of course, because of the SS uniform. He began to grow distinctly annoyed. The role of German officer was evidently going to Sellinger's head.

When the Englishman emerged at last with a paper carrier bag, Halloran saw him ungraciously into his seat and slammed the door. Back behind the wheel, he edged the car into the flow of traffic and then scowled into the mirror.

"What was all that about?"

"Well, I would hardly lunch with my driver," the

other pointed out evenly. "And you could not order for yourself, because you don't speak French. So I got them to make up a lunch. Did you think I was eating on my own?"

The American felt sheepish and grinned, heading out of town on the road to Grenoble. After some miles, they turned off onto a track which led to a small copse. He drove between some bushes and they pulled branches over the vehicle in an attempt to camouflage it before settling down to eat the egg pie and French bread Sellinger had managed to obtain, together with a bottle of wine.

"I'm not sure whether we might have been better to stay in the town with plenty of people around," observed Sellinger. "But we need somewhere to hide, and this might do, if no one spots us."

Both men stretched out in the car and went to sleep. When the rain woke them, it was already dark. Sellinger checked the time on his German-manufactured watch. They still had six hours to wait. The rain fell steadily and the hours passed slowly, cumbrous with boredom and interrupted only once by a bicycle lamp wavering along the track past the trees, carrying a farm worker home. But at last it was time to leave again. Halloran stretched stiff muscles and eased the car into gear.

Lyons, when they returned, was almost deserted, and it was two A.M. when they glided to a stop outside the looming building. Sellinger took a deep breath, stepped out stiffly, and strutted through the door. A solitary duty soldier saluted as they marched past and up the elegant staircase.

The long hallway at the top seemed full of creaks and sighs, and Halloran's eyes darted in fear at every sound. Sellinger's face was stony and the walk to the double doors at the far end seemed endless. They hesitated only fractionally, their glances meeting, before the lieutenant swung them open and the English spy snapped through.

The night-duty clerk, a different one from the one in charge that afternoon, sprang to attention and rapped out, "Good evening, Colonel."

Sellinger addressed him in German in the clipped tones of authority. "There are some papers in the safe for General Wallheim. I would like to make sure they are in order. I brought them here today. Here is my receipt."

The clerk studied the receipt with suspicious eyes. He was a stout man with a face crumpled into a permanent moue of self-importance. Halloran closed his eyes and waited for doom.

"Sir. This is a receipt that you brought the papers in," the clerk exclaimed. "It is not an authorization for you to take them out."

Sellinger drew himself up to full height. He looked impressive and distinguished towering over the other. "Did you hear what I said?" he rasped.

Halloran read their faces and interpreted the staccato tone of their voices and chewed his lip.

The German clerk was slightly intimidated and ducked his head a little to blink defensively over rimless glasses. "I'm very sorry, Colonel—"

"You do as you are ordered," roared Sellinger.

The other's features grew more puglike as he maintained stubbornly, "Colonel, I need authorization—"

Halloran's ears almost fell off as the double doors behind him opened and a soldier came in carrying a manila envelope, which he took over to the clerk. He straightened automatically at the sight of the SS colonel and saluted.

The clerk took the envelope and shifted toward the wire cage in the alcove. Sellinger moved around the desk to follow him, and the soldier relaxed to see the senior officer turn his back. He nodded a relieved greeting to Halloran, who managed to release a frozen smile back.

There was a jangling of keys and a faint scraping of metal as the wire cage was unlocked and the clerk walked through to the safe. Sellinger stood determinedly in the entrance of the cage, and the man wavered, beginning to flush.

"Colonel . . . I . . . I need an authorization to give you the papers."

"This is ridiculous," protested the disguised spy, sighing loudly with annoyance and clicking his fingers.

The soldier had taken out a packet of cigarettes and now offered one to Halloran. There was nothing the American would have rather had in his hand at that moment, except perhaps a machine gun, but he shook his head, wishing the other two would return to the room.

But the clerk had started to release the combination lock on the safe, twisting the dial first one way and then back. There was a click, followed by another.

"Just where am I supposed to get an authorization at this hour?" Sellinger snarled.

The man paused, then spun the dial again to the third number, before answering. "I'm not sure. Captain Winkler is on duty on the third floor."

In the office behind them, the soldier had walked over to Halloran and whispered something in his ear. The American looked back, trying to keep terror from his face. The man grinned. It must have been a joke. Halloran's mouth spread widely in response. The soldier was burly and hearty, with the complexion of a dedicated Bavarian beer drinker.

The sound of the captain's voice speaking angrily in German to the clerk carried clearly from the alcove. Halloran's stomach had turned into a block of cement. He could feel the plan disintegrating while he stood there helpless.

"I can't go traipsing all over this building looking for authorization," Sellinger was insisting.

The German soldier tried to communicate again with Halloran in that incomprehensible guttural whisper, and the lieutenant gave him a sidelong look. The man laughed. Halloran did his best to laugh back, rolling his eyes in the direction of his colonel as an excuse for restraint, but the soldier laughed louder, so he joined in. Their guffaws resounded through the office and the soldier slapped him heartily on the back. Halloran returned the gesture with enough emphasis to knock the other back a pace. They roared in joyful unison.

The clerk had spun the dial to the final number and pulled down the handle. Sellinger watched fiercely, willing him to give in over the formality of the authorization.

In the street below, a German staff car pulled up behind the car used by the two Allied spies. Four soldiers climbed out and were stamping up the entrance steps, relaxed and talking loudly to each other.

The soldier in the room whispered something else to the American, who laughed efficiently. The man looked at him, and he nodded and smiled. The soldier stopped smiling.

"Terrific," muttered Halloran to himself, and swung from the heels as the German reached for his gun. He hit him square on the jaw. The head snapped back under his fist and the body began to sag. Halloran hit him again and he dropped to the floor.

The man at the safe had wheeled around at the sound of the scuffle, but Sellinger's gun was against his neck in an instant. The clerk twitched his hands in the air, his face blotching with fear.

The newly arrived soldiers were clattering across the marble-floored foyer below. They were jovial, as though they had just come off duty after an evening fraternizing with willing French girls. Two of them were straightening their uniforms as they approached the main staircase.

Sellinger had begun to riffle through the papers in the safe, still keeping his gun trained on the clerk, who was shaking so violently that even his jowls quivered. Halloran was dragging the unconscious body of the soldier across the floor and behind the desk when he heard the racket of the approaching soldiers. They sounded like a regiment of horse, their boots echoing on the stairs. He worked feverishly, hauling the soldier onto the clerk's chair, swiveling it around and propping him up against the desk.

The noise of tramping boots was growing louder and nearer. Sellinger was still searching for the papers. Halloran's hands were trembling.

He grabbed the cigarette packet from the soldier's pocket, then searched for the lighter. He spun the wheel against the flint once, but it did not catch. A second time. It lit. He flamed the cigarette and shoved it in the soldier's mouth.

The approaching men had started down the hallway. The clerk heard them just as Sellinger found the papers and spread them on the table beside the safe. Still with his gun cocked, the English spy took a Minox camera from his pocket.

Halloran, itchy on his feet, squinted through the alcove, dived across the cage, and snatched the camera, exploding, "Are you out of your goddamn mind?"

Grabbing the papers and stuffing them in his pocket, he slammed the safe closed and gave Sellinger a shove toward the door. The Englishman's revolver slanted, and the clerk, listening to the voices of the oncoming soldiers, decided to chance it. He opened his mouth to shout. The words never emerged. Halloran hit him in the throat with his gun and then on the back of the head. He went down like a paperweight.

The two men closed the metal cage, with the inert body still inside, and checked the soldier at the desk. He was still unconscious and looked like remaining that way for an hour or two.

The four Germans were only a few feet from the end of the hall when the double doors swung open and Sellinger stormed out, Halloran at his brisk heels. They straightened like boards and saluted. The SS colonel deigned to return the salute curtly, without breaking stride. His aide stared straight ahead. As soon as the soldiers walked through the double doors, the two spies started to run.

On entering the office, the Germans saw the soldier

sitting behind the desk, casually smoking his cigarette. Some papers were in his hands, and he had his back to them.

As Sellinger and Halloran sped along the hall, the first man asked, "Where is Corporal Leiter?"

The soldier behind the desk did not answer. He did not turn around. The smoke from his cigarette curled upward.

"Where is Corporal Leiter?" repeated the other.

Still no answer. Two of the waiting soldiers looked at each other, raised their eyebrows, and shrugged.

"I'm talking to you!" The first raised his voice angrily.

The others walked over to join him, waiting for the insolent desk clerk to answer.

The American and the Englishman had reached the top of the stairs and were trying to hurry down, Sellinger gripping the wooden rail and stumbling with his bad leg, when the first soldier tapped the man at the desk on the shoulder.

The unconscious body fell to the floor, dragging papers off the desk with it.

The two fugitives were about halfway down the stairs when they heard the soldiers burst into the hallway overhead. Paul glanced behind and stumbled, missing several steps and letting out a cry of pain as Halloran caught him and tugged him on.

The soldiers appeared above just as they reached the last two steps. A shot rang out. The bullet ricocheted off a marble tread and angled up into a chandelier with a pleasant tinkle. The second shot splintered the wood on the banister by Halloran's hand.

"Son of a bitch!" he swore, dropping to his knees, wheeling, and firing upward. He caught the first soldier in the thigh, spinning him around. A follow-up shot chipped the stone in front of him, and a third hit the soldier behind in the face. The first tumbled down the stairs, making grunting sounds as he hit each step, and Halloran, with electric reflex, had twisted toward the exit even before the second soldier staggered backward from the force of the bullet, grabbing his face.

The two remaining Germans were firing from the head of the stairs as Sellinger pulled at the door, and its glass panels shattered. Halloran passed him, bounding down the marble steps three at a time, but the Englishman could only tackle each one individually. He was just halfway there by the time the other had reached the car.

Across the street, three other soldiers, responding to the sound of shooting, had come running out of a doorway, and the noise of windows being opened and voices shouting came from high in the building overhead.

Halloran dived into the driver's seat and started the car. Bullets were skipping down the steps around Sellinger as the pursuing men fired through the gaping hole in the glass. As he watched Paul Sellinger limping pathetically toward him, the American wanted to sob. The whole affair had become grotesque. The car engine was throbbing sensuously. In slow motion the three soldiers across the street drew their guns, and bullets began zinging by. Orders and counterorders rang from the windows above. It was like the finale to a mad movie.

The disguised captain finally blundered headlong into the back of the car. Halloran kicked the accelerator to the floor and the vehicle squealed away, the rear door crashing against the side panel. Two bullets smashed through the windscreen, and the car veered up the steps, swerved off, spun, and skidded in the opposite direction past the soldiers who had fired at them, taking the corner into a narrow side street on two wheels.

By this time, the entire city seemed to be in an uproar, with sirens blaring and alarms ringing. They hit an alleyway of cobblestones and bowled along it, Halloran biting his tongue and cursing, and Sellinger struggling to get off the floor and reach the dangerously swinging door.

Forbidden light flickered on in a house, and a woman's voice shrieked something as they passed.

"What did she say?" Halloran asked.

"She was wishing us to hell," mumbled Sellinger.

It was very comforting. They doubled back through narrow sidewalks, scraping the sides of the German car against projecting walls, the lieutenant relying on a gingered-up sense of direction to get them back to their original route. Once, shooting out into a main thoroughfare, they found themselves alongside a military-police car, its siren screeching. Even before Halloran could betray them by braking, Sellinger had stood up in the rear seat and shouted an order, pointing ahead imperiously. The police car scorched off. Halloran jetted down the next street.

"What about backing into a yard or an empty garage for an hour or two, till all this dies down?" suggested Sellinger.

Halloran shook his head. "They'll have this town sealed off pretty soon, and then they'll comb it from end to end," he said, driving through a square of silent buildings.

There was a gap at the far side. He eased the car through it and whooped as they found themselves on the road by which they had entered Lyons that morning. The houses of the city soon left the hunt and merged into a castlelike silhouette behind them.

Headlights approached from a distance, and the American turned off his own and swung from the road. Although the car lurched onto an unfenced field, he did not stop driving. A German patrol lumbered along the road . . . past them . . . and then out of sight. Halloran snapped his headlights back on and continued careering over the rough field.

After leaving the major's office and walking down Whitehall, Margaret Sellinger reached Parliament Square and paused, not sure of what to do next. She intended to travel to the American air base in Hertfordshire, but needed time to prepare herself. The

visit to Trumbo had been a strain, although she had
not betrayed this. In fact, he had been left thinking
her remarkably cool.

On impulse, she made for the Embankment, past
the Houses of Parliament, and walked steadily along
it for some minutes. The sun was a white disk in a
colorless sky, sending down no warmth, but bringing
an enameled shine to the black waters of the Thames.
A line of barges, loaded with planks of wood and
metal pipes, drifted by like a toy. A man and a boy
were skipping from one to the next with surefooted
speed. Margaret leaned against the river wall and
watched them disappear beneath Westminster Bridge.

In summer, small naked boys would jump from the
bridge to swim in the fishless river, risking typhoid
probably, though no one had ever been known to die
after such an escapade. But the river police made
great drama of it and pursued them to the banks in
their motor launches, perhaps because they were so
close to the veranda of the House of Commons, where
members sat with their visitors.

Turning her head, she could see a pair of figures
clinging with some difficulty to the underside of the
next bridge. By the time she reached it, they were
climbing up a small flight of stone steps in the wall,
with squelching shoes and watermarks over the turn-
ups of their pants, and they carried a brace of pigeons
in each hand. Margaret had occasionally wondered
where the restaurants got their supplies for the pie
which appeared so often on wartime menus. She
knew now, but could not smile.

She stared at the moving water and did not struggle
against the meanderings of her mind. The Thames was
full of activity and incident, of passing boats and bobbing buoys, of ducks and remarkably clean white
swans. A barge cargo was being unloaded into a
warehouse opposite. She saw them all and reacted to
nothing. It was as though she was outside herself,
watching herself mourn with downturned face and

limp body, but feeling nothing beyond a dull bleakness.

It was tempting to believe she was being punished, that risking Paul for Halloran had cost her both of them. A gaping crater in the south-bank waterline caught her eye. People might have died there, too, and everyone could not be guilty of secrets like hers. She thought of friends who had been widowed, and she was positive nothing they had done could have deserved such retribution. Nothing she had done warranted such a judgment. Yet, like Halloran, she could not accept that it was all a lottery.

Her slow walk had taken her to the front of the Tate Gallery. It was years since she had been inside. She went up its steps automatically and wandered unseeing through its vast light rooms hung with paintings. There did not seem to be anyone else there, except the ancient men in gallery uniform who dozed in corners near the doorways. The building was a Chinese box of high chambers leading one to the next, without end. The masterpieces on their walls were blurred squares of color. She had no idea which direction she was taking or why she was there, but at last she sat down on a bench and gazed at the picture straight in front. It was a white landscape like the day outside, a small figure in the foreground, a phantom sail and a band of dark grey sea, and in the sky a pinpoint of light: Turner's *Evening Star*.

"There, now, dearie. Don't take on so. We've got to keep fighting, and it'll all be over soon."

The elderly attendant was beside her and patting her on the shoulder. Margaret suddenly realized that tears were rushing down her face again.

"Why don't you go to the cafeteria for a nice cup of tea?" he suggested.

"Yes," she said brokenly. "Yes." And crept away.

In the cloakroom she took out her compact and pressed powder over her skin, drying up the tears and covering the inflammation with a fine white film. Then

she outlined and filled in her mouth with scarlet lip-
stick and combed her shoulder-length hair. Her eyes
looked back from the mirror sternly.

It took two and a half hours to cross London and
make the train journey to Letchworth and through
them she forced herself to study the railway time-
table carefully, and then bought and read a newspaper from end to end, straining to concentrate on each
item, refusing to give her feelings a chance to take
hold again.

A lanky soldier with a crew cut and a schoolboy
face led her to the concrete office building at the
American base, past uniform squares of Nissen huts
and a line of spotless trucks. The place had an air of
rigid order, unbroken by an unpainted window frame,
a discarded chewing-gum wrapper, or a serviceman
with a loose bootlace. Margaret thought of Paul's
comfortable, cluttered office, with all the treasured
objets in pleasant disorder on the chimneypiece and
shelves, and wondered how he could have been driv-
en to this.

When the soldier opened the dark green door, the
American officer was already standing behind his desk,
waiting for her.

"Mrs. Sellinger?" It was a rhetorical formality.

She nodded and held out her hand.

"I'm Colonel Bart," he introduced himself. "Major
Trumbo told me you were coming to see me."

There was a false sincerity about the man which
made her feel she had made a wasted journey. She
felt a little tired. "It is nice of you to take the time to
speak with me."

"Not at all . . . won't you sit down?"

He waved her to the seat where Halloran had been,
and her fingers nervously discovered and began to rub
at the same rough spot on the arm which his had
scratched only a few days before.

"I know I must seem an awful pest," she began,
anxiety giving her a certain hardness. "I just have
to know for myself . . . what has happened."

"Yes, of course." Ronald Bart had a standard voice for the widows and families of lost men. He had not had to use it too often, and an opportunity to practice was quite welcome. He lowered the tone and tried to imbue sympathy, with just a touch of directness, meant to imply that he expected his listener to take it—like the dead man—on the chin.

"Well . . . we still have received no notification of survivors." He said it straight. "We can't send any reconnaissance aircraft to check—for fear of drawing unnecessary attention to the mission. You understand."

"No, I don't," exclaimed Margaret flatly.

"Yes . . . well . . ." Bart, who had expected his pronouncement to be the end of it, looked ruffled. "There's every chance they managed to bail out."

"You don't know for sure . . ." Margaret persisted, leaning forward in the chair and pinning him down with her wide-eyed scrutiny.

"No . . . I don't . . . except I do know that if they did bail out . . ." He cleared his throat in a search for suitable words. "Your husband is in good hands. The pilot—Lieutenant Halloran—is a . . . very determined and resourceful man."

Margaret Sellinger went deathly white and collapsed back in the chair, as though he had slapped her across the face.

Not long before dawn the two fugitives reached the edge of the forest where they had emerged after the struggle from the destroyed aircraft. A path, enclosed by dense undergrowth, ran off from the road. Halloran turned into it, and shouting back to Sellinger to duck his head, rammed the car through a heavy clump of rhododendrons. Then, gathering branches of the evergreens, they filled in the screen again and set off on foot toward the farmhouse.

A thin hem of purple had appeared at the foot of the night sky by the time they had walked over the fields and knocked softly at the back door of the house. A dog shut in a nearby shed set up a cacopho-

ny of rage which sounded treacherously brassy in the
otherwise silent valley. Halloran shifted his feet, and
Sellinger leaned back against the wall, facing away
from the house, on the lookout for attack from the
buildings. As heels clicked on the stone floor inside
and the door opened at last, he turned around.

"*C'est nous*," he whispered to the French girl who
had helped them that morning.

"Apple pie." Halloran nodded, grinning.

She stepped swiftly outside, throwing warning
glances toward the second-floor window above and
motioning them to be quiet. Then she led the way
across the yard to the barn, and as they followed, curtains parted in the window and an elderly man looked
out.

The skinny cows were already on their feet and
pulling hay in dusty tufts from metal mangers at the
head of their stalls. The girl stood at the foot of the
ladder as they climbed to the loft.

"*Je reviens avec du pain et du vin*," she promised.

"*Merci . . . merci*." Sellinger smiled down through
the trapdoor.

As she left, he let out an exhausted sigh and
flopped on the hay near Halloran. A look of euphoria
crossed his face, and he leaned across to punch the
American joyfully on the arm.

"We did it! Well, I'll be damned . . . we actually
did it!"

The lieutenant gave his slow, amused smile, and
ventured, "I don't want to cramp your style or anything, but we still haven't gotten out of France yet."

"Oh, we'll get out, all right," returned Paul, buoy-
ant. "It would be absurd for us to have come this far
and then not get out."

"It would ruin my whole day," agreed Halloran
laconically.

In the farmhouse kitchen, the young French girl
had put a loaf of bread in a basket and was filling
an empty bottle with wine directly from a glass car-
boy in a walk-in cupboard cooled by a small north-

facing window. The old man had tiptoed down the
stairs and was peeking through the slightly open
door behind her. She stoppered the bottle, put it beside the bread, and went through the back door to the
yard.

The old man crept away from the kitchen up the
flagstoned lobby to the vestibule, picked up the telephone receiver, and dialed.

"'Allo," he whispered. "*Je voudrais appeler les gen-
darmes. . . . Vite! . . . Vite!*"

12

Only thirty-six hours had passed since they had first met, and yet, in a strange way, Halloran and Sellinger had grown alike. The Englishman had acquired some of the American's dynamism, and the American had developed some of the human perception and sensitivity of the other man. They had survived more danger together than with anyone else at any other time, and the shared risks had released confidences from Paul Sellinger that he had never disclosed before, not even to himself. There were no failings or weaknesses in either man that had not been revealed under the stress of the mission. Now they felt no restraint. In less than two days they had become like brothers.

"I can go back now. I can be more for her to see," Sellinger was saying, without embarrassment, as they sat back in the hay, waiting for the food.

Halloran glanced at him with interest and observed, "She must be very special."

"She is very special," confirmed the English captain. "Have you ever felt that way about any woman?"

The warm, imageless sense of Margaret hovered in Halloran's mind. "Yes, I do," he declared. "Except, with me, it's . . . different." He searched for the disparity he realized existed between the love he had for his woman and that of Sellinger for his wife. "Ever since I met her . . . I don't know who I am anymore."

The English spy contemplated him openly before emphasizing, "I know who you are. You're a good and a brave man."

"I don't feel very brave," confessed Halloran.

"That's ridiculous," retorted the other. "Look what you've done."

"I didn't do anything except try to stay alive," he admitted. "Whatever I did . . . it was because I was too scared to die."

"The only brave men are frightened men," Paul pointed out. "Men who aren't frightened aren't brave. They're insane." He paused and leaned on one elbow. "You're only brave when you have something to lose, and you still go on trying."

Halloran's hand stirred the dust of husks on the wooden floor beneath the thin covering of hay beside them as he thought about this.

"When we get back, go to her and hold her . . . and never let her go," Sellinger urged. "That's what I'm going to do when I see Margaret."

Halloran's hands stopped moving, and his lungs felt suddenly restricted.

"Tell me about your . . . wife," he said slowly. "What is her name?"

"Margaret. God, I love that name, don't you?" Paul asked illogically.

"Yes," breathed Halloran.

"How do I tell you about her? If there really is such a thing as one woman for a man, it is Margaret for me. I know it sounds like something out of Mother Goose, except it's true," the Englishman explained happily. "We have a daughter, Sarah, who looks like her mother, which is reason enough to think that she's beautiful."

As he talked, he had unfastened his German watch and opened the back of it. A little photograph was fitted inside like a locket, and he held it out to Halloran.

"Here . . . this is Margaret."

Halloran took it and looked at it, and closed his eyes.

"Isn't she lovely?" said the English captain.

"Yes," the American confirmed, not looking.

Light footsteps sounded on the wooden stairs below the trapdoor. Sellinger twisted to his feet and aimed his revolver. Halloran did not move. The door lifted upward, and the French girl put her basket on the floor before climbing through.

"*Mange,*" she instructed.

"*Merci, mille fois,*" the spy thanked her.

She spoke quickly and softly. "*Allez aux montagnes, à gauche. À huit kilomètres, une église, prés de la rive. La résistance est là. Ils attendent, maintenant.*"

"She says there is a church about eight kilometers from here where a group of the resistance is waiting for us," Sellinger translated to the American, who looked blank.

The girl grabbed first Paul's hands and then Halloran's hands, kissed them emotionally, and left.

Sellinger smiled fondly after her, broke off some of the bread, and lifted the wine bottle to his mouth, no longer concerned that it was before eight A.M.

"Here is your watch back," muttered Halloran, holding Margaret's tiny face in the palm of his hand like a pearl.

The Englishman took it and strapped it back on his wrist, eating hungrily and jerking his head toward the basket, urging, "Eat something, old man."

But Halloran had no appetite.

They heard the low growl of engines approaching the farm at the same moment. It galvanized Halloran to his feet from the stunned trance, and he sprang toward the front wall to squint between the slats.

A German staff car and three motorcycles were roaring down the rough track from the main road, and at the gate to the farmyard the elderly man was waiting and gesticulating, twitching excitedly from foot to foot and casting glances over his shoulder toward the barn every few minutes.

"Son of a bitch," Halloran spat as the patrol stopped in an explosion of dust and the soldiers dismounted from the motorcycles. "The girl's fink father called the krauts."

He wheeled around and pushed Sellinger toward the hole in the floor and they scrambled down the ladder to the cowshed below. While the Englishman bolted the main door, Halloran searched his pockets for the lighter taken from the soldier at Gestapo headquarters, flicked it alight, and set fire to a fistful of dried grass, which he flung up into the loft. It quickly ignited more of the great store of hay there, and as that began to burn, he kicked violently at the slatted rear wall until enough of the wood gave way to make a hole big enough to escape through.

The two men crouched behind the cowshed, and after listening for a second, the American gestured the Britisher to wait while he slithered across the wet morning ground on his stomach, along the side of the barn, to a corner where he could see the whole of the farmyard. Little fingers of smoke were beginning to find their way through the cracks as he passed beneath.

The old man had opened the cattle gate and was talking eagerly to the Germans, waving his arms in the direction of the barn. As he turned, smoke began to waft out of the front of the structure and curl up to the sloping wooden roof. Suddenly he saw it and began to bawl hysterically.

The soldiers drew their guns and scrambled forward, two of them hurling themselves against the door, which creaked feebly. They charged again, the rotting old building shuddering and the door cracking at the impact. Under the third attack it crashed inward, catapulting the men forward into the smoke. The rest of the patrol followed with drawn guns.

As soon as they had disappeared inside, Halloran broke from the side of the barn, running for his life. He hared across the dung-covered yard, vaulted the low wooden fence, and leaped into the patrol car, hand feverishly searching for the starter. There was no key.

"Perfect," he muttered to himself, leaping from the car and plunging toward the motorcycles.

He could hear the sounds of shouting and shots coming from the barn behind, as the soldiers milled around in the smoke, coughing and firing at random into the loft and toward the back of the structure. Bullet holes tore through the wood just above Sellinger's head. He crouched lower as, outside, the lieutenant kicked a bike starter and the motor roared into life.

He popped the clutch, the front wheel reared, and the machine snaked across the yard up the side of the barn, sliding to a stop at the back as the sound of the engine brought the first soldier running out. Sellinger had his head down to avoid the stray bullets and did not see or hear the motorbike pull up at the corner.

"Will you move!" Halloran screamed.

He bolted upright, saw the American, and ran as best he could toward him. As he climbed on, the soldier who had appeared at the front of the barn came around the side and saw them.

Without noticing him, Halloran kicked up a cloud of dirt as he spun and headed back to the yard, the only way out. The German took aim. Sellinger was hanging on to the pilot's waist as they splashed through the mud. They were no more than ten feet from the soldier when Halloran saw the barrel of the gun pointing directly at him. There was no time, only that second of recognition before the shot rang out.

The soldier hurtled forward, blood spouting from a hole in his back. Halloran looked up and saw the young French girl holding a rifle in the doorway of the farmhouse. It flashed through his mind that he did not know her name. The other three soldiers came rushing from the barn and hesitated between her and their fallen comrade just long enough for him to squeal across the yard and through the gate. As he hit the track, the gunfire opened up, the soldiers running wildly for their two remaining motorcycles and the staff car.

He drove like a maniac, skidding and swerving, cannoning over rocks and jinking to avoid the bullets. When they reached the smooth tarmac of the road, the machine uncoiled, thrusting forward in an animal leap, almost out of control. Their pursuers vanished momentarily in the exhaust, and after a few hundred yards Halloran screeched off to the left, the bike slanting so that his feet almost scraped the ground. Sellinger's eyes were squeezed shut as they bounded up hills and weaved between trees, whose boughs slashed at them as they passed.

The staff car had branched off, when the going got rough, along the road encircling the heights, but the hornetlike whine told them that the two motorcyclists were still not far behind. Halloran sliced a corner and took off almost vertically to the next crest. The steep incline ended without warning in a sudden drop of about forty feet to the road below.

He braked violently, but the machine continued sliding on, to stop with its front wheel on the very edge of the ridge. Looking down, he saw that the German staff car was already racing along the road. The motorcyclists had broken through the trees and were churning up the first slope after them in clouds of debris. The flier's eyes measured the twenty-foot gap to the other side; he grimaced and pivoted the motorcycle to head back down the hill directly at the two oncoming soldiers. The distance between them narrowed rapidly as he stormed forward about seventy-five yards, then unexpectedly wheeled around without stopping and headed at top speed back up to the top, faster and faster, to the highest point of the ridge.

The staff car had halted in the road directly below. Halloran opened the throttle all the way, the engine straining as it accelerated. He was at full speed as he hit the top. The motorbike left the ground, the back wheel lower than the front, and soared over the twenty-foot gap.

Sellinger's eyes flared open with shock in time to catch sight of the German driver's openmouthed face below as they passed forty feet over his head.

"My God!" groaned the Englishman, leaving his stomach behind and shutting his eyes tightly again.

The back wheel barely reached the other side. The machine wobbled and shuddered, started to spill over, caught itself, and continued careering down the opposite gradient.

The first of the harrying motorcycles had reached the top of the ridge and taken off over the chasm, but without enough speed. A wheel struck the wall of rock opposite and it pitched backward, to fall upside down on the road below, exploding in a black-and-orange burst of flame and smoke in front of the patrol car.

The second German machine tried to skate to a halt, its wheels sliding out from under the driver, who threw himself off just before it screamed over the edge of the ridge and landed in a twisted, burning jumble of metal on the side of the road. The waiting staff car sped off around it with a protesting wail.

"I think I left my kidneys back there," gasped Sellinger as they bounced on down the side of the far hill.

"You've still got your ass," Halloran retorted dryly.

He turned onto the road as the car appeared around the bend less than a hundred yards away. The motorbike erupted under him with volcanic force, blazing forward to roar around the twists and turns ahead, the throat-biting smell of scorching rubber rising from its tires and its engine howling dementedly.

Halloran saw the fragile bridge suspended over the ravine ahead as the first burst of machine-gun fire from the staff car tore up the ground to his left. He swerved to the right and reached the span as the car eeled around the last bend and the machine gun opened up again. Its fire spat up the length of the little bridge; the timbers splintered beneath the wheels of the motorcycle.

The American felt Sellinger's grip weaken and glanced down at his waist to see the clinging hands begin to let go and blood seep from under the captain's uniform cuff and down his fingers.

There was a mortar explosion behind, and the bridge swung convulsively. The bike yawled, adding to the pitching; he hooked it back under control and stared ahead.

A group of men had appeared at the far side, and as they began firing in his direction, he knew it was all over. He opened the throttle and thundered on out of pure cussedness. After an instant, he realized they were not firing at him, but at the patrol car behind. A grin of greeting spread across his face.

Another mortar shell hit the end of the bridge behind him, tearing a hole in the supports, stopping the pursuing Germans in their tracks, and causing the whole structure to tilt so that Halloran found himself riding uphill, as one side of the bridge gave way completely.

Paul Sellinger yielded his last weak hold and his body slid off the bike, to sprawl on the slats and begin tumbling toward the edge. As he rolled over, he managed to catch on to part of the railing, and Halloran reached the other side.

The band of French resistance surrounded the American, keeping up the crossfire with the Germans as he spilled from the motorbike and looked back. There was no bridge left. He stared down at his waist, at the bloodstains from Sellinger's hands, and rushed to the edge of the ravine.

The bridge was dangling from the one remaining support, and Sellinger was holding on to the railing, his feet hanging over the plunging drop. Halloran froze. Boulders and glass-edged rocks lay on a prehistoric riverbed hundreds of feet below. Wood cracked with every movement of the fractured bridge. He stood, staring down, terrified into immobility.

The Germans had begun firing at the injured Britisher, their machine-gun shells exploding on the rock face. Halloran took a deep breath, half-shrugged, and reached for the railing of the dangling structure.

His weight made it grind and totter. He began to climb down under the covering fire from the Frenchmen. The enemy in the staff car saw him and started to zero in. Foot by foot he made his way down to Sellinger, who was staring up with glazed eyes. The remaining bridge support began to give way, and bullets cracked all around them.

Halloran leaned perilously over, reached out his hand, and yelled, "Grab on!"

The veins in the English captain's forehead bulged under a dew of sweat. His face was livid. "I can't!" he gasped. "Go back!"

"I'm too scared to argue with you!" growled Halloran, swinging like a monkey above. "Grab on, dammit . . . before you get us both killed!"

The injured man weakly grasped the outstretched hand and then the wrist above it. Halloran locked his fist over the Englishman's wrist and yanked with all his strength, pulling himself back up with his remaining free hand, inch by inch through the crossfire. Sellinger's legs were scrabbling against the rock face.

"When you get . . . back to . . . London . . . please . . . look up my wife. . . . Her name . . . is . . . Margaret." He struggled to form the words through the great waves of pain as the American lieutenant jerked him up the disintegrating ladder of rails. "Please tell her that . . . her . . . husband . . . died . . . a brave man. . . ."

Halloran wrenched them up to the next hold with a loud grunt of effort, before retorting, "Tell her yourself."

Sellinger's voice was fainter as it carried to him. "It's no use. . . . I'm too weak. . . ."

"Will you shut up!" he snarled back, squinting with some desperation to the top, still about ten feet away.

The German machine-gunner in the patrol car was still firing haphazardly across the ravine, the bullets splashing over the rock like flat stones across water, sending up small sprays of flint. A gorse-covered rise protected the Frenchmen, who were keeping up a constant return of fire. Halloran had five feet to climb. There was no more noise or movement from Paul Sellinger, whose grip around his wrist had slackened. He could feel the man's arm beginning to slip from his own grasp as the body weight grew heavier. Four feet. . . . His breath was coming in noisy sobs. Every muscle and sinew, even his skin, was stretched to splitting point with the monstrous effort. Three feet to go. . . .

A hand reached out and seized him. With a final rush he forced Sellinger up and over, and collapsed beside him on the heather-covered ridge. The waiting team dragged them to cover behind the scrub. There was a brilliant flash of yellow and orange accompanied by an explosion that echoed again and again along the fissure of the gorge as the petrol tank of the German car blew up.

Halloran stumbled to his feet to see it evolve into a smoking sculpture of black metal; then he looked down at the Englishman, his friend. His chest and back were covered with blood.

"I get . . . the wet coat again," Paul whispered.

Halloran shook his head and murmured with a sad, fleeting smile, "No, pal . . . you get the girl."

Sellinger's eyes closed and his face went like paper. The American stared down in horror and dropped onto his hands and knees beside him.

"Oh, no you don't . . . you can't!" he yelled in his ear. "You die on me now, I'll kill you."

There were queues outside food shops on most days, but on Saturday morning the lines of waiting people were several times as long, as whole families engaged in the weekly battle for supplies.

Margaret left Sarah among a group of children and grandmothers outside the baker's to collect the government-authorized national whole-wheat loaves: the sale of white bread was prohibited, because it did not contain enough vitamins. She herself went on to the grocer's, taking her own buff ration book and the child's blue one. Before leaving the house, she had picked up Paul's book, too, from the kitchen drawer, but had quickly replaced it.

Many shop assistants had left to do war work, and the waiting people had grown used to inching slowly up the street to the shop door. It took Margaret nearly half an hour to reach the counter. For once she did not mind. It was a way of passing the time. Around her, the other women talked about the shortage of goods, about their jobs and the value of the new utility furniture, swapped the news about their men, and compared recipes. Margaret gratefully let herself become involved in the exchange, until she was inside the shop at last.

She bought a pound of sugar, a half pound of butter, two ounces of cheese, a quarter pound of tea, some powdered eggs, tinned pilchards, a jar of jam, and a few unrationed items—all she was allowed for two people for one week. Sarah was waiting on the sidewalk when she came out, and they lined up outside the butcher's together, and by the time they had obtained their small ration of meat, the morning was over.

They went home and Margaret cooked a quick

lunch for them both. She forced herself to eat it and smile as she listened to Sarah's continuous prattle about school and friends and games, interspersed with hoary jokes: "Waiter, there's a fly in my soup." "Don't tell everyone, sir, or they'll all want one."

Then the activity was over. The table was cleared, all the dishes were washed up, and rain forced them to abandon their plan to go out. They drifted into the living room.

"Would you like to play cards?" asked Margaret brightly. "I feel like demolishing you."

Sarah had noticed one of her father's handkerchiefs lying on the bureau and ran her finger along the edges of it, her small face suddenly intense.

"You're trying to be cheerful because you're worrying about Daddy," she accused her mother. "And he's going to be all right."

Margaret crossed the room and put her arms around her, bending to rest against her head and whisper, "I love you more than it is possible to love anyone under four feet tall."

At that moment the telephone rang, and Margaret jumped, freeing the child and dashing toward it to snatch up the receiver.

"Hello." The word had an anxious eagerness all its own. She listened to the matter-of-fact voice at the other end, color flooding her face.

"Yes," she gasped, slumped onto a chair, and covered her face with her hands, sobbing uncontrollably.

Standing opposite her, Sarah had gone rigid, still holding the handkerchief and staring at her mother.

"Mummy . . . is it good crying?" she asked in a cautious voice. "Or bad crying?"

Her mother lowered her hands and tried to answer, but could not. Her face was drowned in a waterfall of tears. She tried to smile, and managed to nod to the child.

"I knew it," shouted Sarah, grinning and jumping up and down.

Margaret Sellinger sat on the edge of her seat

throughout the long taxi ride to the hospital in the West End, seeing nothing of the streets through which they passed, but already running along the corridors to Paul's ward in her mind. The driver sensed the urgency and maneuvered through the traffic with that mixture of skill and death-defying madness unique to London cabbies, slicing corners, shortcutting down unknown alleys, and squeezing through impossibly small gaps. He drew up outside the large Victorian entrance with a satisfied screech of brakes and shouted "Good luck" after her as she thrust the money into his hands and sped up the steps without waiting for change.

"Captain Sellinger. What room is he in?" she asked breathlessly at the reception desk. "I'm his wife."

A middle-aged woman in a sweater set and tweed skirt ran a pencil down the roster before replying with the ward number and giving directions. Margaret had started to run even before her sentence was finished. She sped around the corner of the pale green corridor and stopped in her tracks. Halloran was walking through the busy scurry of nurses toward her. He saw her at the same moment and stopped, too.

She ran to him. She was in his arms, her eyes closed, her head buried in his shoulder. This was what he had carried inside him over the Channel, across France, and through all the danger. His eyes shut, and for a long moment they did not speak. Finally he loosened his hold and looked down.

"Hello, old friend," he said, taking her face in his hands and gazing at it. "It's unfair for anyone's eyes to be that color."

"Halloran . . . I . . ." she began, wanting to tell him how much she had missed him, how terrified she had been for him. Instead she began to cry.

But he knew. "Me, too," he said, pulling her against him again.

She was trembling violently, those great silver-blue eyes made even larger by the magnifying tears. She ran her hand across his forehead, brushing his sandy hair back, lingering on his head, before tracing the outline of his face.

"I was lost for a while, but now I'm back," he said reassuringly.

She nodded, still unable to speak.

He put both hands on her shoulders and held her back a little from him, looking down seriously. "There's a man in a room down the end of the hall," he began. "He's a good man. He loves his wife and his daughter —more than he loves his own life."

"When I first heard that you were both shot down together . . . I . . . felt I was being punished," Margaret confessed, haltingly. "Then, after a while, I knew . . . I knew you would take care of him . . . I knew you would come back."

She moved to hold on to him again, so tightly that her arms ached and she could feel his heart beating against her skin.

"I love you enough to let go of you," he murmured into her hair. "Which is more than I have ever loved anyone or anything before in my life."

His jacket was warm and damp where she was pressing her face. "I wish I didn't cry all the damn time," she sobbed, looking up at him. His eyes were tender and frank with totally committed love. "If it means anything to you, I will never . . . care for anyone . . . the way I care for you."

"It means something." He brushed his hand against her cheek.

"Remember, we have a street . . . where we met. It's ours. It will always be there . . . no matter where we are. It will never change. No one can ever take that away from us."

She hung on to his words, oblivious of the bustling people around them and the curious glances, reaching into the still palm of his hand with her face.

"Now go . . . go to him. . . ." His eyes did not waver as he said it. "Go . . . before I change my mind and blow this whole thing."

His hand fell down her face . . . down her shoulder . . . down her arm . . . to her hand. She held onto it. He stepped back. Their hands clung together. She began to move in the opposite direction. Their fingers stretched and reached, and then their fingertips parted. Margaret began to walk toward her husband.

Halloran reached the corner as she reached the door. They both stopped to look back at each other. He smiled that lazy, heartbreaking smile, turned, and walked around the corner. Margaret opened the door to the room and entered.

Halloran moved swiftly past the reception desk and through the swing doors, taking the steps down two at a time, striding along the street and across the square, to turn into Hanover Street.

The boards had been taken away, and the little restaurant had been repaired. A shaft of light shone as its door opened to reveal people sitting at its small tables taking tea. The doorway where they always met had been patched up. There was a cluster of people at the bus stop.

The winter evening settled over London. It weighed more than the afternoon.

ABOUT THE AUTHOR

MAUREEN GREGSON was born in Scotland of Irish/
Scottish parents. Educated in English boarding
schools, she began her career as a journalist on a
woman's magazine. Later she spent several years
working on national newspapers in Fleet Street before entering the film industry as a publicist. Her first
novel, *Wild Honey Time,* won the British P.E.N. club
literary award. She has written a number of novels
since, and *Hanover Street* is her fifth novel based on
a screenplay. Ms. Gregson currently resides on a farm
deep in rural England with her husband and child,
and is working on another original novel.

THE LATEST BOOKS
IN THE BANTAM
BESTSELLING TRADITION

RELAX!
SIT DOWN
and Catch Up On Your Reading!

☐	11877	**HOLOCAUST** by Gerald Green	$2.25
☐	12836	**THE CHANCELLOR MANUSCRIPT** by Robert Ludlum	$2.75
☐	12859	**TRINITY** by Leon Uris	$2.95
☐	2300	**THE MONEYCHANGERS** by Arthur Hailey	$1.95
☐	12550	**THE MEDITERRANEAN CAPER** by Clive Cussler	$2.25
☐	11469	**AN EXCHANGE OF EAGLES** by Owen Sela	$2.25
☐	2600	**RAGTIME** by E. L. Doctorow	$2.25
☐	11428	**FAIRYTALES** by Cynthia Freeman	$2.25
☐	11966	**THE ODESSA FILE** by Frederick Forsyth	$2.25
☐	11557	**BLOOD RED ROSES** by Elizabeth B. Coker	$2.25
☐	11708	**JAWS 2** by Hank Searls	$2.25
☐	12490	**TINKER, TAILOR, SOLDIER, SPY** by John Le Carre	$2.50
☐	11929	**THE DOGS OF WAR** by Frederick Forsyth	$2.25
☐	10526	**INDIA ALLEN** by Elizabeth B. Coker	$1.95
☐	12489	**THE HARRAD EXPERIMENT** by Robert Rimmer	$2.25
☐	11767	**IMPERIAL 109** by Richard Doyle	$2.50
☐	13161	**DOLORES** by Jacqueline Susann	$2.25
☐	11601	**THE LOVE MACHINE** by Jacqueline Susann	$2.25
☐	11886	**PROFESSOR OF DESIRE** by Philip Roth	$2.50
☐	12433	**THE DAY OF THE JACKAL** by Frederick Forsyth	$2.50
☐	11952	**DRAGONARD** by Rupert Gilchrist	$1.95
☐	11331	**THE HAIGERLOCH PROJECT** by Ib Melchior	$2.25
☐	11330	**THE BEGGARS ARE COMING** by Mary Loos	$1.95

Buy them at your local bookstore or use this handy coupon for ordering:

Bantam Books, Inc., Dept. FBB, 414 East Golf Road, Des Plaines, Ill. 60016

Please send me the books I have checked above. I am enclosing $_____ (please add 75¢ to cover postage and handling). Send check or money order —no cash or C.O.D.'s please.

Mr/Mrs/Miss _____

Address _____

City _____ State/Zip _____

FBB—8/79

Please allow four weeks for delivery. This offer expires 12/79.

Bantam Book Catalog

Here's your up-to-the-minute listing of over 1,400 titles by your favorite authors.

This illustrated, large format catalog gives a description of each title. For your convenience, it is divided into categories in fiction and non-fiction—gothics, science fiction, westerns, mysteries, cookbooks, mysticism and occult, biographies, history, family living, health, psychology, art.

So don't delay—take advantage of this special opportunity to increase your reading pleasure.

Just send us your name and address and 50¢ (to help defray postage and handling costs).

BANTAM BOOKS, INC.
Dept. FC, 414 East Golf Road, Des Plaines, Ill. 60016

Mr./Mrs./Miss_____
                          (please print)

Address_____

City_____State_____Zip_____

Do you know someone who enjoys books? Just give us their names and addresses and we'll send them a catalog too!

_____

Mr./Mrs./Miss_____

Address_____

City_____State_____Zip_____

_____

Mr./Mrs./Miss_____

Address_____

City_____State_____Zip_____

FC—9/76